Sadie King was born in in Lancashire. After gra history from Lancaster to West Lothian, Scotland, where she now lives with her husband and children. When she's not writing, Sadie loves long country walks, romantic ruins, Thai food and traveling with her family. She also writes historical fiction and contemporary mysteries as Sarah L King.

Also by Sadie King

Spinster with a Scandalous Past
Rescuing the Runaway Heiress
Hastily Wed to the Duke

Look out for more books by Sadie King coming soon!

Discover more at millsandboon.co.uk.

TRUTH OR DARE WITH THE VISCOUNT

Sadie King

MILLS & BOON

All rights reserved including the right of reproduction in whole or in part in any form. This edition is published by arrangement with Harlequin Enterprises ULC.

This is a work of fiction. Names, characters, places, locations and incidents are purely fictional and bear no relationship to any real life individuals, living or dead, or to any actual places, business establishments, locations, events or incidents. Any resemblance is entirely coincidental.

Without limiting the exclusive rights of any author, contributor or the publisher of this publication, any unauthorised use of this publication to train generative artificial intelligence (AI) technologies is expressly prohibited. HarperCollins also exercise their rights under Article 4(3) of the Digital Single Market Directive 2019/790 and expressly reserve this publication from the text and data mining exception.

® and TM are trademarks owned and used by the trademark owner and/or its licensee. Trademarks marked with ® are registered with the United Kingdom Patent Office and/or the Office for Harmonisation in the Internal Market and in other countries.

First published in Great Britain 2026
by Mills & Boon, an imprint of HarperCollins*Publishers* Ltd,
1 London Bridge Street, London, SE1 9GF

www.harpercollins.co.uk

HarperCollins*Publishers*, Macken House, 39/40 Mayor Street Upper, Dublin 1, D01 C9W8, Ireland

Truth or Dare with the Viscount © 2026 Sarah Louise King

ISBN: 978-0-263-41870-5

02/26

Printed and Bound in the UK using 100% Renewable Electricity
at CPI Group (UK) Ltd, Croydon, CR0 4YY

For my family

Chapter One

July 1820

As ever, the mud-clogged roads of Northern England were utterly merciless. Elspeth resisted the urge to groan aloud at the churning in her stomach as the carriage continued to rumble and jolt, the cushioned red velvet of the seat beneath her doing nothing to ease her discomfort. Outside the rain had started again, its heavy droplets tapping insistently upon the carriage window, noisily renewing the threat of flooding, which would further delay what had already been an interminable journey.

Elspeth glanced to her side, astonished to see that her mother's maid, Temperance, still slept soundly, as she had done ever since they'd left the last inn. Wishing she could do the same, she sucked in a sharp breath and squeezed her eyes shut, trying to ignore both the constant jostling and her nausea as she conjured far more pleasant surroundings in her mind's eye. The cosy library of her family home, Chatton House, aglow with the light of a fire burning gently in the hearth, its air enriched by the scents of leather and wood. Her favourite wingback chair, large enough to curl up in as she indulged in her two greatest pleasures: absolute silence and a good book.

Pleasures which had been regrettably absent from her life of late. But then, she could hardly expect this new, somewhat nomadic existence of hers to offer opportunities for quiet contemplation, much less for serious study. Such things required a space, indeed a room of her own, and currently that was not something she had in her possession. All she had were the rooms of others, and so far, her presence in those rooms had come with certain conditions: the need to be agreeable and sociable, to take tea, to indulge in gossip, to promenade with gaggles of giddy young ladies, and to attend an endless procession of dinners and balls. To smile and chatter and offer herself up to the curiosity of provincial Society.

To obey the laws of visiting, because for the time being, a visitor was exactly what she was. She was a guest in the homes of a succession of her mother's friends as together they toured the north and hoped to find a new direction for themselves. Or rather, a new destination. A new home, fit for a Dowager Duchess and her spinster daughter.

Until that home was found, Elspeth would simply

have to endure the upheaval, as well as the nauseating journeys which made reading all but impossible. She would also have to make peace with the uncomfortable fact that, for the first time in her life, she lacked purpose. At Chatton, she'd always had so much to occupy her, from her charitable endeavours with the local school for girls to her own continual pursuit of learning and self-improvement. Now, having left that life behind, she felt rootless and not at all sure what her future purpose should be.

'I do believe we are drawing near to Hallowford. The roads ought to improve soon,' the Dowager Duchess said, clearly noting her daughter's discomfort.

'Mmm,' Elspeth murmured, gripping the seat as yet another wave of nausea rolled over her. 'I'm afraid my tolerance for travelling seems to have grown worse than ever. It is a pity we could not stay longer on the coast,' she added, trying not to sound wistful. She'd rather relished taking the sea air as she walked along those great stretches of golden sand. Never alone, of course, but still—there had been something almost blissful about it.

'Really?' Her mother arched an eyebrow at her. 'I thought two weeks in the Salmesbury household was quite sufficient. Elizabeth has far too many unwed daughters, and like their mother, they are all very… lively,' she said, choosing her words carefully. Lady Salmesbury was one of the Dowager Duchess's oldest and dearest friends, but her ceaseless chatter and penchant for drama could try the patience of a saint. Without doubt, all five of her girls had been created in her image.

Elspeth smiled. 'Point taken, Mama. Should I dare to hope that the Dunsforth dower house will be more sedate?'

Her question was teasing, since she knew very well that it was unlikely to be peaceful. Their next hostess, Lady Dunsforth, lived with her daughter and young granddaughter, who was no more than five years of age. She also knew how much her mother was looking forward to their visit, because she had not seen Lady Dunsforth for years. As young ladies, her mother and Agnes Blair, as Lady Dunsforth was then, had debuted in Society during the same Season and become firm friends. Their bond, however, was tested by Agnes's marriage to the wealthy but reclusive Marquess of Dunsforth, and perhaps would have been lost entirely had both ladies not been so keen on writing letters. Elspeth could recall the many missives back and forth over the years as the two women, separated by distance and duty, conducted their friendship on the page.

After being widowed several years earlier, Lady Dunsforth had left the isolated family estate for good and settled permanently in Hallowford—the north's answer to Bath, or so it was said, with its natural spring waters and pump rooms. Her daughter, meanwhile, had joined Lady Dunsforth in the town after also becoming a widow, at a far younger age than her mother and, tragically, whilst with child. Elspeth was looking forward to meeting them all, and whilst she doubted their home would be tranquil, she'd wager that one small child could not equal the noise and chaos created by the entire Salmesbury brood.

The Dowager Duchess made a face. 'I would not get your hopes up, dearest.' She sighed. 'As for Agnes—I cannot say how I will find her now. I am a little nervous, if I am honest. It is my fault, I think, for leaving it quite so long to visit…'

Elspeth reached over, placing her hand clumsily over her mother's as the carriage juddered yet again. 'It cannot be helped, Mama. You have had much to occupy you at Chatton until very recently,' she said softly, acknowledging the turmoil the family had suffered over the past years.

Both of Elspeth's older brothers had inherited the dukedom of Falstone and the Chatton estate in turn. The eldest, Perry, had been reckless and dissolute, and had perished after drunkenly crashing his gig as he drove home at dawn. Perry had not married and sired an heir, and so his early demise had forced her other brother, Ted, to leave his beloved vocation as an Edinburgh physician and to accept his new responsibilities. Elspeth was acutely aware of the burdens her mother had borne throughout this time, first in trying to curb the worst of Perry's excesses, and secondly in supporting Ted as he grappled with his unexpected inheritance.

Then, Ted had suddenly decided to marry, surprising everyone, not least Elspeth, who'd been more than a little upset that he'd selected her close friend, Charlotte, as his bride. Subsequently she'd made her peace with it; after all, they did seem to be very much in love, and the fact that there was a new duchess at Chatton did mean that her mother had been effectively granted her freedom. But still, she missed Charlotte, and although she'd gained a sister, she could not shake the niggling feeling that she'd lost a friend. And as Elspeth's lack of rapport with the silly Salmesbury sisters had demonstrated, she did not find making friends particularly easy.

She squeezed her mother's hand, shaking off that discomfiting thought as she fought against the churning in her stomach once more. 'I'm sure Lady Dunsforth will understand, Mama. And at least we are to stay for five weeks—that will allow you both to make up for lost time, and we will be able to become better acquainted with Hallowford and all it has to offer.'

The creases which had formed upon her mother's brow softened and her expression brightened once more. 'I have always enjoyed taking the waters. It is odd, really, that your father and I never once went to Hallowford, but then, he was such a devotee of Bath…'

'Perhaps you will love the town and being reunited with Lady Dunsforth so much that you will want to find a house there,' Elspeth replied, a little too hopefully, the thought of a cosy, quiet library returning to her mind once more.

Her mother grinned mischievously. 'Who knows what we both shall find in Hallowford? You know that I do still hope you will find some happiness for yourself, Elsie…'

'Mother!' Elspeth objected, wincing at both the use of that dreadful childhood name and the bluntness of the remark. She knew exactly what sort of happiness her mother wanted for her, and it was absolutely not the sort she envisaged for herself. Unfortunately, another regrettable consequence of her brother's decision to marry, aside from the loss of her good friend, was that the Dowager Duchess had now decided to turn her attention to the marriage prospects of her only daughter.

Although frankly, to call them prospects at all was laughable. She had learned long ago that she was far too bookish and far too outspoken for the tastes of most gentlemen. It had been a painful, humiliating lesson, learned over many a London Season spent conversing with gentlemen who'd greeted the merest hints of her scholarly inclinations with condescension at best, and derision or mockery at worst. The rules of polite Society meant that they'd avoided personal attacks, of course, but she'd understood the message contained within the barbed generalisations about the dreaded *intellectual lady* clearly enough. Becoming a wife required her to change, to be someone she was not, and she would not do that. She would not sacrifice herself on the altar of matrimony, and so she would remain unmarried and free to nurture her bluestocking tendencies however she saw fit.

Her mother held her hands up in mock surrender. 'Can a mother not hope that the right sort of gentleman might come along and sweep her daughter off her feet?'

'And can a daughter not be left in peace to pursue her own interests and her own form of contentment in this life?' Elspeth countered. The carriage jolted again, and this time she could not stifle her groan as she gripped her stomach. 'I'm six-and-twenty, Mama. I know my own mind well enough to know that I do not require a husband to make me happy. Please do not try to foist one upon me.'

The Dowager Duchess looked affronted. 'I would not dream of it, dearest. I only wish that you would at least try to…' She paused, pressing her lips together and apparently thinking better of what she'd been about to say. 'I do hope that we will like Hallowford,' she said after a long moment, mercifully changing the subject. 'Agnes speaks very highly of the Society—although I'm not sure that some quarters of it deserve quite such high praise.'

Elspeth frowned. 'What do you mean by that?'

Her mother leaned forward conspiratorially. 'Agnes's neighbour is Lord Barden,' she said, giving Elspeth a meaningful look. 'You must surely recall the stories about him. About his poor wife.'

Elspeth gasped as it took the barest moment for the penny to drop. As if she could forget the gossip which had swirled around London Society when she'd been little more than a debutante. Unsavoury tales of a wicked viscount, of an unrepentant philanderer who'd coldly cast his wife aside and exiled her to the countryside, never to be seen in Society again. The pitiable woman had died several years later in obscurity.

Elspeth had never met Lord Barden, which was perhaps just as well, since, as a young lady, she'd found the whispers about him unsettling enough. Those whispers had also served as a cautionary tale about the danger of marrying the wrong sort of man and had reinforced a growing sense that she did not wish to marry at all. A sense which had only become more potent each time she'd dipped her toes in the shallow waters of the marriage mart, only to be left feeling bruised and exposed. To be left feeling as though she was the wrong sort of woman—for any man.

The Dowager Duchess nodded slowly, doubtless reading the look of horror which had fixed itself firmly upon Elspeth's face. 'Yes—that Lord Barden. I remember his father, and regrettably he was much the same. As a young woman in Society, your grandmother gave me strict instructions to avoid him. A rotten apple, she called him.'

'And now the rotten apple's equally rotten son lives in Hallowford,' Elspeth murmured. 'Perhaps the town does not have so much to recommend it, after all.'

'Well, it seems Agnes would disagree. In her letters, she has often said what a thoughtful and attentive neighbour Lord Barden is. She feels that he is much misunderstood. I remain unconvinced, but then, I am not the one who is acquainted with him. He avoids London Society—has done for years.'

'No doubt he does,' Elspeth huffed, 'since such notoriety is bound to be unforgiving. And as for misunderstanding him, I am not sure there is much to misunderstand about a man who sets his wife aside so callously, who takes his pleasure with all and sundry...'

'Elspeth!'

The indignation in her mother's voice disturbed the still-slumbering maid, who let out a loud snore, then muttered something indecipherable in her sleep.

'It is unseemly of you to speak like that,' her mother hissed, glancing warily at Temperance, lest she wake fully. 'Whatever we may think of Lord Barden and his reputation, we must keep it to ourselves. We are to be guests in Agnes's home. Remember that—at all times.'

'Of course, Mother,' Elspeth replied, feeling suitably chastened. She was too forthright with her opinions and would have to keep herself in check. A task which would prove far easier if she could simply lock herself away in a library filled with books and not be forced to speak to anyone.

'Good.' The Dowager Duchess appeared to be satisfied. 'Hopefully we will see little of Lord Barden anyway. He merely lives next door, after all.' Elspeth watched as her mother's gaze shifted towards the carriage window. 'And look, my dear—I think we are almost there!'

Pushing aside all thoughts of rotten viscounts, Elspeth peered outside. The rolling hills of Yorkshire had given way to a townscape now, and she could see that they were travelling along a grand square arranged around fine formal gardens, each side lined with imposing, palatial townhouses which announced the wealth and status of those who dwelt within them. She saw, too, that the earlier torrent of rain had abated to a mere drizzle; a small mercy for which Elspeth was grateful, since she felt the carriage begin to slow and finally, to draw to a halt. She nudged Temperance gently, urging her to wake now. They had indeed arrived.

Before she could gather her wits and remind herself of her duty to be mild-mannered and restrained, the carriage door was flung open. The Dowager Duchess hurried out, urging Elspeth to follow quickly behind her and instructing her bleary-eyed maid to coordinate the unloading of their luggage with their driver. Clearly, the nerves her mother had been experiencing earlier had now been replaced by excitement. The warm, wet summer air greeted Elspeth as she clambered out, swiftly smoothing her hands over the skirt of her deep purple dress in an effort to straighten herself. She glanced up to see a rather severe-looking older woman in a mob cap waiting to greet them at the top of a handful of stone steps which led to the house's front door. The housekeeper, she presumed. She followed closely behind her mother as the woman curtsied, then beckoned them inside and led them along a wide hallway and into a bright, airy parlour, where four people had gathered, ready to receive them.

Two ladies—mother and daughter, wearing matching smiles. One child—a small girl, who bounced up and down excitedly between the two ladies, who each held one of her hands. And a little to the side of them stood a man, his countenance more serious than the rest as he stood stiffly, his hands clasped behind his back. Elspeth's gaze lingered in his direction as she tried to work out who he might be. Lady Dunsforth's son, perhaps? Certainly she had one, although he was the Marquess now, and she was sure that her mother had said nothing to her about him being in Hallowford…

Elspeth felt her breath catch involuntarily in her throat as the man's deep green eyes swept over her, completely devoid of any subtlety as they made their initial assessment. Feeling oddly provoked, she stared back at him and was alarmed to find herself noticing the reddish tint to his otherwise brown hair and the way it seemed tousled, as though he'd just returned from riding. Noticing, too, the way his broad shoulders filled his impeccably tailored coat, and in turn, how he seemed suddenly to fill the room, so that even as her mother darted forward to embrace Lady Dunsforth and the introductions began, Elspeth found that she struggled to tear her eyes away.

What on earth had got into her?

'Agnes, this is my daughter, the Lady Elspeth Scott,' the Dowager Duchess said. 'And Elspeth, this is my dear friend, the Dowager Marchioness of Dunsforth.'

Two slim, warm hands took hold of Elspeth's, and she swallowed hard as finally she forced her gaze to shift to the kindly face of the older woman who stood before her. Elspeth bobbed a brief curtsy as two bright and inquisitive blue eyes made their study of her. 'It is a pleasure to meet you, Lady Dunsforth.'

Lady Dunsforth grinned at her. 'Such dark eyes,' she observed. 'You look just like your father, my dear.' She relinquished Elspeth's hands, gesturing towards the younger woman and the child as she addressed both of her guests once more. 'Allow me to present my daughter, the Dowager Countess of Westhaigh, and my granddaughter, the Lady Matilda Carlton.'

The younger woman stepped forward then, gathering the child into her arms. Both had hair so fair it was almost white and the same bright blue eyes as Lady Dunsforth. It struck Elspeth that Lady Westhaigh looked much as she imagined a goddess might look—tall and graceful, with impossibly pale and flawless skin and a curvaceous figure which filled her sumptuous cornflower blue day dress magnificently. She was the sort of lady whose beauty would draw every eye in a room towards her—the men out of desire, and the women out of envy. Elspeth felt suddenly and uncomfortably plain in her presence.

Lady Westhaigh inclined her head politely, before smiling at her daughter. 'We prefer to be called Lady Melliora and Tilly among friends, don't we, little one?' she said.

'Yes, Mama.' The child giggled. 'I'm Tilly. I'm nearly five,' she said, holding up five chubby little fingers.

Elspeth smiled sweetly at the girl, trying hard to mask her surprise at the goddess's intriguing departure from convention. As an earl's widow, Lady Melliora ought to be addressed by her husband's title. The fact that she preferred to use the title she'd been granted at birth by virtue of her father's rank was more than a little odd.

Elspeth glanced at Lady Dunsforth, but intuited no look of surprise upon her face at her daughter's pronouncement. Instead, Lady Dunsforth turned swiftly to the gentleman, still standing stiffly on the periphery and awaiting his own introduction. Cautiously, Elspeth let her gaze wander towards him again, hoping that initial, strange response she'd had to his presence would not be repeated. She was not used to being so affected by a man, and such a response would not do—especially if the gentleman, whoever he might be, was residing in Lady Dunsforth's house, too.

Unfortunately, as her eyes met his, she felt those same feelings wash over her again. Something akin to provocation, but accompanied this time by a disconcerting warmth, which grew of its own accord in her already unsettled stomach, before spreading upwards through her chest and spilling on to her cheeks. Horrified at the thought that she might by now be glowing scarlet, Elspeth felt her heart begin to race, its furious beat so loud in her own ears that she felt sure that the entire room could hear it. She clasped her clammy hands together tightly, willing herself to calm down as Lady Dunsforth gave the gentleman a broad smile and took him by the arm.

'And this is our dear friend and neighbour, Lord Barden.'

Almost immediately, the heat turned to ice. Despite herself, and despite her promise to her mother, Elspeth felt her eyes narrow at him, felt any hint of a polite smile evaporate and a scowl form in its place. Of course this was Lord Barden. Of course this was the wicked Viscount, the rotten son of a rotten apple.

And of course, of all the men in all the world, it had to be this man who'd caused her to have such an overpowering, mortifying and thoroughly inappropriate response to his presence. At least now that she knew who he was, she could kill such feelings stone dead. Elspeth pressed her lips together, suppressing her scowl as she inclined her head politely towards him and prayed that she looked convincingly impassive. From now on, she promised herself, the only response that Lord Barden would elicit from her would be her indifference.

Chapter Two

Robert had seen that look on a woman's face scores of times before, and he knew exactly what it meant. Dawning realisation, followed swiftly by the horror and disgust which made him feel like a condemned man on his way to the gallows. In fairness to the Dowager Duchess, she hid her feelings well, even managing to smile and utter brief pleasantries in greeting. Her daughter, however, was another matter entirely—indeed, if looks could kill, then he would most certainly be dead. He'd received some hostile receptions over the years, but even so, he was not quite prepared for how awful that scowl had made him feel. How angry—not at the Lady Elspeth Scott, per se, but at the unfairness of it all. At the unfairness of being tried and found guilty, again and again, on the basis of stories and whispers, of rumour and reputation.

Around him, the assembled party settled down to enjoy some tea, while the nursemaid was summoned to take Tilly back to the nursery. He ordered himself to recover his wits, to restore that devil-may-care countenance which he wore like a Spartan shield. This was the price he paid for keeping the truth from Society, he reminded himself. A price he'd committed to paying, long ago.

It didn't help that he'd had the most unsettling response to Lady Elspeth, the moment that she'd walked into the parlour. A response which had only grown more confusing and intense when their eyes had met. A response which had felt disconcertingly like attraction. He supposed he should not be surprised. She was extraordinarily pretty, with her large, dark eyes, button nose, deep brown curls, not to mention her dramatic purple travelling dress—a colour which commanded attention and demanded she be taken seriously. She was exactly the sort of woman who would have appealed to him once, long ago, when he was a young man harbouring dreams of a love match. Before painful experience had shown him just how far beyond his reach such dreams were. Apparently, she was also exactly the sort of woman whose mere presence was sufficient to remind him that, hidden behind that Spartan shield of his, he did still have longings just waiting to be stirred.

No matter, he told himself. She'd shown she disliked him in no uncertain terms, so there was an end to it.

'Well then, what do we all think about this terrible business with Queen Caroline?' Lady Dunsforth asked, turning the conversation to one of her favoured topics of the moment.

When no one else answered immediately, the Dowager Duchess shook her head sadly. 'I think it's clear that the King and Queen have always been ill-suited, and with the passing of dear Princess Charlotte, they lost the shared bond of parenthood. It's all very tragic, really.'

'It is, but...' Lady Dunsforth paused, sipping her tea thoughtfully. 'The King is the King, when all's said and done, but I do find myself vexed by his actions of late. First in refusing to recognise his wife as his queen, and now there is this Bill in Parliament...'

The Dowager Duchess frowned. 'What Bill?' She repaired her expression, giving everyone an embarrassed smile. 'I'm afraid that with all our travelling lately, Lady Elspeth and myself are perhaps not quite so well-informed as we ought to be.'

'The latest bit of news is that the King has charged the Queen with adultery,' Lady Dunsforth explained. 'And the Bill seeks to deprive her of the title of Queen Consort and to dissolve their marriage. It's a dreadful business.'

'Oh, that must have been what was on the front of that broadside.' Lady Elspeth pondered aloud, and despite himself, Robert found his gaze wandering back towards her.

'What broadside?' the Dowager Duchess asked.

'It had been left on a table at the last inn we stopped at. I remember glancing at it and seeing it said something about the King and Queen—but then, when do the broadsides not?' she added with a shrug before returning to sip her tea.

The Dowager Duchess's eyes widened as she regarded her daughter. 'I am surprised you didn't pick it up and read it, dearest. That is quite unlike you.' She sighed as she turned to address the rest of the group. 'Oh dear, I fear this will affect the plans my son, the Duke, had made. He was hoping to spend the summer at Chatton with his new Duchess,' she explained. 'But I suppose he may have to attend the Lords now.'

Robert felt his heart sink in sympathy with that. Upon hearing the news of the Bill, he had thought the same for himself. Since becoming *persona non grata* in the eyes of the *ton*, he had absented himself from London Society, and that meant he'd seldom attended the Lords. For something as important as this, however, his attendance may yet be required.

Wonderful.

'I suppose I did not think much about it,' Lady Elspeth continued, and Robert's wayward eyes wandered back to her once again. 'I had been trying to read my book, you see, and then...'

'Ah! There we have it.' Lady Dunsforth clapped her hands together, apparently satisfied. 'The lure of the novel. One should never underestimate the power these stories have over young ladies' minds.' She glanced at Lady Melliora. 'You struggle to tear yourself away from those Gothic tales, don't you, dear?'

Lady Melliora inclined her head in agreement. 'It is true—I am an admirer of Walpole's Gothic novel, in particular. However, I hardly think I can be called a young lady, Mama...'

Lady Elspeth shook her head fiercely. 'No indeed, neither can I. Nor was I gripped by a novel. I—' She paused abruptly, as though thinking better of what she'd been about to say.

Her protest, and subsequent hesitation, made Robert even more curious. 'What do you have against the humble novel, Lady Elspeth?' he asked before he could think better of it.

She bristled. 'Nothing, my lord.'

'I see. But you were not gripped by one.' He sat back in his chair, lacing his fingers together theatrically. 'But whatever reading material you were gripped by must have been engaging indeed—far more interesting than tittle-tattle in a broadside,' he mused.

He saw the merest hint of a frown gathering between her eyes. 'Not at all, my lord,' Lady Elspeth began through what sounded suspiciously like gritted teeth. 'It is just that...' She paused, as though considering her answer carefully, then smiled sweetly at everyone—except him—as she picked up her teacup once more. 'Actually—Lady Dunsforth is right. Now that I think about it, the novel I was reading did thoroughly distract me. It must have caused me to overlook the news about the King's Great Matter.'

Robert smiled wryly as Lady Dunsforth laughed, congratulating herself on her own skills of deduction. The King's Great Matter, indeed—a reference to the divorce of Henry the Eighth from Catherine of Aragon, if he was not mistaken. A reference which was not lost on him, and one which hinted at an opinion Lady Elspeth did not wish to explicitly convey. Nor had it escaped his notice that she had deftly avoided sharing the name of the novel which had allegedly held her so completely under its spell. It was not clear why, and that only made him more curious.

What was clear to him, however, was that Lady Elspeth was as clever as she was pretty. A lethal combination, if ever there was one.

As the conversation moved on to other subjects, their eyes met again, just briefly, and this time he saw the indignation burning in her dark gaze. Indignation at having been questioned. Indignation, perhaps, at knowing she'd been read and understood—by him, of all people. Unable to resist provoking her further, he gave her a triumphant smile. She might despise him, but he could already see that she would prove a worthy adversary over the coming weeks. An adversary with whom the prospect of crossing swords seemed suddenly very appealing indeed.

* * *

'How many wooden blocks do you have now, Tilly?'

Robert watched as the girl pointed a finger at each block in turn, counting them under her breath. Her nursemaid sat quietly nearby, only interrupting periodically to curtly remind Robert that it would be time for the child to have her dinner soon. In other words, that it was almost time for him to leave.

With each reminder he'd nodded politely, resisting the temptation to sigh. He was already aware that the minutes he'd secured with the girl were stolen ones, snatched from a reluctant Lady Dunsforth, not long after they'd all finished their tea and her guests had retired to their rooms to rest awhile. He knew that by requesting a short visit to the nursery, he was breaching their agreement. For the duration of the Dowager Duchess and Lady Elspeth's stay, Lady Dunsforth had asked him to be a less frequent visitor at the house. Not because of his reputation, of course—she'd been vehement in her protest when he'd suggested that was the root of her concern—but for the sake of propriety.

'It does not matter a jot whether the world thinks you are a saint or a sinner,' Lady Dunsforth had said in whispered tones, lest the servants overhear them. 'As an unattached gentleman, your regular presence here might appear odd to the Dowager Duchess and her daughter, and frankly, I believe we're all old enough and wise enough to know that such attention would be best avoided.'

She'd gone on to remind him that he was merely a neighbour and needed to behave as such. He'd acquiesced, of course, not reminding her that there was considerably more to his connection to their family, and to Tilly, than that. After all, the exact nature of that connection was never acknowledged out loud—they'd all agreed upon that, long ago. The Great Secret was too dangerous for words; it had to remain behind a wall of silence, even if that silence meant that Tilly might never know who her father really had been. Even if the child might always believe that her father was an old, dead earl and not Robert's younger, deceased brother, Rafe. Even if it meant that she might only ever know Robert as the man who lived next door, and not as her uncle. Keeping the truth from Tilly pained him, and a part of him hoped that one day, perhaps when she was grown, she might be permitted to know. However, that was not his decision to make.

The decisions rested entirely with the Dunsforths— including, unfathomably, to invite him for tea that day, despite knowing that their guests' arrival was imminent. And despite knowing him well enough to understand that he would never return home without saying goodbye to Tilly first. A prolonged goodbye, which usually involved him sitting still on pain of death while she drew him, or helping her to practise her letters or her numbers.

'Fifteen!' Beside him, the child squealed her delight, clapping her hands together. 'That right, Robert?'

'It is indeed, Tilly,' he replied, giving her an affectionate smile. He glanced at the nursemaid, who gave him another of her stern looks, then rose from his seat. 'We will practise again soon—up to twenty next time.'

Swiftly, he bid Tilly farewell and strode towards the door, deep in thought. She was a bright child, and it was high time that Melliora employed a governess to begin her formal education. He had raised the matter previously, but for whatever reason, so far her mother had seemed reluctant. He promised himself that he would raise it again soon, and this time he would try to understand the cause of her reservations, to see if there was something he could help with. On the other hand, he reasoned, it might be best to wait until Lady Dunsforth's guests had departed before broaching the subject. It would seem odd to her visitors if they overheard him, a mere neighbour, discussing Tilly's education with Melliora.

Lady Dunsforth was right—he did need to make himself scarce. The Great Secret had to be guarded, just as his own secrets had always been. Whilst he lived and breathed, the world would never know the truth of Tilly's parentage, just as it would never know the real reason why his marriage had been doomed from the start. That it was not his unfaithfulness or callousness which had caused him to separate from Lucy, but her love for someone else, her misery, and her unyielding desperation to be set free. That he'd brokered their agreement to live apart out of respect and compassion for a woman who'd wanted the marriage their fathers had arranged for them no more than he had.

That he'd borne the scandalous rumours and the blame which Society heaped upon him because he'd known that he could withstand it, when Lucy could not. As a young man he'd grown accustomed to being talked about, to being automatically associated with the terrible conduct of his father. Not that his own conduct before marriage had done anything to help matters; he grimaced now to recall his indiscreet dalliance with a dark-haired beauty from the London stage, conducted in that youthful haze of first love. In hindsight, it had probably been lust rather than love which had driven him to be so reckless with his already fragile reputation, but he'd been too naïve to understand that at the time.

'The rotten son of a rotten apple,' Society's gossips had crowed as they'd feasted on the scandalous reports about old Lord Barden's heir and the actress. Of course, when later his marriage had fallen apart,

those same gossips had found it all too easy to condemn him.

Indeed, he was glad that they had. Being a man who was regarded as a rake was bad enough, but for women, the stakes were always higher, and for Lucy, the besmirching of her reputation would have been too much to bear. So, he'd guarded Lucy's secret and continued to do so, even though she'd been dead these past four years. Just as he guarded Melliora and Rafe's secret, even though he knew that meant keeping the truth from Tilly herself.

Still consumed by his thoughts and walking at a pace, it took him longer than it should have to see someone emerge from one of the rooms on the second floor. At the last moment he started, almost colliding into the person as they hurried out into the hallway. A very female, very pretty person, her earlier deep purple travelling dress replaced now by one fashioned in a paler blue, the dark curls of her hair neatly rearranged and the fresh scent of lavender wafting around her as she let out a startled sound. Goodness, she was lovely, and goodness, he needed to cease paying quite so much attention to that fact.

'Lady Elspeth—forgive me,' he said. 'I did not mean to alarm you.'

She raised a single dark eyebrow at him—half curious, half disapproving. 'Still here, my lord?'

Her directness took him aback. 'Yes—Tilly had left

one of her dolls downstairs. Everyone was busy preparing for dinner, so I told Lady Dunsforth I would return it to the nursery.' He concocted his story hurriedly, praying it sounded convincing.

That single eyebrow lifted a notch higher. 'I see,' she replied. 'And are you joining us for dinner this evening, my lord?'

'No.' He grinned at her, recovering himself. 'You will be pleased to hear that you will be spared my company this evening.'

His teasing earned him a curt nod. 'Very well,' she replied, before turning on her heel and stepping towards the stairs. 'In that case, I shall bid you farewell, my lord.'

'I am curious, Lady Elspeth,' he called after her, suddenly and unfathomably unwilling to let that be the end of their conversation, 'to know the name of the novel you were reading—the one you found so diverting.'

Lady Elspeth turned back to face him, and he could see that, despite her efforts to appear unflustered, her cheeks had begun to colour a little at his question. 'Why do you wish to know?' she asked.

He shrugged. 'Perhaps I am in need of a little diversion myself.'

'Indeed?' This time she raised both eyebrows at him. 'I daresay you need no recommendation from me concerning how to divert yourself, my lord.' Before he could respond to that particular barb, she continued: 'But if you must know, it was not a novel. I was reading a book called *The Pantheon of the Heathen Gods and Illustrious Heroes.*'

Now it was his turn to raise his eyebrows. 'You are interested in the myths of the Greeks?' he asked.

She seemed to hesitate. 'Yes.'

He grinned at her. 'Then we have that in common, Lady Elspeth, since I too have an interest in mythology.'

'Indeed,' she replied flatly, as though she could not imagine that they could ever have anything in common.

Unthinkingly, he stepped towards her. 'Why would you not be drawn on what you were reading when it was discussed earlier at tea?' he asked. 'I am curious, that's all.'

He heard her draw a sharp breath, then watched as she gave him a withering look. 'You are curious about a great deal, my lord. And as I recall, the only person who was interrogating me at tea about my choice of reading material was you. Now, if you'll excuse me, Lady Dunsforth will be expecting me.'

Her blatant hostility took his breath away, but he was determined he would not be defeated so easily. If Lady Elspeth Scott wanted to go to war with him, then so be it—he would rise to the challenge. The ruder she was, the more maddening he would be. The more irritatingly curious and engaging—perhaps even charming.

Yes—charming. Annoyingly so.

'The King's Great Matter,' he called after her as she took a handful of steps down the stairs. 'Remind me, was that not what Henry the Eighth's court called his quest for a divorce from his first queen?'

She glanced over her shoulder at him. 'I believe so.'

'And do you believe that such a historical reference might be used to express an opinion on current events? An opinion which does not favour our current King?'

She curled her lip at him. 'It might.'

He nodded briskly, trying his best not to show that he sensed a small victory was within his reach. 'That is what I thought, Lady Elspeth.'

She inclined her head politely, then turned and hurried down the sweeping staircase. He followed a little behind her, intent upon making a swift exit now and leaving the family and their guests to dine in peace. As Lady Elspeth reached the bottom step, however, he saw her hesitate, looking left and right down the long hall, as though she'd lost her way.

'The drawing room is this way,' he said, catching up with her and gesturing to his right. 'Everyone will be assembling in there. Would you like me to escort you?'

The thunderous expression on her face told him that was the very last thing on God's green earth that she could ever have wanted. Before she could give voice to her objection, however, Robert offered her his arm, along with the most gracious and charming smile he could muster. He meant to exasperate her, he knew that. He sensed how gravely his mere presence offended her, and that made him want to get under her skin even more. And yet, as Lady Elspeth reluctantly accepted his offer, threading her arm through his, he realised that the joke was on him. Her touch, her warmth, her proximity—all of it was intoxicating, stirring that longing he'd felt when their eyes had first met in the parlour that afternoon. Stirring the sort of desires he believed he'd buried long ago.

'I apologise, if you felt I was interrogating you earlier,' he said as they walked together, sounding suddenly and worryingly sincere. Apparently, his powers of provocation had disintegrated, the moment her arm had come to rest against his. 'I was merely intrigued. Indeed, I am still intrigued.'

She glanced at him, frowning. 'About what?'

'About why you did not simply say that it was a book of Greek myths, which you found far more interesting than troubling yourself with the contents of that broadside.'

She huffed a breath, rolling her eyes. 'I did not say it was a book—any book—which caused me to overlook it. Others made that assumption, just as they assumed it was a novel I was reading, and in the end, I decided not to bother correcting them on either count.'

'Why?'

Lady Elspeth relinquished Robert's arm as they reached the door to the drawing room, leaving him feeling strangely bereft. 'Because sometimes it is better to satisfy the expectations of others than it is to contradict them,' she replied.

How true that was. How painfully accurate. Immediately Robert thought of Lucy, of how he'd allowed Society's opinion of him to go unchallenged because the consequences of everyone knowing the truth would be far worse. He felt the weight of every word hanging between them as their eyes met, and for a moment he found himself wondering what it would be like to lose himself in that dark gaze.

'But if you had been disposed towards contradiction, what would you have said?' he asked in a low voice, no longer sure if he was trying to tease her or not.

Judging by the fierce look she gave him, however, she'd interpreted his question as goading. 'If you really must know, my lord, I would have said that I barely managed to read anything at that last inn, because the journey had made me feel so unwell,' she replied hotly. 'That it was not a book which caused me to ignore the latest gossip about the King and Queen, but the ceaseless waves of nausea which I had suffered throughout that interminable journey. Nausea which, by the journey's end, refused to abate even when we stopped. Nausea which hardly seemed like a suitable topic of conversation while taking tea in polite company and with people I'd only just met. Are you satisfied now, my lord?' she asked, her face glowing scarlet as she glowered at him.

Robert stared at her, completely taken aback by her sudden candour. 'No—yes, forgive me, I…'

She raised a hand in protest. 'Do not trouble yourself to apologise. Nothing vexes me, my lord, not even you,' she insisted, even though she looked very vexed indeed. 'Now, if you'll excuse me, I must join the others for dinner and pray that my poor stomach can tolerate it.'

And with that, she slipped inside the drawing room, leaving Robert standing in the hall, feeling every bit the blockhead he clearly was.

Chapter Three

Nothing vexes me, my lord, not even you.

Elspeth pressed her hands against her cheeks, feeling the heat rising in them at the memory of those words. She had wandered over to the window of her well-appointed bedchamber on the second floor, determined to survey the view as she greeted the bright new day outside. Her mind, however, appeared to have other ideas, continually dragging her thoughts back to yesterday evening. To that heated conversation. To her insistence that she was not vexed, when it must have been abundantly clear that was not true. She'd been very vexed indeed.

Why did Lord Barden have to be so insufferable? And so impertinent? And—most annoying of all—did he really have to be quite so perceptive?

It was bad enough that she'd had that unsettling response to him when they'd first met. That, in those moments before they were introduced, she'd found herself paying quite so much attention to his handsome face and undoubtedly fine physique. But then they'd spoken, first at tea and then on the stairs, and she had the unnerving sense that the wretch had read her, just like the book which he'd been convinced had been the cause of her distraction.

He'd been wrong about that—it had been that intolerable sickness, which thankfully had finally abated—but his suspicion that she'd been reticent to speak about her current choice of reading material had not been entirely without foundation. She knew from bitter experience that polite Society had little tolerance for bluestockings, and she tended to guard her pursuit of knowledge closely, especially in the company of those she barely knew. Better to let her hosts believe she'd brought with her a light-hearted novel which was considered suitable for ladies, rather than choosing to read about Hades stealing Persephone away to the underworld.

Sometimes it is better to satisfy the expectations of others than it is to contradict them.

Elspeth shook her head fiercely, as though she could shake off those words, and indeed, everything else she said to Lord Barden yesterday. She'd been hostile and rude, and when she was not being either of those things, she'd been worryingly frank and honest. The man was a rotten apple and she would do well to remember that. She would do well to give him no credit whatsoever—not for seeming to understand her, nor for his apparent lack of disapproval at her interest in Greek mythology.

An interest he'd professed to share, had he not?

He had, but it did not matter. Lord Barden was wicked—doubtless he'd only said that to irritate her. After all, almost every word he'd spoken to her yesterday had been armed with provocation, and his actions had been no less goading. Why else would he have turned on the charm as he did, offering to escort her to the drawing room, except to amuse himself at her expense? Well, he could find his fun elsewhere from now on, because certainly she would not accept his arm again! Holding on to him like that had been far too...unsettling.

Elspeth huffed a breath, turning away from the window and making her way out of her bedchamber and down the stairs. As was her usual habit, she'd woken and dressed early, intent upon taking a little air before the rest of the household rose for breakfast. From her bedchamber window she'd spotted a garden, situated between the rear of the house and the lane which provided access to both the stables and the rolling fields which lay beyond. It looked small but private enough to be suitable for her to take a turn in, unaccompanied. She made her way there quickly, as though worried that Lady Dunsforth herself was about to spring up and interrogate her. Silly, really. Surely their hostess would not begrudge her an early-morning walk in the Dunsforth garden.

Would she?

That was the trouble with being a visitor—it was so difficult to feel at ease in someone else's home. Just as it was difficult to meander around a neat little townhouse garden, enjoying the peace and quiet, without hankering after the sprawling parkland of Chatton House. At Chatton, she could walk a mile or more alone before breakfast and no one ever batted an eyelid. How fortunate she'd been, to spend so much of her life there. And how wilful she'd been, in refusing to confront the fact that one day she would have to leave it behind…

A dull thudding noise interrupted Elspeth's thoughts, causing her to startle. What the devil was that? She stood still, listening as the noise came, again and again. A regular, rhythmic sound which seemed to emerge from somewhere near to the stables, and yet it was no sound she'd ever heard that she'd associate with the business of caring for horses. Curious, she crept out of the garden and on to the lane, making a swift study of the neat row of stables and outhouses which served the Dunsforths and their neighbours. She spied no ostlers going about their work, no horses being readied for an imminent departure, or indeed anything else which might explain the sound.

How strange.

The noise continued, growing louder now; she followed it, much like a hound would catch a scent, until she reached an unassuming outbuilding, its narrow wooden door tantalisingly ajar. Unable to resist satisfying her curiosity any longer, she tiptoed closer, peered inside, and immediately clapped her hand over her mouth to stop herself from gasping aloud.

It was Lord Barden, hitting what looked like a large bag which had been strung up from the rafters. He had his back turned to her, which was just as well because that back was completely and unashamedly bare. For several moments Elspeth could do nought but stare in wonder at those magnificent broad shoulders and perfectly sculpted arms, watching every sinew and muscle strain as his fists met his target, again and again. Lord Barden was a wicked man, and he had been built wickedly to match—not moulded by Prometheus from clay, but fashioned from flesh by Zeus himself. A body made for sinning, that was for certain.

She felt hot and flustered, all over and everywhere as she ordered herself to blink, to recover her wits, and to slip away unseen. To not make any sound which might betray her presence. And absolutely to not catch the door with a trailing arm as she stepped away, so that it creaked loudly and caused Lord Barden to spin around...

'What the devil!' he cried. 'Lady Elspeth?'

Oh no.

It took far longer than it should have for Elspeth to lift her gaze to meet his. Not really because she was mortified, although of course she was, but because her eyes were stubbornly fixed upon his gloriously bare chest and stomach—taut and perfectly defined and embellished with the merest dusting of brown hair, which drew a neat line down his stomach before disappearing beneath the waist of his pantaloons. She swallowed hard, commanding her traitorous eyes to cease feasting quite so brazenly. Yesterday, the wretch had vexed her with his words. She could not allow him to see that the mere sight of him bothered her, too.

'I... I was merely curious,' she stammered, gathering her wits and wishing she had a bucket of ice to hand, to cool the fire currently raging in every part of her.

The wretch smiled, just briefly. 'I can see that,' he replied, grabbing his shirt and pulling it over his head.

She bristled at his insinuation. 'No—I mean, about the noise. I was taking the air in the garden, and I heard a thudding sound. I was curious to know what it was.'

He shrugged. 'I suppose it was your turn.'

'For what?'

'To be curious, and for that curiosity to get you into hot water. Yesterday, it was me. Today, it is you. I daresay this makes us even.'

He was trying to annoy her again, she was certain of it. 'To be clear, I did not know that this was your outbuilding, or that it was you in here. If I had, I would have given the place an extremely wide berth,' she replied hotly. 'I have no need to see you, or this, or whatever it is you're doing…'

'Boxing,' he said. 'It's called boxing. It's a form of sport. Although, strictly speaking the sport usually involves hitting an opponent, not a bag.'

She curled her lip. 'I know what boxing is, my lord. It is rather ungentlemanly, is it not?'

Lord Barden chuckled. 'You'd be surprised how many gentlemen enjoy it, although most prefer to wager on fights rather than participate in them.'

'Do you fight?' The question slipped from her lips before she could stop it.

He grinned at her. 'Only with a bag, these days.' He pressed a hand casually against the bag beside him, causing it to swing. 'Would you like to give it a try, Lady Elspeth?'

'Certainly not!' she replied, glaring at him. 'Why on earth would I want to do that?'

He shrugged. 'I don't know—because you are naturally curious? Because you are the sort of lady who likes to learn about the world?'

'Why do you say that?' she asked, her hackles rising further at the shrewdness of his observation.

Another shrug. 'Well, the fact that you read books on Greek mythology, for a start. I'm not really a betting man nowadays, but if I was, I'd wager that you're a lady who has learned a great deal from books.'

Elspeth stared at him, feeling her temper flare. The nerve of the man—assessing her, scrutinising her, then using the conclusions he'd drawn to mock her! Because that was what he was doing, wasn't it? Sniffing out her intellectual achievements then sneering at them, just like so many gentlemen had done, time and again, until in the end she'd turned her back on the marriage mart in despair. Hearing such mockery from prospective husbands had been bad enough, but to hear it from a rotten apple like Lord Barden…

'You know nothing about me, my lord,' she said hotly, taking a step back from the doorway, determined to take her leave of him now. 'Now, if you'll excuse me, I must go inside for breakfast. I can tolerate a lot of things, but being mocked on an empty stomach is not one of them.'

'I was not mocking you.'

Lady Elspeth's response to his observation took Robert by surprise. Without thinking, he hurried towards the door, catching hold of her arm as she turned her back on him. His touch seemed to surprise them both in equal measure; for a long moment, their eyes fixed upon the impertinent hand, which had apparently acquired a mind of its own, until eventually Lady Elspeth snatched her arm away, as though burned. As though she'd felt the strange fire which was currently coursing through his fingers, too.

'I was not mocking you, Lady Elspeth,' he repeated, holding her gaze and somewhat taken aback by the fury he saw blazing in those dark eyes. 'If that was how it seemed, then I assure you, that was not my intention. I was merely…'

He swallowed hard, suddenly and uncharacteristically at a loss for words. What had he been doing, exactly? One minute he'd been throwing punches at that bag, just as he did most mornings when the hour was still early and when the world was still silent. When his thoughts were in the direst need of quietening, because he'd lived this solitary life of his for long enough now to know that the mornings were the worst, and that working up a sweat in an outbuilding was preferable to rumination. The next minute, he'd turned to see Lady Elspeth staring at him from the doorway, looking flustered and alarmed and beautiful, and…

Any space he'd had in his mind for those usual thoughts, the ones about Lucy, about the Great Secret, about Rafe, had gone—consumed entirely by the very cross, very resplendent female who was still standing in front of him, hands planted on her hips, her entire formidable countenance awaiting his explanation.

'You were merely…?' she prompted him.

He smiled at her, recovering himself. 'Merely getting myself into hot water—again,' he replied. 'I hope you are feeling better now,' he said softly, deciding that a swift change of subject was required.

She nodded curtly. 'I am, thank you. Unfortunately long journeys have never agreed with me. However, yesterday's malady was particularly acute.'

'I am sorry to hear it. I have known others who have suffered similarly.' Lucy. He bit his tongue, refusing to allow either his mind or his words to be drawn in that particular direction. 'Have you tried taking ginger?'

'I have tried everything, my lord, but to no avail,' she replied. 'It is just something I must bear.'

'At least you will be able to enjoy some respite from it now,' he said. 'Lady Dunsforth tells me that you are to stay for five weeks, and I doubt she will arrange any lengthy outings in her carriage. She is a great devotee of Hallowford and rarely leaves it. I know she will be keen to show you all that the town has to offer.'

'You seem to know Lady Dunsforth and her family very well,' Lady Elspeth remarked, her brows lifting at his commentary.

He shrugged, praying to God that he appeared nonchalant. 'I suppose I do. Our families have owned these houses for years,' he explained, gesturing towards the adjoining townhouses. 'I've known the Dunsforths since I was a child, spending my summers here.'

She nodded slowly. 'And still you spend your summers here,' she mused.

'Nowadays I spend most of my time here,' he corrected her. 'As does Lady Dunsforth. She settled here permanently, after her husband, the Marquess, died. I believe Hallowford suits her very well. She likes the Society and taking the waters, of course.' He bit his tongue again, resolute that he should say no more. He did not know how much Lady Elspeth knew about Lady Dunsforth's marriage, about her isolated life with a cruel and controlling husband, or about just how profoundly widowhood and Hallowford had liberated her. In any case, none of it was his story to tell.

'Hallowford must suit you very well, too, if you choose to spend so much time here,' Lady Elspeth observed, and Robert could not decide if she was trying to irk him or not. Her reaction upon their introduction yesterday told him in no uncertain terms that she knew exactly who he was, or at least, the man he was reputed to be. She must have known that his life here was a form of exile, even if she could never decipher why he'd banished himself to Hallowford in particular.

'I have my own reasons for being here,' he murmured. How true those words were. More true than Lady Elspeth could ever know.

He watched as those dark eyes of hers narrowed, and it was clear she was ruminating on something. 'I hope that Hallowford suits my mother well enough. She is on something of a mission, to find a new home—a nice dower house, somewhere. She is right to do so, of course—now that my brother, the Duke, has married, he will doubtless have an enormous brood of children soon enough. He can hardly be expected to put up with us forever…'

'Us?' he interjected. 'You will be living in a dower house, too?'

She folded her arms across her chest, somewhat defensively. 'Of course. Where else would I go?'

He blinked at her, unable to muster a response which would not get him into further hot water. A lady like her—intelligent, beautiful, and a duke's daughter, no less—was the answer not patently obvious? Most would desire an adoring husband, an army of children, and a home of their own. However, he suspected such a response would not be welcome.

She sighed at him, apparently exasperated by his latest silence, then glanced over her shoulder. 'I ought to go inside. My mother will think I have gone missing. If she sends out a search party and they find me talking to you…'

'Of course,' Robert replied, bristling at the emphasis she placed on *you*. A reminder, as if it was needed, of her low opinion of him—an opinion formed on nothing more than scandalous rumour, but an opinion he would not, indeed could not, contradict. 'Being seen alone with me would be a grave matter indeed,' he added pointedly. 'You have my word that this conversation never took place.'

He saw her cheeks colour slightly at the frankness of his response, and then she gave him another one of her brisk nods before turning away. For a moment he leaned against the doorway, just watching her, his eyes transfixed as hers had been by the sight of him boxing, bare-chested and sweating. Her flustered reaction to him had been intriguing but then, he supposed, he ought not read anything into it. She was an unwed Society lady, after all; she'd likely never seen a man looking like that. But still, the way she'd stared...

'Lady Elspeth,' he called after her, some part of him apparently unwilling to let her go just yet.

She spun around quizzically, then immediately folded her arms as she took several steps back towards him. 'Yes, my lord?'

'Who is your favourite god, or goddess, from the Greek myths?'

She raised her eyebrows, clearly surprised by his question. 'Oh—well, Artemis, I suppose.'

The goddess of the hunt, the wilderness, and virginity—amongst other things. Interesting. 'Now you have me worried, Lady Elspeth,' he said. 'If you are as adept with a bow and arrow as your favoured goddess, then I am in grave trouble indeed.'

'Only if you give me just cause.' Her tone was serious, but he could see the ghost of a smile playing upon her lips.

'Ah—then I fear that I am a condemned man already,' he retorted, meaning to sound teasing, but instead perturbed by the bitter note he heard in his own words.

Judging by how quickly her smile faded, Lady Elspeth had noticed his tone, too. 'What about you, my lord?' she asked. 'Do you have a particular favourite?'

For several moments he regarded her carefully, as though giving his answer considerable thought. In truth, as interesting as he found them and their stories, he was not keen on most of the pantheon—they were too tyrannical, too cruel, and too vengeful for his tastes. However, an answer like that would certainly not do, for it was not the sort of answer Lady Elspeth would expect from the man she believed him to be. After all, a man as purportedly wicked as Lord Barden would surely not condemn Zeus for his many infidelities and repeated betrayals of his wife. Just like the rest of Society, Lady Elspeth believed he was a libertine, and that was what he must always be—to guard the truth and to protect Lucy. His wife might be dead now, but the spilling of her secrets still threatened harm, especially to the person she'd loved more than anyone in the world.

'Dionysus,' he replied in the end, giving her the most mischievous grin he could muster. 'The god of wine and a good time—what more could a man possibly need?'

The look she gave him was disapproving, but thoroughly unsurprised. 'I am sorry I asked,' she said with a sigh, before turning on her heel and marching away from him once more.

This time, Robert resisted the urge to call her back.

Chapter Four

Elspeth sniffed the water in her little cup, wrinkling her nose at the sulphurous odour emanating from it. Around her, Hallowford's pump rooms bustled, the early-morning crowd having gathered to take the waters before breakfast. In one corner a trio of violinists sat, playing a repertoire of cheerful tunes, as though music alone could mask the grim taste of what every patron was currently sipping in the name of good health. Well, almost every patron. For her part, Elspeth had not yet managed even the smallest taste of the water. Frankly, the smell of it alone was enough to turn her stomach, which still remained stubbornly delicate and vulnerable to the slightest provocation, even though that horrid journey was now several days in the past.

'I only ever pretend to drink it,' Lady Melliora whispered, clearly noticing her reticence. 'Mama swears by the waters, says that they cleanse the body, but I cannot abide the taste and I am not convinced of the benefit of taking them at all.'

'You think the water does nothing?'

Lady Melliora shook her head, sending her white-blonde curls into a brief affray. 'I did not say that. Certainly it has an effect, although in my experience, it is not usually a pleasant one.' She made a face and pointed towards her stomach. 'I swore off it for good when I was with child. Frankly, the maladies which accompanied pregnancy were bad enough, without drinking that. Usually I managed to make an excuse not to accompany Mama here—until my confinement, of course. Then excuses were no longer necessary.'

'I recall my mother telling me that your husband passed away while you were with child,' Elspeth replied. 'It must have been a very difficult time.'

Lady Melliora nodded, giving her a pointed look. 'That is one way to describe it, I suppose. The Earl's passing was sudden. He was a good deal older than me, and I was his second wife. His first had borne him a son who inherited the earldom and estate. Let's just say that the new Earl was not well-disposed towards me, and so I wrote to my mother, asking if I could join her in Hallowford. To my enormous relief, she agreed.'

'Thank goodness for your mother,' Elspeth replied, offering her a sympathetic smile and resisting the temptation to air her views on just how poorly the new Earl had apparently conducted himself. 'I am sorry for your loss, and for it to happen at such a time.'

A sorrowful look flickered briefly in Lady Melliora's blue eyes, but she composed herself quickly. 'Thank you,' she replied. 'Oh, look, there is Lord Barden. What a surprise! He never comes here to take the waters. He is far too clever for such folly,' she whispered conspiratorially, her countenance brightening again now.

Elspeth forced a smile as her gaze wandered reluctantly to the imposing figure of the man who was now engaged in conversation with Lady Dunsforth and her mother. A man whose presence once again seemed to fill the room, and who, she was loath to admit, had been given more than a passing thought these past days. She had not seen him since their encounter near the stables, but that had not stopped her seeing that chest of his in all of its taut, defined, and very naked glory every time she closed her eyes. Honestly, she did not know what had got into her, and it was truly infuriating. He was infuriating and impertinent and dissolute and thoroughly wicked and…

Standing right in front of her.

Elspeth blinked as Lord Barden bowed in greeting, giving her one of those wretched charming smiles. 'Lady Melliora, Lady Elspeth—good morning to you both. It is a pleasant day, is it not?'

'It would be all the more pleasant if my mother had

not ordered us to get up with the larks so that we could come here to drink this,' Lady Melliora retorted, holding up her cup. 'I do not know what Lady Elspeth must think, being dragged out at such an ungodly hour.'

Elspeth shrugged. 'Do not worry on my account. I am more of a lark than an owl.'

'Are you, indeed?' Lord Barden was about to tease her again—she could tell by the wicked glint in his eye. 'Then we have that in common, Lady Elspeth, since I also like to rise early and take a little exercise before breakfast.'

The veiled reference to their early-morning encounter made Elspeth's stomach fizz with nervous indignation. So much for behaving as though it had never taken place! The memory of sweating, shirtless Lord Barden hitting that bag with his fists crept unbidden into her mind, and she was sure her cheeks must have been glowing scarlet.

Fortunately, she was not required to answer him, as Lady Melliora interjected first. 'Perhaps we should all learn from your example, my lord, and embrace exercise instead of drinking this pungent water. I was just telling Lady Elspeth how surprised I was to see you here. You never visit the pump rooms.'

'Ah—yes, that is true. Certainly, a drop of that odorous elixir will never pass my lips.' He gave Elspeth a cautious look before addressing Lady Melliora. 'You have warned your guest about the possible consequences of drinking too much of that?'

Lady Melliora grinned at him. 'With as much delicacy as I could manage, my lord.'

Elspeth's gaze flitted between the pair of them as they laughed. There was an easy familiarity between them, of the sort that people shared when they'd known each other for a long time. But then, had Lord Barden not said that they'd been neighbours for years? He would have known Lady Melliora since childhood and certainly would have seen a lot of her these past years, since she took up permanent residence in Hallowford with her mother. Perhaps they had grown close during that time.

So what if they had? It was really none of her business. She was merely a visitor, a guest in the Dunsforth house. The nature of the acquaintance between the wicked Lord Barden and the goddess-like Lady Melliora did not matter a jot to her...

Of course it didn't.

'You should join us for dinner tonight, Lord Barden,' Lady Melliora continued.

'Oh—no, thank you,' he replied, appearing uncharacteristically ruffled by her invitation. 'You have guests already. I could not possibly impose upon your mother's hospitality...'

'Nonsense—it is only dinner, and she will be glad to have you,' Lady Melliora insisted, before glancing regretfully at Elspeth. 'Besides, if the number of cups of water the Dowager Duchess has consumed this morning is anything to go by, I fear we may be one less in number at dinner tonight. I'm afraid that my mother has rather led her astray.'

Elspeth looked over at her mother and inwardly groaned. Another unwanted encounter with Lord Barden was on the horizon, and worse still, if Lady Melliora's prediction proved to be correct, she would have to endure it without the reassurance of her mother's company. Wonderful. An evening spent gritting her teeth while Lord Barden made sport of his impertinence, without so much as the watchful eye of her mother to dissuade him. What could possibly go wrong?

Robert nodded obligingly at Evans, the Dunsforths' butler, as the man asked him to wait for a moment in the hall. He felt on edge tonight, although he was struggling to understand why. He must have had dinner with the Dunsforths hundreds of times over the years, and yet somehow this evening felt different. It was probably because they had guests; guests who would expect him to behave like a guest, too, and not a member of the family. Not a man who'd been bound to them by blood and secrets.

More than likely, his discomfort was also due to his awareness that by accepting Melliora's invitation, he was transgressing his agreement with Lady Dunsforth again. These past few days, he'd managed to keep his side of the bargain and had stayed away. In truth, he had been relieved to do so; after that early-morning encounter with Lady Elspeth, he'd been feeling decidedly off-kilter. Everything about it had been unsettling, and not only because she'd seen him half-naked. Indeed, he feared that was the least of his worries. Far more haunting were her words to him, so many of which had been either shrewd, direct, or cutting. And as for those looks she'd given him—mostly indignant, often downright disapproving, and on one occasion, utterly furious…

And yet, despite all that, he'd called her back. He'd asked her more questions. He hadn't wanted their conversation to end. It was blatantly obvious that the lady despised him, but still he wanted to see her, to talk to her. To tease her, to cross swords with her. If he was honest with himself, that temptation had drawn him into the pump rooms today, hadn't it? He'd spied her through the window, clutching her cup of water, and the prospect of a few brief words with Lady Elspeth had immediately diverted him from his business in town.

Well, more fool him, because those very few, very brief words had earned him far more time in her company than he'd anticipated. Thanks to Melliora's invitation, he would now spend the evening being lavished with Lady Elspeth's contempt. He suppressed the urge to sigh out loud. Really, what had Melliora been thinking, given he was meant to be making himself scarce? Then again, he knew her well enough to know that the lady who'd won his younger brother's heart was as impulsive as she was warm and caring. Rafe had been the same—kind and soft-hearted, but with a thoroughly reckless streak. It was this impulsiveness which had proven dangerous when combined with their deep and abiding love for each other, leading them to conduct the affair which had ultimately resulted in Tilly.

If life had been fair and aristocratic marriages made on the grounds of love rather than titles and money, then Rafe and Melliora would have wed long ago. It would perhaps not have prevented Rafe's untimely death, but at least they would have been happy. But then, if life was fair, he and Lucy would not have found themselves trapped together in matrimony, either.

'Oh—you are here already, I see.'

The sound of Lady Elspeth's customary disapproval caused Robert to turn around. She was standing at the foot of the stairs, looking utterly breathtaking in another purple gown, its sleeves short and full, and its neckline sweeping temptingly across her décolletage. She might detest him, but damn it all, she was so very beautiful. He bowed in greeting, taking the opportunity to drink in the sight of her once more before instructing himself to exercise some restraint. He would not give the slightest hint of his attraction to her, of the effect she had upon him. He would not be irked by her dislike of him, either. Tonight, he decided, he would resist the temptation to rile her, to engage her in battle. Instead, he would be pleasant, polite, and completely disarming. He would pour water on the fire which thus far had raged between them, in the hope that he might extinguish the futile longings she'd stirred in him, too.

'Good evening, Lady Elspeth,' he said. 'You are looking very well.'

She frowned slightly, as though unsure whether to accept the compliment. 'Regrettably the same cannot be said for my mother. She is indisposed, I'm afraid, and will not be joining us for dinner.'

'I am sorry to hear it,' Robert replied. 'Hallowford's waters work their wonders yet again, I fear.'

Lady Elspeth gave him one of her withering looks. 'Something like that. Anyway, I am sure Lady Dunsforth and Lady Melliora will be here presently, although I think Tilly is giving her mother some trouble tonight.'

'Oh?' Robert stepped forward, gripping the carved wooden banister to prevent himself from darting upstairs to assist. 'I am sorry to hear that. Is the child unwell?'

To his relief, Lady Elspeth shook her head. 'I believe

it is rebellion rather than illness which disturbs the peace in the nursery this evening. Little Tilly seems to think that she should be permitted to join the adults rather than go to bed,' she added with a wry smile.

Before Robert could say anything further, the sound of quick little footsteps on the floor above them intruded, followed by the exasperated voices of Melliora and the nursemaid as they called out to the child, instructing her to return to the nursery. Instructions which were not heeded, since moments later the girl appeared on the stairs above them, wearing an enormous grin on her face.

'Robert!' she called out, breezing past Lady Elspeth as she raced towards him. 'Where you been?'

He chuckled as the tiny girl launched herself into his arms. 'Next door, Tilly, where I usually am.'

Tilly pouted at him. 'You've not come here for aaaages,' she said dramatically. 'I counted more numbers. Up to five-and-twenty now.'

'That is excellent, Tilly.' He glanced up the stairs, just in time to see Melliora appear. 'However, I think you have made your mama cross. You must do as she says and go to bed now.'

Reluctantly, the girl nodded. 'Will you come soon for more counting?' she asked, giving him a hopeful look.

'As soon as I can.' He smiled indulgently as he put

her down and ushered her back towards her mother. 'Now, be a good girl for your mama and your nurse.'

Apparently satisfied with his answer, Tilly wandered back up the steps, albeit more slowly than she had come down them. The girl might look like her mother, but when it came to that wild and wilful streak she possessed, she was undoubtedly Rafe's child. Remembering that he was meant to be behaving like a guest, Robert forced himself to stand stiffly, straightening his face and offering Melliora a curt nod as the child returned to her charge. Although, as he glanced at Lady Elspeth and read the quizzical expression on her face, he feared it was already too late for that. She'd witnessed the little girl's informality with him, and from her chatter had doubtless surmised that he was a frequent and familiar presence in the house—one who taught the girl her numbers, no less. Thanks to Tilly, that particular Pandora's box had creaked open, no matter how determined Lady Dunsforth had been to keep it shut.

'Forgive me, both of you, but I will need to settle this little one,' Melliora said, gathering Tilly into her arms and giving her an exasperated look. 'And Mother is late—as usual. Please, do have a seat in the parlour. I will ask Evans to attend to you right away.'

He saw Lady Elspeth's lips part, as though poised to object, before she pressed them together, apparently thinking better of it as she descended the remaining few steps to join him. Determined once more to honour his unspoken pledge to cease warring with her, Robert held out his arm, offering her a smile as she took it and trying to ignore how yet again every nerve in that particular limb seemed suddenly to be aflame. Trying to ignore the way her lavender perfume wafted seductively around him as they walked towards the parlour, or the way her hip occasionally brushed against him, giving him ideas he absolutely ought not entertain.

The sort of ideas which no doubt Lady Elspeth would fully expect from a man with his reputation, he thought glumly. Ideas which were ultimately futile and which, if she ever caught wind of them, would certainly make Lady Elspeth despise him even more.

Chapter Five

Elspeth sipped her wine, letting the silence hang between her and Lord Barden as they sat opposite each other in the cosy parlour. At first she'd been inclined to request some tea, but Evans's offer of a pleasant glass of hock while they waited had proved too tempting, and she had accepted. She'd reasoned that it might help to calm the nerves which were currently fizzing horribly in her stomach, and had been ever since she'd wandered down the stairs to find Lord Barden standing there, looking far too divine for comfort in his dark evening attire. Nerves which had not been helped by Lady Melliora's insistence that they wait in the parlour—together! At least a maid had been dispatched to sit discreetly in the corner and to act as a chaperone of sorts. In spite of the ongoing chaos upstairs, someone had clearly remembered the need for propriety, to not leave Elspeth alone with a gentleman—especially one such as Lord Barden.

A wicked man. A dangerous man. A man who, try

as she might, she seemed entirely unable to tear her eyes from.

What was wrong with her? Had she taken complete leave of her senses?

'This wine is very nice,' Lord Barden remarked, apparently determined at last to make conversation.

Elspeth inclined her head in acknowledgement. It had not escaped her notice that so far, he'd behaved differently towards her tonight. More restrained and polite, and certainly less irksome. She hardly knew what to make of it, much less how to respond. Nor did she know what to make of the interaction she'd witnessed earlier between Lord Barden and Tilly. The way the child had embraced him and spoken to him so familiarly. The fact that she'd referred to him by his Christian name. Robert. A name which suited him and made him seem far less like the rotten apple that she knew him to be.

'Lady Dunsforth's taste is impeccable,' he continued after a moment, examining his glass. 'The selections which appear from her cellar never fail to impress.'

'I daresay your own cellar is not neglected, my lord,' she replied. Apparently her mouth had now decided how it was going to respond to him—tartly.

She expected some clever retort, but instead he merely shrugged. 'There is only me and my servants in my home, and I seldom entertain. What I have is sufficient, but I have no need of a vast bottle collection.'

She arched an eyebrow at him, somewhat surprised by this revelation. 'Dionysus would be disappointed to learn that, I am sure. Since by your own admission, you are such a devotee of his.'

'Ah.'

Those deep green eyes of his levelled their gaze at her, filled with understanding but not, she was surprised to note, with amusement. That was different, too. Until now, whenever they'd sparred, she'd sensed he was enjoying himself, but there was no hint of relish from him tonight. She wondered then if he'd simply wearied of teasing her, or if there was something else troubling him.

'Ah?' she asked.

He gave her a tight smile. 'I can see I am going to be dodging your arrows again all evening, Lady Elspeth. Or, should I say, Artemis?'

It was a half-hearted attempt at teasing her, and Elspeth could not fail to notice how raw it sounded. She watched Lord Barden closely, trying now to detect whether something was indeed amiss. His countenance, however, remained difficult to read, and in the end, she concluded that she would be wise to err on the side of caution. She might have a sharp tongue, but she intended no harm or malice towards anyone. No matter what she thought of the man, she would not compound whatever was bothering him. If he could be polite and pleasant company, then so could she.

She could suspend hostilities between them, if only for one evening.

'No, indeed, I have put my bow and arrow away,' she replied smoothly. 'Since I doubt Tilly would ever forgive me, if I wounded you. That little girl clearly thinks highly of you,' she added.

Lord Barden chuckled at that. 'I think what Tilly thinks most highly of is delaying her bedtime. I was merely a convenient means to that end.'

Elspeth gave him a pointed look. 'A convenient means who teaches her to count and permits her to call him Robert.'

'I live next door. I've known the child all of her life. She likes to count with anyone who will indulge her.' He gave a shrug, draining his glass now. 'And she's barely five years old—I think a little informality is permissible at such a young age.'

Elspeth nodded slowly, unconvinced by his protest. It was clear from observing Lord Barden with Tilly earlier that he had an affectionate regard for the child—an observation which, though she was loath to admit it, went very much in his favour. It was difficult to square the man she'd glimpsed tonight, a man who'd behaved so kindly and gently towards that girl, with the man who was reputed to be so wicked and callous, he'd exiled his wife to the wilderness and left her there to perish.

And yet, he'd done exactly that, hadn't he? All of

Society knew that, and she would do well to remember it. Being polite and making conversation was one thing, but revising her opinion of him simply because he was nice to Tilly was another. Besides, anyone could feign niceties, she reminded herself. She was certain that even the devil himself had the capacity to be charming, otherwise how would he tempt mankind to fall from grace? Clearly Lord Barden had worked his charms on the Dunsforths to great effect, if Lady Dunsforth's opinion that he was merely misunderstood was anything to go by. Well, Elspeth would not be similarly deceived. Hell itself would freeze over before that happened.

'Have you read anything diverting of late, Lady Elspeth?' Lord Barden asked, changing the subject now.

She shook her head. 'No, in truth I have read little since arriving in Hallowford. My days are so full that I do not seem to find the time.' That was true enough. These first few days with the Dunsforths had been such a whirlwind of social activity that most nights, Elspeth had gone to bed with her head spinning.

'And that bothers you?'

His astuteness made her bristle, and yet again she sensed he was reading her. 'As a guest, it would be ungracious for me to say that. I would merely observe that my routine is very different to the one I kept at home. Here I enjoy outings, tea, dinners, conversation, whereas at home I confess that I liked nothing better than the quiet of our library and the shelves filled with good books.'

'Then I hope that your mother finds a dower house which contains both.' A smile hinted on his lips. 'In the meantime, you are welcome to use my library. It is very peaceful, and I think you will find plenty to read which is to your liking. I have collected a good number of works on mythology which I think would be of interest to you.'

His offer surprised and unsettled her. 'Oh—no, my lord, thank you, but I could not possibly impose...'

'It is no imposition. Bring your maid, of course,' he continued. 'Despite what you might think of me, Lady Elspeth, I am not suggesting anything improper.'

The way his emerald eyes seemed to blaze as he said that discomfited her even further. But then, she supposed, she hadn't had any success in hiding her opinion of him, no matter how often she swore to herself that she would seem indifferent. He'd proven far too bothersome for that—until tonight, at least. Tonight he'd made his disinterest in provocation clear and had been the epitome of gentlemanly sincerity instead. She considered his offer more seriously then. The lure of a good library was one which had always been irresistible to her, and she was as desperate for some new reading material to engage her as she was for a little peace and quiet. Surely there was no harm in accepting, as long as she was chaperoned...

'In that case, my lord, I will gratefully accept,' she said in the end.

He nodded briskly. 'Very good. Tomorrow, after luncheon?'

'As long as my mother is feeling better and can spare Temperance to accompany me, then yes.'

Just as they reached their agreement, Lady Dunsforth and Lady Melliora breezed in, immediately lacing the air with a multitude of apologies for their tardiness. Lord Barden rose to greet them both, effortlessly playing the charming gentleman as he repeated his earlier favourable comments about the contents of the Dunsforth cellar. Elspeth busied herself with finishing her wine, trying and failing to instruct her wayward eyes not to roam approvingly over the man. She needed to give herself a stern talking-to, because having her head turned by a man like Lord Barden was not like her at all. Usually she was more than capable of noting that a man's good looks, indeed of appreciating them, without letting that awareness seep under her skin and affect her the way he clearly did.

This evening, Lord Barden had been disarmingly pleasant company, and she'd been at serious risk of softening her view of him on more than one occasion. That would not do at all. Nor would it do to allow herself to enjoy looking at him quite as much as she evidently did. She was a committed spinster, and he was a rogue. She would do well to remember that and to keep her eyes fixed firmly on his bookcases when she perused the contents of his library tomorrow.

Robert huffed an irritated sigh as he adjusted his cravat, his restlessness growing with each passing minute. Lady Elspeth would be here soon, in his home and in his library, and God only knew how he'd allowed that to happen. One moment he'd been making polite conversation, eschewing the deliberate provocation he'd hitherto indulged in. He'd resisted the urge to vex her, even when those arrows of hers took their aim. Even when he remembered, with a sinking heart, that it would never matter how pleasant he was towards her, because in her eyes, he was already condemned. The next moment, however, she'd seemed to relent, dropping her shield to match his and talking to him sincerely—about Tilly, yes, but he felt he'd managed those awkward questions well enough.

Then, in amongst those tricky enquiries, she'd said his name—in that factual, direct way of hers, of course, but his name nonetheless.

Robert.

Looking back on it, he suspected that had been his undoing. He was not able to put his finger on any other reason why he might have lost his mind and invited her to his home. Certainly, hearing her refer to him as Robert, however indirectly, had haunted his dreams last night. Hot, fevered dreams in which Lady

Elspeth was not only in his home but in his bed, the deep brown curls of her hair cascading over his pillow and those dark eyes of hers imploring him as she cried out his name over and over. Dreams which he had absolutely no business having about a woman who had nothing but contempt for him. A woman whose low opinion of him was impossible to change, because to do so would involve betraying his secrets, and that was something he could never do.

He sighed again, meeting his own eye disapprovingly in the mirror. He was two-and-thirty, for goodness sake. He knew better than to fall prey to desire, or to let a woman inhabit his dreams. He'd been unhappily married, unhappily separated, then unhappily widowed in turn, and all of it had cost him a great deal. All of it meant that he could never contemplate developing tender feelings for a woman, because to do so would be futile when no woman would ever return them. In the eyes of Society he was tainted and irredeemable, the sort of gentleman who might enjoy a fleeting liaison with a woman from time to time, but who could never have anything more.

Moreover, he told himself, he did not want anything more. His marriage to Lucy had not been his choice, but he'd dutifully abided by his father's wishes. Not that he could have done anything else, since attempting to disobey his cruel and callous sire was always as futile as it was costly. So he'd committed himself to the marriage, convincing himself that in time, he might grow to love his bride. But Lucy had not wanted his love, because she'd already had that of someone else—someone who she loved so deeply that she could not bear their separation. He'd freed her from their union, and her despair, but the wounds his marriage had inflicted upon him had cut deep. The scars had faded with time, but nonetheless he was resolute that it was best to remain alone. Even if a woman did ever desire him for her husband, he could hardly condemn her to a life in which she'd be tainted by him and by his reputation. That detestable reputation would trap her just as it had imprisoned him, because he could not contradict it—not without spilling to the world the secrets of what had really happened during his travesty of a marriage, and this he would never do.

Robert stiffened his posture, giving himself a mental shake. His attraction to Lady Elspeth was merely a reminder that his resolve wavered from time to time, and nothing more. Clearly, he had an itch he needed to scratch, so to speak, but he was out of his mind if he thought he could do so with a Society lady like her, and a duke's daughter, no less! A casual liaison, however, might be sufficient to satisfy his appetite and get Lady Elspeth out of his head and out of his dreams, for good. After all, it had been some time since he'd had one of those…

'Your guest is here, my lord. I have shown her into the library, as you instructed.'

His butler, Chadwick, made the announcement with the same raised brow that the man had worn since Robert had informed him of Lady Elspeth's visit last night. An expression which betrayed the man's surprise and curiosity—apart from occasionally inviting the Dunsforths to dine with him, Robert never received visitors, and certainly not female ones. Doubtless his faithful servant was wondering about his master's motivations now, too.

Wonderful.

Robert hurried down the stairs and into the library, to find his guest already casting a scrutinising eye over his crammed shelves, filled from floor to ceiling with books. Many of his favoured volumes had been brought long ago from the Barden estate to Hallowford, meaning that the modest townhouse library contained far more books than it was ever designed for. Better that, though, than leaving them to rot in the draughty, coastal country seat he'd grown up in; one which he'd left locked up and in the care of his steward ever since he and Lucy parted ways. That house contained far too many memories—most of which he was keen to forget.

'I do not even know where to begin, my lord,' Lady Elspeth said, dispensing with the usual formal greetings as she turned around to face him. As usual, her choice of dress was striking, a deep blue which complimented her dark hair and brown eyes. And as usual, the sight of her left him feeling rather breathless.

He nodded dumbly, his eyes shifting briefly to the maid, who'd seated herself dutifully in a corner, her sewing strewn across her lap as she watched his every move. 'There is rather a lot of choice, I suppose,' he began, 'which is why I was confident you would find something…'

'No.' Lady Elspeth shook her head, sending her near-black curls into a frenzy. 'I mean, quite literally, I do not know where to begin. You do not have any sort of organisation on these shelves, my lord. No system, no categorisation, no alphabetisation.' She planted her hands on her hips and regarded him severely. 'What you have is chaos.'

Despite himself, he smiled. She was right, of course—half the time, he did not know where anything was, but he was not about to concede the point. 'I daresay that of all the ways in which I offend you, Lady Elspeth, this is the most grave.'

'This is no laughing matter, my lord,' she huffed. 'Libraries must have order, otherwise they are not serving the scholar as they might.'

He quirked an eyebrow at her. 'The scholar?'

She bristled, as though realising that she'd said something revealing. 'The reader, then. Or indeed, anyone who wishes to find anything without spending a full day searching for it.'

'All right—well, perhaps if you tell me what sort of book you are looking for, we might search for something suitable together?' he ventured.

If the wrinkle in that button nose of hers was any indication, however, this suggestion did not please her. 'I will not know what I am looking for until I find it, my lord. That is part of the pleasure—perusing a well-ordered shelf, allowing the books to tempt me with their subject matter...'

Robert cleared his throat, which felt suddenly constricted at the sound of Lady Elspeth's talk of pleasure and temptation. Words which she'd used in such a prim and scholarly manner, but which sent his thoughts in an entirely inappropriate direction nonetheless.

'I suppose I could try to bring this place to some sort of order,' he said, looking around somewhat helplessly.

'I will assist you.'

Her offer took him aback. If, indeed, it could be called an offer, because it sounded far more insistent than that. He blinked at her. 'You will?'

'Yes, of course,' she replied crisply. 'If there is one thing I know intimately, it is the library. And besides, I do enjoy a good project.'

'You do?' he asked, his mouth growing dry as he tried and failed not to think about what else he'd imagined her knowing intimately, during his sleeping hours.

Another flinch, as though once again she'd said more than she'd intended to say to him. 'Yes, I do.'

She marched purposefully back towards his bookcases, her skirts swishing as she walked the length of them. She paused in front of the one situated at the far side of the room, and although she had her back to him, he could sense that critical eye of hers was hard at work, making a study of the contents. Then, after a moment, she began to carefully remove the books, making neat piles on the floor.

'What are you doing?' he asked, glancing again at the maid, who seemed entirely unmoved by what was unfolding as she occupied herself with her sewing.

Lady Elspeth turned around and gave him a withering look. 'I am making a start, my lord,' she replied, determination lingering in her dark stare. 'Someone needs to sort out this mess, and there is no time like the present, after all.'

Chapter Six

Elspeth sat down on the floor of Lord Barden's library, swiping away the curls which had stuck to her forehead with a weary sigh before glancing over to the window. The day outside was sunny and bright, and for a moment she regretted her decision not to join her mother and the Dunsforths on their afternoon promenade. However, there was still much work to be done here, and in truth, Elspeth was relishing the peace and quiet far too much to tear herself away from it. And so, when the appointed hour had arrived at which her mother's maid needed to return next door to help the Dowager Duchess get ready for her walk, Elspeth had declined to return with her—much to Temperance's horror.

'Your mother instructed me not to let you out of my sight,' the maid had insisted. 'She said that you must not be left alone with Lord Barden for even a moment.'

'A moment alone with Lord Barden would prove difficult, since he is not at home at present,' Elspeth had countered. 'He has gone to town and expects to be away for some time. I am in no danger, Temperance. Please inform my mother that Lord Barden is currently out and assure her that, if he returns, I will ask one of his maids to sit with me.'

In the end, Temperance had reluctantly relinquished her role as guardian of Elspeth's virtue and left. Elspeth had no doubt that she'd be on the receiving end of one of her mother's lectures later. The Dowager Duchess had already made it abundantly clear that she disapproved of Elspeth's visits to the home of the wickedest man in England. Nor did she understand, even when Elspeth had explained that his library was in such a state of disorder that it had not even been possible to find a suitable book to borrow.

'You are missing my point, dearest,' she'd said. 'This is not about books—this is about that man's reputation. Visiting once to borrow a book was one thing, but visiting him frequently is another matter entirely. Quite apart from the dubious matter of his honour, there is the risk that people will talk.'

'My visits will be chaperoned, Mama, so my virtue will be quite safe,' she'd insisted. 'And no one is likely to notice, since I will only be visiting over a matter of days, so I daresay the risk to my reputation is negligible, too.'

She'd resisted the temptation to remind her parent that she was not a naïve debutante, but a mature spinster of six-and-twenty. She was quite capable of repelling any unwanted advances from Lord Barden. Not that he had made any—indeed, during the hours he'd spent working with her, he'd been nothing but courteous and gentlemanly towards her, accepting her instructions without complaint or even the merest hint of teasing as he undertook most of the physical work. If anything, over these past few days she'd been the one who'd frequently fallen prey to inappropriate ideas, enjoying the sight of him with his rolled-up sleeves and loosened cravat a little too much. More than once, she'd caught herself considering whether she preferred the unbuttoned Lord Barden in the library or the half-dressed one, shirtless and boxing in an outhouse.

Each time she'd given herself a mental shake, reminding herself that it was the lure of a library and the love of a good project which had brought her here, and not any temptation offered by Lord Barden. Predictably, she had found the execution of her project invigorating, relishing the renewed sense of purpose it had given her. One by one, she was bringing Lord Barden's bookcases to order, categorising his books by subject matter, then ensuring each section was arranged in alphabetical order by the surname of the author. She hauled herself off the floor, determined to finish one more bookcase before returning next door.

Given her mother's concerns, she knew that it would be sensible to leave before Lord Barden came home.

'The problem is, my lord, I think you have more books than you have the space for,' she muttered to herself as she stared down at the remaining piles. 'No wonder your library was in such a mess.'

She picked up the book which topped the latest pile she'd decided to tackle, her heart leaping as she opened it to see that these were the ones they'd loosely categorised as mythologies when first emptying the shelves. She smoothed her fingers gently over the title page, struggling to resist the temptation to sit down and peruse its contents. There was much to be done, but still—a moment's curiosity could not hurt...

'*Northern Antiquities*,' she read aloud. '*A Description of the Manners, Customs, Religion and Laws of the Ancient Danes...*'

'It is a book of Norse mythology.' The deep timbre of Lord Barden's voice made Elspeth startle, and she spun around to see him standing in the doorway. 'My apologies—I have been gone far longer than I expected. There were some matters I had to attend to.'

'It is fine,' she said, waving away his apology. 'I was quite content by myself.'

'I can see that. You really do relish a project, don't you?'

Elspeth shrugged. 'I like to keep myself busy, that's all.'

'Is this the sort of project you undertook at home—reorganising the library?'

Elspeth felt her eyes narrow briefly at Lord Barden as she tried to determine what lay behind his question. 'No, not really. I had other interests to occupy me.'

He quirked an eyebrow, and she could see immediately that he was not going to let this matter go. 'Such as?'

'Such as the School of Industry I'd helped to establish for the education of local girls. My mother and I were its patrons,' she replied, clutching the book she held ever tighter, as though it was a shield. 'I was not a teacher, but I spent a good deal of time there. It was important to me, I suppose, to oversee what the girls were learning...' She pressed her lips together, resolving to say nothing further. She was hardly going to tell Lord Barden just how passionate she'd been about advancing the girls' education beyond basic reading and domestic skills. About just how much she'd wanted to make scholars of them all. Instead, she watched his expression closely, trying to discern his response to what she had said. His countenance, however, remained frustratingly impassive as he leaned against the doorframe.

'I imagine you enjoyed that,' he mused. 'I imagine you miss it, too.'

Elspeth felt her breath catch at the astuteness of that remark as Lord Barden finally sauntered into the room, casting his eye around as though he was subtly trying to assess her progress. When his gaze reached the now-vacant chair where Temperance had been sitting earlier, she saw him frown. 'Where is your maid?' he asked.

'Next door. She had to attend to my mother.'

'Then I'd better ask one of my maids to chaperone you, rather than risk your mother's wrath.'

His evident concern for propriety was unexpected, and Elspeth found herself both moved and confused by it. It was hardly the sort of behaviour a woman would expect from a man who was reputed to be one of the most rotten and wicked in the kingdom. Again, much like his endearing behaviour towards Tilly, she could not square it with what she knew of him.

'Do as you see fit, my lord,' she replied. 'However, I do recall that when you first invited me to visit your library, you did insist that you were not suggesting anything improper.'

He raised his eyebrows, the ghost of an amused smile playing on his lips. 'Are you taking me at my word, Lady Elspeth?'

She shrugged. 'You've given me no reason to doubt it—so far. Besides, I can always fetch my trusty bow and some arrows, should you start to give me any trouble.'

'Consider me warned,' he replied, chuckling. 'Sorting books in peace with Lady Elspeth seems infinitely preferable to waiting for Artemis to take her aim—especially since she never seems to miss,' he added, giving her a pointed look.

A teasing note had crept into their exchange, but nonetheless there was a sharp edge to Lord Barden's words which told her that all her barbed quips and disapproving looks had had an effect. She caught herself feeling momentarily remorseful, before reminding herself that Lord Barden had always more than matched her whenever they'd crossed swords. Although, thinking about it now, such sparring between them had been mostly absent in recent days. Instead, as Lord Barden had observed, they had worked peacefully together, and Elspeth was forced to acknowledge that she had begun to grow comfortable in his company. So much so, in fact, that often she found herself forgetting what she knew about him and about the sort of man he was. That was probably why she had not immediately insisted upon him fetching a new chaperone, when really, she should.

'Have you read this, my lord?' she asked, holding up the book.

He nodded, walking closer to her now. 'Not recently, but yes.'

'And would you recommend it?'

'I would, and you are very welcome to borrow it.' He paused, and she saw a small frown hinting upon his brow. 'Although, if my memory serves me, I believe that one section of the book is in Latin, so perhaps it is not...'

His observation, and all that it implied, made Elspeth's temper flare. 'It may come as a shock to you, Lord Barden,' she interrupted sardonically, pushing the book into his hands, 'but some ladies do have a working knowledge of the language.'

She detected the slightest hardening of his jaw as he regarded her. 'I am aware of that,' he replied, his voice clipped. 'But those ladies are exceptions, not the rule, as I am sure you must know. All I meant was...'

'Oh, I know exactly what you meant!'

Unthinkingly she stepped closer to him, placing her hands upon her hips as she surrendered entirely to her ire. To the thought that the man standing before her was just like so many others she'd encountered over the years, believing that a woman's education should amount to little more than the training required to manage a household. That, for a female, knowledge of classical languages was not only unnecessary, it was utterly beyond the pale. Of course a man like Lord Barden believed that! A man who had such a propensity for wickedness. A man who'd cast his wife aside as though she was nothing...

'I'm sure you must find their rule-breaking deeply offensive,' she continued. 'I'm sure you must think such ladies are the most odious creatures in all of Society!'

* * *

Robert gazed down at the fierce, dark-haired beauty standing in front of him, trying his damnedest not to allow his temper to match hers. Her hot words had offended him, but worse than that, he felt more than a little devastated by them, too. These past days, working together in the library, their short acquaintance seemed to have found some sort of equilibrium, even if he had to concede that it had been the constant presence of Lady Elspeth's watchful maid which had forced him to mind his tongue, and his wayward gaze. Moreover, the truce they'd both appeared to quietly declare in Lady Dunsforth's parlour had seemed tantalisingly close to becoming a permanent peace. But it was clear now that he'd been fooling himself—all it had taken was a few ill-chosen words on his part for warfare to resume. This was how it would always be, he told himself. Lady Elspeth would always think the worst of him no matter what he did, because his reputation preceded him and that reputation had to remain unchallenged. Her presumptions about his views on female education, however, did not.

'I know you do not wish to give me any credit, Lady Elspeth, but even so I must protest. I am not a man who objects to the education of women. Nor am I surprised in the slightest that you have a knowledge of Latin. In fact, I would not be at all astonished if you were to tell me that you taught yourself to read it.'

She blinked at him. 'But you just said...'

'I did not say anything. Before you interrupted me, I'd been about to say that I did not know whether or not you had any knowledge of Latin—that was all.'

She quirked an eyebrow at him, apparently unconvinced. 'That was all?' she repeated.

'Yes.' He sighed heavily. 'And I was going to suggest that if you had not received any schooling in Latin, I would check to see if I had an English translation of that part of the book.'

Those hands of hers dropped from their position on her delectable hips, and he sensed she was beginning to relent. 'I see. Well, that won't be necessary but it is...would have been...very generous of you.'

He gave her a curt nod, aware suddenly of the scant distance between them and of the air, so thick with tension. Of the darkest depths of her eyes as she continued to regard him and of the pink colour of the lips on that tart mouth, the one which uttered words so capable of wounding him, and yet at the same time looked so tempting and kissable...

Robert turned away and walked over to the window, staring vacantly at the street outside as he sought to dampen his desire. Kiss her, indeed! As if he would dare! Such an act would only make her hate him even more, since it would prove to her that he was exactly the sort of wicked libertine she believed him to be. He might not be able to refute his reputation, but he would not seek to confirm it, either. Better to let it hang between them, unaddressed and unresolved, just as it was with the rest of polite Society.

'I am sorry, Lord Barden,' Lady Elspeth said after a long moment. Her tone was contrite, and Robert realised she'd interpreted his withdrawal from her as an indication of his displeasure.

For a moment Robert pressed his eyes shut, composing himself. There was something he needed to say, he realised. Something which did need to be addressed, if he was going to survive these weeks of Lady Elspeth living next door with his wits intact.

He opened his eyes and turned around. 'You do not have to like me, Lady Elspeth,' he began. 'Indeed, you do not have to think anything of me. But the fact is that for the foreseeable future, we are neighbours, and due to our mutual acquaintances, we are going to encounter each other. Therefore, I think it would be best if we tried not to rile each other quite so much and simply endeavoured to get along instead. Wouldn't you agree?'

She nodded, attempting a half-smile. 'I daresay you are right.'

'Well, there is a first for everything, I suppose,' he said drily. He walked towards her again, holding the book out to her. 'A peace offering, of sorts. I hope you manage to find some quiet moments in which to enjoy it.'

Their fingers brushed momentarily as Lady Elspeth accepted the book from him, and Robert tried not to notice how his skin seemed to burn at her touch. His attraction to her was potent, and it really had to stop. Perhaps now was the time to pursue that fleeting notion he'd had, days ago, of indulging in a casual liaison. Surely there was no better way to stop himself dreaming of nights of passion with Lady Elspeth than to indulge in such a night with someone else…

'Thank you, my lord—as do I,' she said soberly. She ran a careful hand over the book's fine leather cover. 'And I look forward to learning about the Norse myths, since I know little of them.'

He smiled at that. 'I would know little of them either, were it not for my brother. That was his book.'

'Was?'

Robert nodded, a lump growing in his throat as he wondered what on earth had prompted him to mention Rafe to her. He thought about his brother every day, but he seldom spoke about him—not even to Melliora. He told himself that it was part of his duty to guard the Great Secret, but in truth, it was easier that way. Easier not to dwell on how his brother's passing had left him entirely alone and cut adrift in the world.

'Yes—he died, five years ago.'

'I'm sorry, my lord,' she replied, her voice almost a whisper.

'Thank you. He, uh…he was a scholar, rather like

yourself. He had a talent for languages, always loved to work on a translation. That was why I thought that I might have an English translation for the Latin portion of that book, tucked away with all of his papers.' He smiled sadly. 'It would have been just like Rafe to have done that.'

Lady Elspeth reached out, touching him gently on the arm. It was a sympathetic gesture, but he felt it everywhere. 'You speak very fondly of him, my lord. You must have loved him a great deal. I know how that feels, I… I lost my eldest brother, Perry, in an accident. He was not always a good brother, nor did he conduct himself well at all, but he was my brother and I loved him, nonetheless.'

Unthinkingly, Robert placed his hand over hers. 'It seems we have found common ground at last, Lady Elspeth, even if it must be in our grief for brothers lost.'

She smiled wryly, and it did not escape his notice that she made no attempt to remove her hand from beneath his. 'What about the interest we share in the Greek gods and goddesses? Surely that must count, too?'

He nodded, welcoming the lighter note she had introduced to the conversation. He'd already said far more than he'd ever intended to say to her, and at that moment he was not sure whether he could trust himself not to say a great deal more, if invited. The tension in the air, the empathy in her dark gaze, the feeling of her ungloved hand under his—all of it threatened to undo him entirely, if he allowed it.

He would not allow it. He could not allow it.

'I should go,' she breathed, retreating from him now. 'My mother will have an apoplexy if she returns from her walk to find that I am not next door. I will have to tell her that I was chaperoned by one of your maids, if she asks. Would you mind if...?'

He gave her a tight smile. 'You were chaperoned throughout your time here, Lady Elspeth. You have my word.'

'Thank you.' She rolled her eyes. 'I do wonder how much older I must be before I can own the title of an old maid in earnest and the freedom which comes with it. I envy gentlemen, coming and going as you please.'

'You intend never to marry?' The question fell from his lips before he could prevent it.

She shook her head. 'I learned some years ago that marriage was not for me, my lord, and at six-and-twenty, I daresay that ship has sailed in any case.'

He wanted to ask why she felt that way, but something caused him to hesitate. Something which cautioned him against discussing the subject of marriage, lest he lose his mind completely and begin to discuss his own. 'Six-and-twenty is far too young an age to be considered an old maid, I'm afraid,' he said instead.

She inclined her head politely at the compliment. 'In that case, interminable chaperoning it is,' she said.

She clasped her hands together, her attention shifting to the remaining piles of books on the floor. 'Will I return to continue our work tomorrow? Chaperone permitting, of course.'

Robert felt himself hesitate. Should she return tomorrow? After today, after their proximity, after their frank exchanges—heated one moment and heartfelt the next—could he bear it? Could he trust himself not to surrender his sanity completely and begin to tell her things about himself, and his past, which ought never to be discussed?

'No,' he answered, his heart lurching as she furrowed her brow in confusion. 'I uh… I have matters I must attend to over the next few days, and besides, given your mother's obvious concerns, I think it would be wise for us to call a halt to the project, for now.'

She crossed her arms defensively, still frowning. 'I see,' she said, in a tone which let him know that she did not see at all.

'Good. The books can wait. Perhaps we can resume our work at another time.'

'As you wish, my lord.' Her clipped words stung him. She offered him the briefest, least sincere curtsy he'd ever seen, then marched towards the door. 'I shall see myself out.'

Those final words to him were cast over her shoulder, with no last look to accompany them, and when he heard his front door slam a few moments later, he was left in no doubt as to the depths of her displeasure. So much for simply getting along with Lady Elspeth. So much for peace—there could never be any such thing between them. If sparring with her had made the air between them fizzle, then speaking to her candidly had all but set it on fire. It was clear now that he could not trust himself around her, and that certainly, he could not have her in his home, alone with him in his library, ever again. Lady Elspeth was altogether too tempting—to kiss, yes, but more dangerously, to talk to. He had to keep his distance. There was far too much at stake, if he did not.

Chapter Seven

'Please try to look as though you are enjoying yourself, dearest. No gentleman is going to ask you to dance while you're wearing an expression like that.'

Elspeth resisted the temptation to roll her eyes at her mother's gentle rebuke, instead forcing a smile as she surveyed the candlelit Assembly Rooms from the peripheral position she'd occupied ever since they'd arrived some time ago. These days, she never had any desire to dance at balls, as her mother knew only too well. But the Dowager Duchess was an eternal optimist and still clung to the hope that one day, at one of these events, a gentleman would come along and charm her daughter so thoroughly that not only would Elspeth waltz with him, she would marry him.

A hope which she seemed to be entertaining with increasing fervour this evening. Not only had her mother seized upon Lady Dunsforth's suggestion that they attend tonight's ball, she had also recruited her friend to her cause. As a result, Elspeth now had not one but two ladies urging her to fill her dance card, which remained stubbornly and mercifully blank. Indeed, all Elspeth had succeeded in filling tonight was her glass of very enjoyable and very potent punch—several times. A choice which may not have been wise, since she was now feeling more than a little lightheaded.

Worse still, the contrast between her dance card and Lady Melliora's could not have been more pronounced. The goddess-like widow had thoroughly shown her up, attracting gentlemen like bees seeking out the brightest flower in bloom, and securing a succession of willing dance partners within moments of arriving. Although Elspeth did not wish to dance, it was impossible not to feel slighted at having been so overlooked. Perhaps her mother had a point—perhaps the look on her face was to blame.

A look which she did not doubt was forbidding, since she was not in a favourable mood. In truth, she knew that she had spent these past few days stewing over that last encounter with Lord Barden in his library and over the way they'd parted. No matter how hard she tried, she could not stop turning it all over in her mind, trying to decide if she felt contrite or simply cross with the dratted man. She had been defensive and far too quick to make assumptions about his views on learned women. She'd allowed her bitter memories of the marriage mart, of all those gentlemen who'd been either critical or downright churlish about her bluestocking traits, to combine with her awareness of Lord Barden's reputation and lead her to assume the worst of him. That had been unfair of her, but she had apologised to him, and he'd accepted that, hadn't he? He had appeared to—insisting that they should try to get along, giving her the book as a peace offering, telling her about his brother.

Calling her a scholar.

The way he'd said that word—without a hint of mockery, or a hint of judgement—it had warmed her heart, and Lord help her, but she really had begun to contemplate whether she liked the man then. Because, despite everything she knew about him, Lord Barden had started to seem eminently and unfathomably... likeable. Drat him.

But then he'd told her not to come back to his house the following day. Nor had he sent any word to her since about continuing their project, and now she was completely confused. Had he brought their library project to such an abrupt halt because he was still upset with her for thinking the worst of him? Or was he being the wicked man he was said to be, drawing her in, then pushing her away and toying with her like a cat with a ball of string? Try as she might, she struggled to believe that was the case, not least because the heartfelt way he'd spoken about his brother had seemed genuine. But then, she supposed, even a blemished apple might have a tender core...

One he did not wish anyone to see.

Ugh! Yet again she was thinking about him, and yet again she found herself tempted to give him far too much credit, to think more favourably of him. He occupied her thoughts far more than he deserved, considering he'd all but ended their acquaintance and had forced her to leave her library project frustratingly unfinished. He deserved her ire for that, at the very least.

Not that he was here to receive it. Indeed, as far as she could tell, he had not been anywhere these past days—he'd paid no calls to the Dunsforth house, and she had not spied him leaving his home. Were it not for the regular, thudding rhythm she heard coming from that outbuilding early each morning as she took a turn about the garden, she would think that Lord Barden had disappeared off the face of the earth.

'You've stopped smiling again, Elsie.'

This time her mother's chiding did provoke an eye-roll. 'My glass is empty. I think I will fetch another drink,' she said, this time making no effort to fix a more pleasing look upon her face.

The Dowager Duchess began to shake her head. 'Oh, but dearest, don't you think...'

Elspeth marched away, pushing her way through the crowds before she could hear the rest of her mother's lecture. She knew well enough what she'd been about to say—cautionary words about leaving the punch well alone now. Her mother was right, too. It was unbecoming for a lady like her to drink too much, but then, it was hot in here, wasn't it? And she was thirsty and besides, who was she trying to impress?

No one.

Her dance card was empty, and when it came to gentlemen, her heart was empty, too. She'd willed it so, a long time ago, and no one could possibly come into her life and change that now.

'Lady Elspeth.'

Even in the midst of the throng and the chatter, the familiar, deep timbre of Lord Barden's voice startled her. Momentarily, she gripped the edge of the punch table, trying to anchor herself as again her head began to spin. It was odd; these past days she'd spent so much time thinking about Lord Barden and imagining what she might say to him, what pithy remark she would muster at their next meeting. Yet now, in this noisy, crowded place, her mind addled by the punch, she felt suddenly on edge—as though she did not know where to put herself, much less how to behave towards him. What was the matter with her?

Elspeth sucked in a breath, then turned around. 'My lord.' She gave the smallest, most wooden curtsy, praying that she appeared sober. 'I did not know you were attending tonight.'

Her words sounded like an accusation, even to

her own ears, and judging by how he bristled, Lord Barden had noted that, too. 'A last-minute decision,' he replied. 'I arrived only a short time ago.' She watched as he glanced left and right at the jostling bodies surrounding them. 'Could we perhaps—could we talk? Not here, but somewhere a little more private?'

She gave him a quizzical look, then nodded. Reading her silent signal, Lord Barden led her towards a quiet alcove, far away from the dancing and far away from where her mother and Lady Dunsforth stood. That was a small mercy; this evening, her mother was undoubtedly frustrated enough at her lack of effort where gentlemen were concerned. The very last thing she needed was to be caught giving the wickedest man in England the time of day.

'Forgive me,' he said, dragging his hand through his red-brown hair. 'I promise I will be brief. I do not wish to keep you from the dancing.'

Elspeth tucked her hands behind her back so that he would not see the blank dance card tied to her wrist. 'I suppose I can permit you five minutes, my lord.' She arched an expectant eyebrow at him. 'Well?'

'I realise that we parted ways rather abruptly at our last meeting, and I neglected to thank you for all of your assistance with the library. That was rude of me, and I wish to apologise.'

'I see,' she replied crisply. 'And how is the library? Finished now, I presume?'

She watched as he shuffled uncomfortably. 'Not quite. I began to follow your system for reorganising the place, but it seems that I have rather too many books and too few shelves upon which to arrange them in an orderly fashion.'

'I could have told you that, my lord. In fact, I believe I was going to, before I was summarily dismissed.'

Lord Barden gave her a pained look. 'You aren't going to forgive me for that, are you, Lady Elspeth?'

'That depends,' she huffed.

'On what?'

'On whether you are intending to properly explain yourself.'

Those emerald eyes of his flashed with something she could not quite read. 'I thought I already had, at the time. I've been busy of late, but more importantly, from what you'd said it was clear to me that your mother was concerned about your visits. You do have a reputation to consider, Lady Elspeth. As much as you may wish to be, you are not an old maid yet. A lady as intelligent as you are knows that beautiful, noble ladies of marriageable age cannot go wandering freely into gentlemen's houses, especially the homes of gentlemen like me.'

She blinked at him, her lips parting in surprise. Had Lord Barden just called her intelligent? And beautiful? 'If that's the case,' she began, deciding to set his compliment aside. 'Then why suggest that we might continue the library project together another time? Why not simply tell me that you planned to finish it on your own? Why lie to me?'

He offered her a grim smile. 'I admit—I did lie, but I was trying to be courteous towards you, whilst doing what I knew to be right and honourable.'

'Honourable?' she replied tartly. 'That is hardly a trait you are renowned for, my lord.'

The moment those words fell from her lips, Elspeth wished she could take them back. Lord Barden's eyes flashed again, and this time the hurt she saw within them was unmistakable. He raked his hand through his hair, exhaling slowly.

'I am sorry,' she began. 'I...'

'Why?' he countered. 'You are only saying what everyone thinks. You are only echoing what the world knows to be true—that Robert Barden, the fourth Viscount Barden, is a heartless and wicked man, just as his father was before him. A man who abandoned his wife, who indulged in his vices while the poor woman suffered and perished alone. A man capable of only depravity and dishonour. A man who a lady like you should avoid at all costs.'

Elspeth stared at him, taken aback by the vehemence of his words. Taken aback, too, by the maelstrom of emotions she could see gathering like storm clouds in his green eyes. Was it usual for wicked men to look so hurt and so angry when confessing to their wickedness? If, indeed, it was a confession at all…

'I had no right to speak to you like that,' she tried again. 'No right to judge you…'

'You'd passed judgement upon me before we'd even met,' he replied. 'I could see it on your face the moment we were introduced.'

Elspeth felt the heat of shame creep onto her cheeks. Of course he'd read her expression at that first meeting. After all, he'd been reading her like a book ever since. 'Perhaps I was too hasty in forming my opinion,' she confessed. 'After all, Lady Dunsforth once told my mother that you are a good neighbour who is much misunderstood, and I have seen for myself just how lovely you are to Tilly…'

Momentarily, Elspeth could have sworn she saw a tender look flicker across his face. Whatever it signified, he buried it quickly, his jaw hardening as his green eyes grew steely and unreadable once more. 'Well, Lady Dunsforth is mistaken, and dear little Tilly's affection for me is misplaced,' he insisted. 'I am exactly the sort of man you believe me to be, Lady Elspeth. Down to every last dreadful detail. Now, if you'll excuse me.'

Lord Barden bowed curtly, then spun around and marched away before Elspeth could utter another word. For a long moment she simply stood there, dumbstruck, staring after him as he disappeared into the crowd. What on earth had just happened between them? How had matters spiralled so quickly and so irrevocably out of control? And what had possessed her to be so unforgivably rude? She'd all but called him dishonourable to his face; an assertion for which she had absolutely no basis beyond second-hand whispers about his reputation. Throughout their short acquaintance Lord Barden's only transgression had been to tease and to vex her, but he had been a perfect gentleman otherwise—considerate, generous, and noble. Little wonder he'd looked so hurt when she'd raked up the rumours about him.

And yet, he had not refuted those rumours, had he? If anything, he'd sought to confirm them, to reject Lady Dunsforth's good opinion and insist that it was all true—unequivocally and without even a hint of shame or remorse. Nonetheless, she could not shake off the bluntness of those words and the niggling feeling that uttering them had troubled him.

None of it made any sense.

Elspeth drew several deep breaths, trying to calm her racing pulse and her whirring thoughts before returning to her mother. There was something about Lord Barden that she was missing, something she could not quite put her finger on. Some mystery concerning that man's past and the reputation it had earned him. Something more than simple scandalous rumour, something painful, something which caused that hurt look she'd glimpsed in his eyes.

Whatever it was, he did not wish to share it, and certainly would not do so now. Frankly, after her outburst tonight, she doubted Lord Barden would say anything meaningful to her ever again.

With a defeated sigh, Elspeth left the alcove and began to make her way through the crowd and towards her mother and Lady Dunsforth. Suddenly she wanted nothing more than to go home. Not back to the Dunsforth dower house, either, but to Chatton. Back to the peace and quiet of her sprawling, rural family estate, far away from all the balls and the dinners and the soirées. Far away from a certain infuriating, confounding gentleman—a gentleman who, despite everything, she found her gaze drawn towards each and every time he walked into a room. A gentleman whose charming smile, whose bright green eyes and whose fine, bare torso occupied her thoughts far more than they should. If she wasn't careful, she'd begin to believe she'd developed a tendre for the wretch…

'Oh! There you are! Your mother was beginning to worry.' Lady Dunsforth's blue eyes shimmered with merriment as she took hold of Elspeth's arm.

'Forgive me, Lady Dunsforth, I was just…'

'You were hiding, my dear. I know,' she interjected, giving Elspeth a pointed look before examining her empty dance card disapprovingly. 'Well, this simply will not do. You cannot come to a Hallowford ball without dancing at least once! Fortunately, I know the perfect gentleman, who will be only too happy to oblige.'

Elspeth frowned. 'Who? Really, Lady Dunsforth, this isn't necessary...'

Her protest fell on deaf ears as Lady Dunsforth urged her towards where the Dowager Duchess stood. Elspeth felt her stomach lurch as by her mother's side she spied Lord Barden, making polite conversation, looking as though nothing was amiss. As though the heated exchange he'd had with Elspeth only minutes ago had never happened.

'My lord, this lovely young lady requires a dancing partner,' Lady Dunsforth announced, beaming at him as she clasped her hands together excitedly. 'And I do believe the next dance is a waltz.'

Elspeth caught the look of alarm which swept across her mother's face at that. 'Dear Agnes, Lord Barden does not have to...'

But Lady Dunsforth was resolute. 'Oh, he does if I decree it. And I do decree it. These young people should be dancing! It is how things ought to be.'

She took hold of the pair of them, urging them towards the middle of the room, where the next dance was about to begin. Elspeth stole a glance at Lord Barden, and for a moment, she thought she saw him emit a sigh. Then, without looking at her once, he offered her his hand. Like her, it was clear he realised that they had no choice. To refuse to comply with Lady Dunsforth's order that they dance together would only provoke comment, and perhaps even questions which neither of them would wish to answer.

Wordlessly, Elspeth accepted Lord Barden's hand and let him lead her. Although she wore gloves, she was shocked at the effect his touch had upon her, how it sent a strange heat coursing from her fingers to her toes. What a ridiculous response to a gentleman who she'd insulted just moments ago. A gentleman who, had it not been for Lady Dunsforth's interference, would never have danced with her at all.

That ridiculous response, however, was nothing compared to how she felt when they began to dance. Because, as Lord Barden took her in his arms and gazed into her eyes, Elspeth was sure that the rest of the world simply melted away like the wax of the candles which made the ballroom blaze. There were no other dancing couples and no more jostling crowds. There was only her and him, twirling together as the violins played and as Elspeth dared herself to wonder what it would feel like if Lord Barden closed the scant gap between them and stole an impertinent kiss.

Chapter Eight

He really needed to stop thinking about kissing her.

Robert swallowed hard, trying to concentrate on his footwork and not the tantalising, dark-haired beauty he currently held in his arms. Not the depths of her brown eyes, nor the way her waist curved temptingly beneath his hand. And certainly not her lips, because every time his eyes strayed towards that pink, tart mouth of hers, his mind conjured ideas that it had absolutely no business entertaining. Especially considering that a short while ago, that same mouth had uttered words which had wounded him to his core and forced him to give voice to a lie, to confirm what was profoundly untrue. To explicitly fulfil all of Lady Elspeth's worst expectations and assumptions, in the name of guarding his secrets.

Damn Lady Dunsforth for forcing him to dance. In fact, damn Chadwick for talking him into coming here at all. As ever, his butler was far too perceptive for comfort and had lost no time in pointing out that his master had spent rather a lot of time at home of late, licking his wounds. Wounds which, he was bold enough to assert, would be best tended to by some pleasant company.

'Whatever has provoked this sour mood of yours, my lord,' Chadwick had continued, giving him a look which left little doubt that the man knew exactly what—or rather, who—had been the cause, 'it will not be solved by staring at piles of books for hours on end. Is there not a ball tonight, at the Assembly Rooms? Now, there's an idea—a bit of dancing, my lord. That'll lift your spirits.'

In the end Robert had acquiesced, tempted out of the house not so much by the promise of dancing but the possibility of a casual liaison which would hopefully exorcise his longing for Lady Elspeth for good. In his experience, the ballroom was an excellent place to find such a tryst and so, dressed in his best evening attire he'd gone out, determined to be sociable and charming and to slip away and into the bed of a discreet and obliging lady as soon as he could.

That had been the plan. But then he'd walked into that ballroom and spied Lady Elspeth standing by the punch table, and all thoughts of his plan had flown out of the window. He'd meant to speak to Isabelle Stephenson, a pretty blonde widow who had previously proven susceptible to his charms and whose feline eyes had been unashamedly beckoning him.

Instead, he'd walked towards Lady Elspeth, suddenly possessed by the desire to talk to her and to make things right between them. In the end, all he'd managed to do was make matters a whole lot worse. Now he was miserable, and he only had himself to blame.

Years ago, when he and Lucy had first separated and the rumours about him had begun to swirl, he'd held his tongue. He hadn't refuted a single tawdry tale about himself, or the comparisons with his cruel and philandering father. He'd remained silent, and over time he'd decided that it would be best for all concerned if he was no longer seen, as well as no longer heard. His complete withdrawal from London Society and his silence had been taken as admissions of guilt, of course. He'd decided he could live with that, because he knew that Lucy couldn't, and that the truth would have done far greater harm to her than the fiction could ever do to him.

Tonight, however, he'd been forced to go a step further than silence. Lady Elspeth's insinuation about his lack of honour had inflamed him, and he had been so close to denying it. So close to expressing the anger, the horror and the disgust he felt at the mere thought of his terrible reputation. So close to imploring her to believe that he was not the man she thought he was, but someone else entirely. A man who'd tried to do the right thing, to help and to protect a woman he'd been bound to before an altar and before God. A man who'd paid a heavy price ever since.

He'd stopped himself, just in time, and after that there had been only one choice left: to confirm the rumours, to say that what she'd heard was true. To embody that wicked man he despised. To wear that horrid mask and to allow it to shield his secrets, and if he was honest with himself, to shield his heart, too. Because that was what he'd been doing for all of these years, wasn't it? By allowing the world to think the worst of him, he'd been able to justify keeping himself apart from everyone, too. He'd been able to remain steadfast in his commitment to remaining alone, nursing the wounds inflicted by his marriage until the scars had faded to little more than reminders, etched upon his skin. Reminders that his loveless, solitary existence was for the best, that within it he'd carved out a sanctuary for himself. Reminders that by not remarrying or siring an heir, he would bring his own accursed dynasty to an end. The title, the country estate, the houses in London and Hallowford—all of it would pass to some distant relation, one who was far enough removed that they would not be easily associated with either him, or his infamous father.

His reputation had always served as a veil for his secrets, but it had been a suit of armour for him, too. A detested, ill-fitting suit of armour, but he was beginning to realise just how vital it was for him to wear it.

Just how vital it was for him to bolster his defences, because ever since Lady Elspeth had arrived in Hallowford, those had seemed worryingly depleted.

So depleted, in fact, that he'd found his resolve wavering again, just for the merest moment, when Lady Elspeth had spoken of how he behaved towards Tilly, and of Lady Dunsforth's insistence that he was misunderstood. A tactful euphemism indeed, and one which made him realise how deeply he was yearning for Lady Elspeth to know the real Robert Barden— the man whose existence Lady Dunsforth had confirmed when she'd prised the truth about his marriage from him several years ago, not long after the news of Lucy's death had reached him.

'I lived with a cruel and heartless man for years, my lord,' Lady Dunsforth had said after dinner on that fateful evening, as she'd plied him with generous glasses of a very potent port. 'I can spot them a mile away, and I am telling you now, I know for a fact that you are not one of them. I have known you since you were a boy, spending your summers in Hallowford with your dear mother and brother. You're every bit as good and gentle as they were, God rest them both.'

'I may have been a good boy, but how can you be certain that as a man I haven't turned out like my father, after all?' Robert had countered. The question had tasted like poison in his mouth and he'd swallowed it down, along with the remainder of the strong drink in his glass.

'Because I remember the look on your face each time the summer came to an end and the three of you had to return to Barden Hall,' Lady Dunsforth had answered. 'You know that I was your mother's confidante, just as she was mine. I know more than most about exactly what you all had to endure at the hands of your father.'

Those words, and the memories they provoked, had made Robert wince. While Society had feasted upon the endless scandals provoked by the wicked Viscount's infidelities, a darker story had unfolded behind closed doors. The ceaseless parade of mistresses and harlots his father had entertained over the years had been bad enough, but his violent temper and aptitude for cruelty had been worse.

'He humiliated my mother and terrorised us all,' Robert had said, his voice barely a whisper as he'd stared into the bottom of his empty glass.

Lady Dunsforth had reached over to him then, giving his hand a gentle squeeze. 'I know,' she'd replied. 'And I know that by the end of his life, you could barely tolerate being in the same room as him. The idea of you emulating that man in any way is frankly inconceivable. You are no wicked lord, Robert Barden, but you are now a part of our family, are you not?'

Family—a word which would have warmed Robert's heart, had the whispered way it'd been uttered not served to remind him of just how dangerous it was. His gaze had shifted briefly to Melliora, spying the pained look which had flickered across her face at this barest reference to all that connected them and all that she'd lost. His thoughts, meanwhile, had wandered to Tilly, then only an infant, sleeping upstairs. Rafe's child. His niece. Solemnly he'd nodded his reply: 'I am.'

'Well then,' Lady Dunsforth had concluded emphatically, 'if you cannot confide in family, who indeed can you turn to?'

That had struck a chord with him, and he had shared his sorry story with Lady Dunsforth and Melliora, on the condition that the truth of it did not leave the walls of the Dunsforth house. Lady Dunsforth had been right, after all; they were the only semblance of a family he had left, after Rafe's passing, and thanks to the Great Secret, they already shared a considerable bond of trust. Allowing them to share his secret could be justified, but burdening Lady Elspeth with the knowledge of it was another matter entirely. She was a visitor to the Dunsforth house and that was all. Theirs was a fleeting acquaintance which would all too soon be at an end—hardly grounds for telling her truths he'd sworn to take to his grave.

Why then did it grieve him to think of them parting without her ever knowing who he truly was? He supposed it was all that longing he felt, driving him out of his wits. The same longing which caused him to spend his nights dreaming about her, tangling with him beneath his sheets, and his waking hours considering what it would be like to taste her lips...

'Lady Dunsforth is watching us like a hawk, my lord,' Lady Elspeth hissed. 'I think we would be wise to at least pretend to have a civil conversation.'

'Your mother is watching us in horror,' he retorted. 'So perhaps it is wise if we don't.'

'Wonderful,' Lady Elspeth replied, rolling her eyes. 'Well, this is not my fault. I thought I'd made my feelings about dancing abundantly clear.'

The perturbed look on her face intrigued him. 'And what feelings are those?'

'That if you strip away all of the performed politeness and delicacy, then what you are left with is a mating ritual—one which I have no desire to participate in.'

Robert laughed awkwardly. The remark was funny, but also uncomfortably true. After all, he could hardly deny that waltzing with Lady Elspeth had given him ideas that he ought not entertain.

'I do not jest, my lord,' Lady Elspeth continued, giving him a severe look. 'Ever since I came of age, my mother has made it her business to cajole me into dancing with gentlemen at every opportunity, in the hopes that I will marry one of them. It is tedious.'

'Is dancing with me tedious?' The question slipped out before he could prevent it.

She wrinkled her nose, considering for a moment. 'I suppose it is tolerable.'

'Take care, Lady Elspeth. That almost sounded like a compliment. However, I daresay your mother would never have cajoled you to dance with the likes of me. This is entirely Lady Dunsforth's doing. I was leaving the ballroom when she accosted me.'

She nodded, cautiously meeting his eye. 'You were leaving because of me. Because of what I said to you.'

He drew a deep breath, apparently unable to either confirm or deny it. 'We are still being observed—keenly,' he said instead, his eyes shifting briefly sideways. 'In fact, I think Lady Dunsforth is trying to read our lips.'

She arched an eyebrow. 'In other words, I should take care what I say.'

He grinned. 'Or you could say something which will shock her and teach her to mind her own business.'

A faint look of amusement flickered across her pretty features. 'I do not believe I am capable of saying anything shocking, my lord.'

Without thinking about what he was doing, Robert tugged her closer to him. 'I doubt that is true, Lady Elspeth,' he whispered to her. 'You are far too clever to be incapable of controversy. I daresay you could call upon any number of strident opinions.'

Those big, dark eyes of hers regarded him carefully. 'Such as?'

'Well, your views on dancing and marriage, for a start. If Lady Dunsforth discerns your strength of feeling against getting wed, it may even help your cause with your mother, to whom she will surely repeat every last word.'

In his arms, he felt her bristle. 'Somehow, I doubt that. Ladies like me inspire little sympathy, since we are apparently so contrary to nature.'

He stared at her, aghast. 'Your mother told you that?'

She shook her head, her dark eyes ablaze with an unmistakable anger. 'No—a gentleman did. Actually, there have been several who have said the same, or similar.'

Robert continued to regard her in astonishment. 'What—because you refused to dance with them? Or because you declined their marriage proposals?'

She shook her head again. 'I believe it was my conversation which caused the offence. It seems that I have rather too much to say for myself, and that I have read far too many books.' She appeared to think for a moment, her jaw hardening. 'Not all were so strident in their opinions on learned women, though. Most of them would simply laugh dismissively before saying something thoroughly condescending, as though they believed ladies talking about scholarship was just a novel form of flirtation.'

Robert felt the heat of indignation claw at him on her behalf. 'Unfortunately, there are many fools among my sex. And a great many whose opposition to the education of women speaks volumes about their own insecurities,' he added, shaking his head.

'Fortunately for me I never had any interest in marrying any of them anyway,' she replied, giving him an obstinate look.

Then the penny dropped. 'Now I understand why you grew defensive with me about your knowledge of Latin, that day in the library,' he said.

She dropped her gaze from his, the colour rising a little in her cheeks. 'Yes, well, a man with your reputation did not seem to be a likely candidate for enlightened views on female education.'

This time, it was his turn to bristle. 'Like most people, I am complicated.'

'And unlike most people, I am not convinced by what is said about you,' she countered.

'I told you, it is the truth.'

'You did,' she agreed, lifting her chin and holding his gaze. 'And yet, now I find myself doubting it more than ever.'

Startled by her assertion, Robert felt his lips part in readiness to protest, although he had no earthly idea what he could say in response. The waltz ended, and around them dancing couples began to melt away from the centre of the ballroom. He knew that they ought to move too, and yet for some reason his brain would not communicate that message to his limbs. Instead, he stood there, frozen on the spot, his arms around Lady Elspeth as their eyes remained locked. Searching, assessing, scrutinising.

'My lord…' she whispered. 'Robert…'

The way she breathed his Christian name brought him back to his senses, and he forced himself to let her go. If she was perturbed by the potency of the moment which had passed between them then, she did not show it, instead marching back towards Lady Dunsforth and her mother in her habitual purposeful way. Robert followed behind her, trying desperately to gather his wits, which had been left scattered in the aftermath of that intimate waltz, and in the wake of her declaration. She did not believe him. He had addressed the matter of his reputation directly; he had confirmed the rumours and insisted every bit of gossip about him was true. He had broken his customary silence on the matter, given voice to the lies which shrouded his secrets and yet now—she did not believe him.

What the devil was he going to do about that?

'Well now, what a fine pairing the two of you made!' Lady Dunsforth clasped her hands together in delight, clearly pleased with herself. 'Wouldn't you agree, Anne?'

'Yes indeed—they acquitted themselves well.' The Dowager Duchess gave a tight smile, although Robert found himself wincing as she shot a stern look in his direction before returning her attention to her daughter. 'Perhaps at the next ball you might even dance a little more, dearest. With other gentlemen, of course,' she added, giving Robert another severe glance.

'They acquitted themselves very well in conversation as well as dancing, I would say. One has to wonder what you found to talk about,' Lady Dunsforth continued, eyeing them both keenly.

'Actually, Lady Dunsforth, we were debating all of this terrible business with the King and Queen,' Lady Elspeth interjected, and Robert tried not to smile at how adeptly she led Lady Dunsforth towards a favoured topic of conversation.

'Oh! Well, the newspapers and the satirists are enraptured daily by it all, of course. Some of those caricatures of poor Queen Caroline…' She shook her head disapprovingly. 'Anyway, tell me, my dear, what did you and Lord Barden make of it all?'

Robert watched Lady Elspeth closely as she prepared to recite parts of a conversation which had not actually taken place. 'I think it's possible that there is wrongdoing on both sides,' she replied. 'However, as I told Lord Barden, the Queen does have my utmost sympathy. Whatever she may or may not have done while living on the Continent all these years, I do not believe she deserves this present humiliation.'

Lady Dunsforth nodded approvingly. 'I quite agree, my dear. Pray tell then, Lord Barden,' she said, turning to him now, 'what was the matter of debate? Since I cannot imagine you objected to anything Lady Elspeth has said?'

He sensed Lady Elspeth's dark gaze fixed intently upon him as he considered how best to answer. Of course, he could simply concur with the popular compassion for Queen Caroline's plight, a sympathy which he did share, and move on—preferably in a direction which would lead him out of the ballroom as soon as possible. Clearly, that was what Lady Dunsforth expected him to do, but then she knew him—truly knew him for the decent and honourable gentleman he was. A gentleman whose existence Lady Elspeth had apparently begun to sense, too, if her sudden doubts about his bad reputation were anything to go by. Doubts he needed to quell, and soon, because if he did not, there was every chance that Lady Elspeth and her formidable, clever mind would continue to examine those doubts and edge closer to discovering the truth—and his secrets.

He had to prevent that from happening, and his heart sank as he realised that left him with only one choice—banish the good Lord Barden and inhabit the wicked one. Earlier tonight he'd given voice to the lies about him, and now he had no choice but to breathe life into a man who, until now, had only existed in the scurrilous rumours and fevered imaginings of Society. His reputation had to be more than armour; it had to become a second skin, impenetrable enough to obscure the man beneath it. He had to shield the truth about his marriage, and he had to preserve his own sanity and protect Lady Elspeth, too. It was clear that his attraction to her threatened to lead him astray, to lull him into confiding in her, and it would not do. No good could come of his drawing close to any woman, and especially not a Society lady whose good name and reputation must never be tainted by the wicked lord which all the world believed him to be.

The wicked lord he had to be—or at least, appear to be.

'Actually, Lady Dunsforth, as I told Lady Elspeth, I find myself firmly on the King's side of this matter,' he replied, as smoothly as he could. 'No good deed goes unpunished, after all, and therefore neither should a bad one. If the Queen is found to have committed adultery, then, of course, the marriage should be dissolved and she should not be crowned.'

Lady Dunsforth's bright blue eyes widened in shock. 'Lord Barden, you do surprise me,' she hissed, clearly affronted. 'You cannot mean to judge our queen so harshly, and yet you say nothing of the infamous behaviour of our king and his many indiscretions…'

Robert shrugged. 'On the contrary, Lady Dunsforth, I mean to do exactly that.' He glanced at Lady Elspeth, trying to ignore how his heart lurched as he spied the astonished look on her face. This was how it had to be, he told himself again. She had to believe wicked Lord Barden existed, even if wearing that costume pained him. Even if every single one of his character's horrid words seemed to burn his tongue. 'The rules are different for men and women. A woman must be beyond reproach, whereas a man can do as he pleases. We all know that, do we not?'

Lady Dunsforth blinked furiously, regarding him in stunned silence for a moment. Then she began to laugh. 'Oh, my lord, you are being deliberately vexatious!' she declared, wafting a dismissive hand in his direction before turning away.

'Just because a man can behave a certain way, my lord, does not mean that he should,' Lady Elspeth said, her quiet disapproval suggesting that she'd taken his remarks far more seriously.

Robert forced himself to look at her and to hold her horror-filled gaze without so much as flinching. Somehow he managed to muster a smile; a wide, amused grin, of the sort he imagined might spread itself across the face of the awful, rakish devil he was pretending to be. His jaw ached with the effort of it.

'That is a distinction which many men do not trouble themselves to make. You'd do well to avoid such creatures, Lady Elspeth,' he whispered to her pointedly, each syllable feeling like a hammer blow to his chest. 'They might appear pleasant, kind, even charming—but beneath the surface, I can assure you, it is all vice.'

Robert turned away swiftly, praying that Lady Elspeth had been too gripped by shock at his words to spy the truth, which he knew would be evident in his eyes. The truth that, in his case, there was no vice, no reprehensible behaviour, no doing as he pleased. There was only a man who'd sworn long ago to remain alone, preserving himself and his secrets within a disguise fashioned for him from the whispers of others. A disguise he had no choice but to embrace, if he was going to succeed in keeping Lady Elspeth at a safe distance and ensure that those scandalous whispers which had long since engulfed him could never harm her, too.

Chapter Nine

'Tilly, darling, please do not climb on the wall!'

The sound of Lady Melliora's gentle admonishment of her daughter startled Elspeth from her thoughts, which she was alarmed to realise had strayed towards Lord Barden yet again. It was a fine and bright Sunday and, having attended church earlier that day, Elspeth had elected to accompany Lady Melliora and Tilly on a promenade around the immaculate gardens shared by the residents of the surrounding houses. Or at least, for the two ladies it was a gentle stroll; for the wayward child whose nursemaid was elsewhere, enjoying her afternoon off, it constituted the freedom to run around and get up to all sorts of mischief.

'She is a little wild,' Lady Melliora said, laughing affectionately as she regarded her daughter. 'But then, I'd be lying if I told you that I was not the same as a child. In fact, I recall running around these same gardens with my brother and our friends and driving all of our neighbours to distraction.'

'Did you spend a lot of your childhood here?' Elspeth asked, determined now to keep her mind focussed on their conversation and not allow her thoughts to keep wandering to the man whose home was but a stone's throw from where they stood.

Lady Melliora nodded. 'Every summer, without fail. My mother has always loved Hallowford. Coming here was a reprieve, I think, from our country estate.' She wrinkled her nose. 'She was never particularly suited to the quietness of life there, with my father.'

That latter remark piqued Elspeth's interest. 'Did your father share Lady Dunsforth's enthusiasm for Hallowford?' she asked cautiously.

'No, he preferred his estate and so never joined us here.' Lady Melliora's expression darkened. 'To be frank, I think that for my mother, coming to Hallowford was a reprieve from my father, too. He was not a good husband.'

'Oh—I see. I am sorry to hear that,' Elspeth replied, unsure what else she should say.

Lady Melliora sighed. 'Such is the reality of many a match made on the marriage mart, is it not? Too many parents pay attention only to the title and not to the man behind it. As a result, young ladies are thrown to the wolves, married off to men who are at best, thrice their age or neglectful or at worst, cruel or philandering.' She glanced at Tilly again, smiling as the girl conducted a one-sided conversation with the doll she held in her arms. 'That is not a mistake I shall make, when it is her turn.'

Lady Melliora's words were surprisingly frank, and Elspeth could not help but wonder how much she spoke from personal experience. 'Was your marriage an unhappy one, too?' she asked searchingly.

Lady Melliora grimaced. 'The Earl was my father's choice. My mother, as usual, was given little say in the matter. The Earl was old, unkind and thoroughly disinterested in me. My marriage was a lonely time, and to be honest, I prefer not to be reminded of it. That is why I choose to be Lady Melliora among friends, and not Lady Westhaigh.'

Elspeth inclined her head towards Tilly. 'At least you have your daughter. She must bring you a great deal of comfort.'

'Yes, she does,' Lady Melliora replied brightly, although Elspeth could not fail to notice the sadness which lingered in her eyes. It was the same look as Lady Melliora had worn the last time they'd spoken of her marriage, that morning at the pump rooms. A look which, Elspeth realised now, clearly owed less to grief and more to the misery which matrimony had caused her.

'You know, the more I hear about marriage, the more relieved I am to have avoided it,' Elspeth continued.

Lady Melliora quirked a curious brow at her. 'You're not an old maid yet,' she countered.

'Now you sound like Lord Barden,' Elspeth quipped, then immediately regretted it. She'd already spent too much time thinking about him today; it would not do to begin talking about him, too.

'Oh, do I?' Lady Melliora's eyebrows rose further. 'And might I ask why you were discussing marriage with Lord Barden?'

Elspeth felt an uncomfortable heat creep into her cheeks. 'It was perfectly innocent, I can assure you. It was a passing remark, that was all.'

Lady Melliora gave a nod, which was distinctly insincere. 'I see. A remark he made when the pair of you were waltzing at the ball on Friday evening?'

'No, and please, do not remind me about that,' Elspeth replied, stifling a groan. 'I only danced with Lord Barden at your mother's insistence, and my mother has been apoplectic about it ever since.'

She felt her heart begin to pound as she recalled how her mother had interrogated her in the aftermath of that ball. How, as well as grappling with her own discomfiting, confusing thoughts about that waltz, she'd had to contend with being questioned about the nature of her acquaintance with Lord Barden and warned in no uncertain terms to keep her distance from the man. There were to be no more visits to his library, even with an army of chaperones, and certainly no more waltzes. As far as the Dowager Duchess was concerned, the man was disreputable and a danger to Elspeth's virtue.

Although, if Elspeth was honest with herself, the way that waltz had provoked her mother's concern was not the only reason she did not wish to be reminded of it. The fact of the matter was that dancing with Lord Barden had provoked feelings within her too—feelings which she'd be unwise to examine too closely. The man was forbidden fruit; a handsome wretch who, by his own admission, was guilty of every charge Society had ever levelled at him. He'd been one of those terrible husbands Lady Melliora had spoken of; the sort of man who embraced his vices and who had no qualms about defending the right of other men—and kings!—to do the same. Hearing him speak like that had troubled her, but not half as much as that warning he'd delivered—the one which had told her, in no uncertain terms, that she should avoid him.

Indeed, given his warning and her mother's concerns, she knew that she should avoid him. And yet...

She could not shake the plaguing sense that there was more to Lord Barden. That he had another side—a kind and honourable side, entirely at odds with his wicked reputation. A side which she'd glimpsed, and which had seeded her doubts about the veracity of the stories about him. A side which he seemed determined to deny and to obscure from view. Ever since that waltz, Elspeth had found herself pondering the same questions, again and again. Who was the real Lord Barden? What was the truth about his marriage, and his reputation? And just how complicated and contradictory was it possible for one man to be?

'Your mother is alarmed because in all likelihood she observed the frisson between the pair of you,' Lady Melliora replied, forcing Elspeth's thoughts back to their conversation. 'I know that my mother certainly noted it.'

Elspeth bristled. 'There is no frisson between us.'

'I do not mean to upset you,' Lady Melliora said, chuckling as she reached over and squeezed Elspeth gently on the arm. 'You're allowed to enjoy dancing with a handsome gentleman, you know. I enjoyed dancing with several that evening—it does not mean that I will marry any of them! But it is nice to be charmed, and I know that when he puts his mind to it, Robert can be very charming.'

Elspeth raised her eyebrows, surprised to hear Lady Melliora refer to Lord Barden by his Christian name, when she had never done so before. A slip, surely, but one which was telling, pointing to their connection over many years and many childhood summers. After all, Elspeth did not doubt that Lord Barden had been one of those friends Lady Melliora had run around with in these gardens, all those years ago. She found herself wondering then if there had ever been anything more than friendship between them. If, as they'd grown up, the handsome and charming Robert Barden had found the fair-haired goddess living next door impossible to resist…

The mere idea of it made her stomach churn, and she pushed the thought aside. What on earth was the matter with her?

'Robert!' Tilly cried out, pointing in the direction of Lord Barden's home. 'Look! He's waving, Mama!'

Elspeth looked up to see that sure enough, Lord Barden was standing at a window on the first floor of his home. Even from this distance, she could see that he was smiling at the child as he waved. She felt her breath catch in her throat as she sensed his gaze wander towards her, and felt her heart begin to beat faster as she dared herself to meet it. Dared herself to recall their last meeting and how it had felt to move around that ballroom in his strong arms, his hand resting firmly upon her waist. Dared herself to remember the way she'd spoken to him as their waltz had ended.

My lord… Robert…

She had not meant to call him Robert, but the word had found its way into her breath and had slipped out, nonetheless.

'Speak of the devil,' Lady Melliora said wryly, returning his wave by giving a playful one of her own.

'Is he?' Elspeth asked, the question leaving her lips before she could prevent it.

'Is he what?' Lady Melliora blinked at her, confused.

'Is he the devil?' Elspeth asked, quieter this time as she felt her usually unassailable confidence falter. 'Only, given everything that people say about him…'

For a long moment, Lady Melliora simply stared at her, her expression as unreadable as her silence. Then, in the end, she answered: 'Well, what do you think? Surely you've spent enough time in his company now to draw your own conclusion.'

Elspeth shook her head. 'I do not know,' she began. 'He appears to be so good-natured, so incapable of such wickedness, and yet he insists it's all true…'

'He told you that?' Elspeth did not miss the look of surprise which flickered across Lady Melliora's face. A look which implied that she knew a great deal more than she was willing to say.

'He did, but the more I consider it, the more it does not make sense to me. How can that man be the same man who your mother regards as a good neighbour, whose company you all evidently enjoy, and who Tilly clearly adores?'

At the mention of her daughter Lady Melliora jolted, her eyes darting around. 'Where is Tilly?'

Elspeth looked all about her, frowning. 'She was here just a moment ago…'

'Tilly? Tilly!' Lady Melliora cried, rushing along the path as she began to search for her daughter.

Quickly Elspeth joined her, calling the child's name as she peered under the thick shrubbery, looking for any sign of the girl. 'She cannot have gone far,' she tried to reassure Lady Melliora. 'She must be hiding somewhere.'

'Tilly!' Lady Melliora was growing frantic now. 'This is not funny. You must come out this instant!'

They reached the gate which led from the gardens and on to the street outside. Elspeth felt her heart begin to beat faster as she noticed that the gate had been left ajar, as though someone had exited through it in a hurry. She glanced at the latch, doubting that it would have proved a sufficient obstacle to a wilful and resourceful little girl. And since they were the only people in the gardens at present, it seemed likely that Tilly had indeed opened the gate and left. Elspeth felt herself join Lady Melliora in her panic then. The girl was barely five years old, and could be anywhere by now...

'Melliora! Lady Elspeth!' A familiar voice intruded, mercifully putting an end to her spiralling thoughts. 'It's all right. She's here.'

The two ladies darted out of the gardens, and immediately Elspeth heard Lady Melliora cry out in relief. There, across the street, was Lord Barden, standing atop the steps which led to his front door, with Tilly clinging to him for dear life as he held her in his arms.

* * *

Robert had never seen Melliora so angry. She hurried across the street towards him, her face flushed as her relief turned to fury, then hauled the little girl out of his arms and into her own. Her words were rapid and tearful as she chastised everyone—the child, herself, and him—in no uncertain terms. The only person she had no cross words for was Lady Elspeth, who stood at her side, looking sombre as she tried in vain to urge Melliora to calm herself.

'How could I lose you?' Melliora wept, burying her nose in Tilly's hair. 'You must never leave my sight again, Tilly—never.'

The girl pouted. 'I was only saying hello to Robert, Mama.'

'You should not have…' Melliora shook her head, then levelled her stormy gaze at him. 'This is your fault, Robert. Your influence upon her…'

Robert held his hands up in gentle protest. 'She ran into my house, Melliora. Opened the door and let herself in. I only realised she was there when I found her in my library, and I brought her straight back outside.'

'Clearly your waving encouraged her.' Melliora's blue eyes blazed at him. 'You know how much she adores you.'

Robert bit his lip, his gaze sliding briefly to Lady Elspeth, who looked increasingly perplexed by what was unfolding. Now was not the time for a frank exchange concerning Tilly, irrespective of just how tempted he was to remind Melliora that he was the girl's uncle, that her father had been his beloved brother, and he was damned if he was going to feel guilty about fostering a close bond with the child. It was bad enough that Tilly would likely never know him as her family, that he had to content himself with being regarded as no more than a neighbour to a girl who was the only real kin he had left in the world. Probably the only kin he would ever have, since he would not remarry or have children of his own. As always, that particular thought jarred with him. Not because he felt any guilt at not fulfilling his duty to the Barden lineage by producing an heir. He'd made his peace with being the last of his dreadful father's lineage, and had come to regard it as a sort of justice served upon a man who had never answered for his sins when he was alive. Rather, that thought reminded him of everything else the solitary life he'd committed himself to had denied him. Love. Affection. The feeling of waking up each day beside another. The sound of childish squeals echoing through his home. The joy of being a husband and a father.

Of course, he could not say any of that. Not on his doorstep. Not in front of Lady Elspeth. Not ever, in fact.

'You're right,' he said, deciding that in the circumstances, the path of least resistance was the wisest choice. 'I am sorry. I shall refrain from waving in future.'

His assurance seemed to placate Melliora. 'Good. Thank you,' she replied, holding Tilly closer as the girl whimpered in her arms. 'We should get you inside, little one. I should think that is quite enough excitement for all of us, for one day.'

'But, Mama…' Tilly sounded close to tears. 'I left my doll.'

'Where? In the gardens?' Melliora asked, looking flustered again as she glanced back across the street.

Tilly shook her head and pouted, pointing towards Robert's house. 'In there.'

'Oh, for goodness sake.' The exasperation in Melliora's voice was unmistakable. 'Well, can you remember exactly where?'

The child shook her head again sorrowfully. 'She's hiding.'

'Don't worry,' Robert interjected, giving mother and daughter a reassuring smile. 'She must be in my library. I will go and look for her now.'

Melliora nodded her thanks, then to his surprise she turned and looked pleadingly at Lady Elspeth. 'Would you mind helping? That doll really must be found—Tilly will not settle into bed tonight without it.'

Robert watched as Lady Elspeth's eyes widened with alarm at the request, and for a moment, he thought she might object. But then she nodded, giving

Tilly a reassuring pat on the shoulder. 'Of course. Fear not, Tilly—Lord Barden and I will find your doll.' He noticed that she did not glance at him, not even once.

Clearly still overcome by the events of the past few moments, Melliora swiftly thanked them both then hurried back towards her home, still clutching Tilly in her arms. With a resigned sigh, Robert beckoned Lady Elspeth inside his home and towards his library, where, amongst the disarray of their half-finished project, Tilly's doll presumably awaited. Truly, if Zeus and the rest of the pantheon existed, then they were laughing at him now. Indeed, he would not be surprised if the gods had orchestrated this entire situation, simply to torment him.

'I will ask a maid to join us,' he announced as they reached the library door. 'For propriety's sake.'

'Surely a man as avowedly wicked as you does not care a jot about propriety,' Lady Elspeth retorted as she sauntered inside the room. She turned to face him then, her dark eyes at once stormy and challenging. 'Unless you are telling me that you are not so wicked, after all?'

Robert felt his jaw clench. 'I told you what I am,' he replied.

Lady Elspeth arched an eyebrow at him. 'So, no maid then.'

He watched for a moment as she began her search amongst the unsorted piles of books, before forcing himself to focus similarly on the task at hand. He perused the bookshelves, praying that they would find this damnable doll quickly. In truth, he was not sure how much time spent in close confines with Lady Elspeth he could bear. Every time he looked at her, memories of their waltz came flooding back—that intoxicating, bewitching dance which had occupied his waking and his sleeping thoughts ever since. But worse still, every time she looked at him, he got the unsettling sense that she was trying to peer into his soul. That she was trying to solve a riddle, and the riddle was him.

'I see that you still have a lot of work to do in the library,' she observed.

He nodded. 'As I said, I have too many books. I plan to acquire some more bookcases, although goodness knows where I am going to put them.'

'Would it not be wiser to simply have fewer books here?' she asked him. 'Surely you have other properties—a country house, where some of your books could be kept?'

The thought of returning to the Barden estate for any reason made his blood run cold. 'The reason I have so many books here is because I am never at my country estate,' he countered, before he could think better of it.

He could see immediately that Lady Elspeth had caught the thread of something significant in his words. 'Why not?' she asked. 'Surely you must go there sometimes, to attend to your business, to ensure things are properly managed?'

'I have a diligent steward who carries out my instructions to the letter,' he snapped. 'But I prefer to be in Hallowford, because this is where I have chosen to make my life, since…' He pressed his lips together, ordering himself to be silent. Once again, he was alone with Lady Elspeth in his library, and once again, he'd become dangerously tempted to lower his guard.

Lady Elspeth regarded him thoughtfully. 'Hallowford appears to be the sort of place people choose to escape to. Lady Melliora told me today that Lady Dunsforth did that for years. All those summers spent here were her reprieve from a life endured with a terrible husband. But I suspect you already know that.'

He drew a deep breath, nodding. 'A town like this can be a refuge, that is for certain,' he replied, wondering what else Melliora had told Elspeth. Surely nothing about her own reasons for choosing to spend her widowhood here, far from the scrutiny of Society.

Curiosity shimmered in the brown depths of Lady Elspeth's eyes as she stepped towards him. 'Is that what Hallowford is for you, my lord?'

Unthinkingly, he stepped closer, too. 'Robert,' he said quietly. 'Call me Robert, just as you did when we danced.'

'You did not answer my question, Robert.'

He shrugged, trying not to notice how the sound of his name on Lady Elspeth's tongue made his blood heat. 'A place of refuge. A place of exile. Perhaps both.'

'A man who has banished himself from Society and sought sanctuary in a northern town does not sound like a particularly nefarious creature to me,' she observed.

'Perhaps his idea of sanctuary is merely a new place in which to be wicked,' Robert replied, giving the first answer which came to mind. He swallowed hard, suddenly conscious of the scant distance which separated them.

She took another step nearer, drawing so close now that their hands were almost touching. 'Or perhaps he was never a wicked man at all.'

'As I have already told you, Lady Elspeth, I am the very worst of men. An unrepentant rake and a dreadful husband, just like my father before me. A man who seduces ladies for sport.' Even to his own ears, the words sounded woefully hollow.

She stared at him, those dark brown eyes of hers at once daring and provocative. 'If that is the case, then prove it,' she whispered.

Her challenge was his undoing. Before he could consider his actions, before he could recover his wits and realise that all his lust and his longing for Lady Elspeth had finally driven him mad, Robert pulled her into his arms. Then he cupped her cheek with his hand and allowed his lips to meet hers—wickedly, decadently, and without a moment's hesitation.

Chapter Ten

Elspeth had never been kissed like this before. In fact, she'd barely been kissed at all, save for one or two uninvited pecks on the lips snatched by gentlemen who'd been both brave and impertinent enough to do so. This kiss was entirely different; slow and searching at first, then deeper and more delicious as the two of them embraced the moment with reckless abandon. She heard herself moan against Robert's lips, greeting his tongue with her own as she allowed her hands to explore those broad shoulders and strong arms she'd once spied, gloriously naked as he boxed in his outhouse. Her touch seemed to have an effect on him, and she heard him growl as he trailed kisses down her cheek, then her neck, and across her collarbone.

She opened her eyes briefly as she clattered backwards against a bookcase, then felt them flutter shut once more as she indulged in the sensual pleasure of feeling Robert's lips and hands everywhere. A delightful shiver ran through her as he explored the curves of her waist, her hips, her bottom, before moving to caress her breasts. She moaned again, straining wantonly against her stays as, even through her clothing, the feeling of his fingers brushing over her nipples caused them to pebble and a curious heat to gather between her legs.

A heat which hinted at so much more, if she permitted it. But of course, she could not permit it. She had already allowed matters between them to stray far beyond what was proper. She had taken leave of her senses and all but dared him to seduce her, and in doing so, she'd strayed dangerously close to ruin. Because what she had not bargained for, when she'd uttered her provocative challenge, was just how much Robert's touch and his kisses would prove to be her undoing. Just how reluctant she would be to end their tryst, and just how ardently she would wish that she did not have to tell him to stop.

In the end, however, she did not have to say a word. With a groan that sounded oddly akin to frustration, it was Robert who tore himself away from her first.

'You should go.' His voice sounded strained. 'Before I lose my mind completely and have you in my library.'

'I thought that was rather the point of being a wicked man,' she replied. She had no earthly idea how she'd managed to muster that tart tone with him when her entire body was still humming with awareness at what had just passed between them. 'To have whatever and whomever you like.'

'You're a duchess's daughter. A duke's sister,' he murmured. 'Even I am not foolish enough to ruin a lady like you and risk the wrath of the Duke of Falstone. I'm certain your brother would have no hesitation in calling me out and pointing a pistol between my eyes.'

'That's if my mother didn't get to you first,' Elspeth replied. 'She has already warned me to keep away from you.'

'Another reason that you should leave, then.' For a moment he stepped towards her, his hand outstretched as though poised to run his fingers down her cheek. Then he retracted it, and Elspeth decided she must have misread his intention. 'I think you have had your proof, Lady Elspeth,' he added, his green eyes seeming to darken as they regarded her. 'Only a devil of a man would take you and kiss you like that.'

'You really just kissed me to prove a point?'

She stared at him, trying and failing to read the look in his eyes. Trying and failing to draw any conclusion beyond the worst one—that he really was the wicked Lord Barden, the rotten son of a rotten apple. The conclusion she'd been so keen to resist of late, when she'd been so determined to believe that there was another, better side to this man. She had always trusted her powers of reason and deduction when deciding what to make of people and of situations, but perhaps this time, those skills had failed her. Perhaps she had been wrong, after all.

He shrugged. 'You issued your request for proof and so, I fulfilled it. Not that you seemed to mind,' he added pointedly.

Elspeth felt her temper flare. The man was beyond infuriating and impertinent! And so acutely, painfully accurate in his assessment of her, since she had not minded being kissed by him at all. In fact, she'd revelled in it.

'You merely caught me by surprise,' she huffed, trying to ignore the flush of embarrassment she could feel creeping on to her cheeks. 'I won't be fooled twice, my lord, so consider yourself warned, should you ever find yourself tempted to kiss me again.'

Momentarily his eyes seemed to heat as they regarded her, so much so that Elspeth could have sworn that she'd spied desire in his gaze. But then, weren't wicked men always wont to look at ladies like that?

'Duly noted,' he replied drily. 'The very last thing I want or need is to be on the receiving end of one of Artemis's arrows. Or worse, turned into a stag and left to be hunted by hounds, as your favoured goddess did to Actaeon. I am certain that would spoil all my fun.'

'Ah yes, and of course, you are all about fun, aren't you?' she replied sardonically. 'That is why you cast yourself as Dionysus. Except, you forget that I have seen you at a ball, and you did not much look like you were enjoying the revelry, or seeking to indulge in vice. In fact, if I recall, you arrived late, appeared to be perfectly sober, and only danced once—with me, and only because Lady Dunsforth forced you to do so.'

'It is difficult to look cheerful when a beautiful woman is insulting you in an alcove,' he countered sharply.

Elspeth sucked in a breath, wondering for a moment if she'd heard him correctly. Had he really managed to both compliment and admonish her in the same sentence? 'Insults which you insist are true,' she replied. 'Since you keep telling me that you are the most dishonourable and dreadful wretch to ever grace God's earth.'

Again, that jaw of his clenched. 'I am.'

'So dishonourable, and yet you hide yourself away in Hallowford instead of keeping company among the innumerable rakes of London,' she countered, planting her hands on her hips. 'So dreadful, and yet the Dunsforths are clearly fond of you—especially Tilly. That little girl seems to regard you as almost her family, if her antics today are anything to go by.'

She saw him bristle. 'Nonsense. She's not even five years old—it was mischief, pure and simple.'

Elspeth frowned at him. 'Was it? For a man so wicked, you have a wonderful manner with the child.

You look far more at ease in her company than you ever looked all evening in that ballroom.'

Those green eyes blazed at her, and she sensed that her words had got under his skin now. Was that because she was right, or because she was wrong?

'You do not know anything about me, Elspeth,' he growled. 'I was not at that ball to dance with young ladies, to drink punch, or to exchange pleasantries. I was there in search of other pleasures. Ones which, in my experience, usually take place between the sheets of the maturer sort of woman who is only too happy to be seduced.'

Elspeth stared at him, too shocked by his admission to really care that he'd taken the liberty of using her name so familiarly. 'You are saying that only to vex me.'

'No, I am saying it because it is the truth.' He glanced towards the door. 'Now, I really would heed your mother's warning, Elspeth, and keep your distance from me. No matter how much that clever mind of yours wants to make its study of me, I can assure you that I am a closed book—one that, trust me, you do not want to open.'

Elspeth shook her head at him, her disbelief mingling with another, hotter feeling—one which felt very much like fury. Fury at this fresh evidence of his rakish behaviour. Fury that she'd ever been tempted to give him the benefit of the doubt. Fury that just like all those other women, she'd fallen so easily for his powers of seduction.

Fury that she'd enjoyed his kisses quite so much.

'Fear not, Lord Barden,' she said cuttingly as she marched towards the door. 'After that unsavoury revelation, I do not think you are a book I'd wish to open, either.'

With a sad smile, Robert gently picked up Tilly's doll, retrieving it at last from its hiding place behind the curtains. For the past half hour his search had kept him busy, although apparently not preoccupied enough to stop him from thinking just how much of an insufferable fool he'd been. What the devil had he been thinking, kissing Elspeth like that? Had he not heeded the warning issued by his ridiculous lust for her—lust which had grown immeasurably, despite the fact that he'd known her for little more than two weeks? He ought to have understood that the moment he crossed that line and pressed his lips against hers, he would be powerless in the face of his passions. That the embers of longing which had burned ever since they'd first met would ignite. That there would be fireworks. And God, had there been fireworks…

Especially when she'd returned his kisses with fervour. When she'd pulled him close to her and moaned against his mouth. When she'd been every bit as fiery and passionate as he might have hoped; indeed, he would have hoped, if he was another man, with another life, at another time. As it was, he could not allow himself to hope for anything, even after a kiss like that—a kiss which had hinted at so much. A shared connection. Mutual attraction. Hints which were futile because a man like him could never embrace those possibilities. Lady Elspeth Scott was forbidden fruit, and as tempting as she was, he had to resist. She could never countenance being with a wicked man, and he could never countenance telling her that he was no such thing. Could he?

No. But that did not mean that having to redouble his efforts to make her believe his lie hadn't been painful. The look on her face when he'd ascribed their kiss to his simply offering proof of his wickedness had wounded him. And as for the sheer horror in her eyes when he'd confessed to attending the ball to hunt for carnal pleasures—that would haunt him until the end of his days. He had not even meant to tell her that, but hearing her speak so perceptively about Tilly, about family, and about what made him happy had terrified him, and he'd blurted out the first deflection which came to mind. Despite his insistence that he was a closed book, he knew already that she'd read him, that she'd begun to understand him.

He'd had to put a stop to it, hadn't he? He'd had to end their embrace, to sever their connection, to embody the wicked Lord Barden and give her no choice but to recoil from him. He'd had to live up to his horrid reputation and to allow it to act as a barrier between them—for the sake of protecting his secrets, yes, but to shield his own heart, too. That kiss might have been driven by his lust, but it had awoken him to the very real possibility that, if he allowed Elspeth to truly know him, far deeper feelings might develop. Feelings which would lead only to heartache, because even if Elspeth shared them, he knew that he could have no future with her. Lady Elspeth Scott was clever, beautiful, and a Society lady with an unblemished reputation. The idea of her binding herself to a man who the entire world regarded as little better than the Devil himself was frankly unthinkable.

No—it was better this way. Better to keep the truth about his reputation to himself, to allow his solitary life in exile in Hallowford to serve its only noble purpose—shielding not only the painful story of his marriage from the world, but guarding the secret about Tilly's parentage closely and thereby protecting both her and Melliora. Better to recommit himself to his fate, and to let Elspeth believe the worst about him. And it was not as though everything he'd said in the aftermath of their kiss had been a lie, had it? Indeed, he had been seeking to satisfy certain appetites that night at the ball, if only to try in vain to overcome his growing passion for Lady Elspeth Scott. A burning passion which he had no hope of extinguishing now. Not after that kiss.

Robert sighed, making his way downstairs with Tilly's doll in his hand. He would go next door now and return the child's prized possession discreetly, and hopefully while Elspeth was getting ready for dinner and therefore unlikely to cross his path. Then he would return home and spend a quiet evening alone. Perhaps later he would go to his outhouse before it was dark and punch that bag a few times. At least that would be productive and would prevent him from being tempted to drown his sorrows in a bottle of brandy. He'd never succumbed to those sorts of temptations before and would not do so now. He needed to be sensible and to keep a clear head. What was done was done, after all. Like everything else, he merely had to live with it.

'Do come in, my lord.' Evans, the butler, answered his knock with a convivial smile. 'I will let Lady Dunsforth know that you are here.'

'Oh, there is no need, I merely came to…'

Robert's gentle protest went unheard as the butler marched away, and within a matter of moments Lady Dunsforth appeared, rushing towards him with an anxious expression on her face. When she spied the doll in his hand, she grinned, letting out an audible sigh of relief, then wordlessly beckoned him into the parlour, closing the door behind them.

'Tilly will be overjoyed—and her mother, more than a little relieved.' She tilted her head, giving him an affectionate smile. 'I understand that Melliora was rather sharp with you earlier. I know she is sorry for it.'

'She was panicked and upset,' Robert replied. 'In the circumstances, her reaction was perfectly understandable.'

Lady Dunsforth patted his arm. 'You are a good man, Robert Barden.' Her expression darkened as she stepped closer, regarding him carefully. 'However, I am afraid I must ask. Is there something amiss between yourself and Lady Elspeth? Only, when she returned earlier she did not seem quite herself, and I understand she'd been next door, assisting you in the search for the doll?'

Robert felt his heart begin to race. He shrugged, feigning nonchalance. 'She did come to the house at Melliora's request and assisted briefly with the search. However, I had more than enough help from Chadwick and several maids, and so I suggested that she should go home.' He smiled tightly, hoping that Lady Dunsforth would not detect his lies. 'Too many cooks spoil the broth, as they say.'

Lady Dunsforth nodded slowly. 'I see. Well, perhaps that is why she was put out. She's a determined young lady, that is for certain.' She sighed deeply. 'On reflection, it was unwise of Melliora to ask Lady Elspeth to assist you at all. I'm afraid that the Dowager Duchess has embraced that popular poor opinion of your character and is holding fast to it. She seems to regard you as a threat to her daughter's virtue, a fear which is not in any way assuaged by the amount of time you have spent in Lady Elspeth's company of late,' she added pointedly.

'I can assure you, I pose no threat to the lady's virtue,' he replied, praying to God that the heat he could feel creeping up his neck was not visible as the image of him almost ruining her against his bookcase crept unbidden into his mind. 'And I would remind you that you are the one who insisted that I waltz with her at that last ball,' he added, giving Lady Dunsforth a stern look.

The older lady, however, was unrepentant. 'That was done in all innocence. I had no idea that there was such a frisson between the pair of you, or that it would be quite so apparent.'

'There is no frisson between us,' he protested, trying to ignore how his heart pounded and his mind immediately conjured the sound of Lady Elspeth moaning against his lips. No frisson, indeed. A tempest, more like.

Lady Dunsforth held her hands up in mock surrender, although it was clear she remained unconvinced. 'I am merely cautioning you to tread carefully,' she said, keeping her voice low. 'The Dowager Duchess does not know you as we do, and I presume, neither does Lady Elspeth. If you do not intend to rectify that, and I assume you do not, then you'd be wise to have less dealings with the young lady, that is all.' She paused, narrowing her eyes slightly as though trying to discern something from his expression. 'Unless...'

Robert frowned. 'Unless what?'

The older lady continued to regard him carefully. 'Unless I am wrong, and you have already confided in Lady Elspeth about...certain matters.'

'Lady Elspeth knows only what the rest of Society believes about me, Lady Dunsforth, and that is how it shall remain,' he replied, somewhat more sharply than he'd intended. 'I have no intention of confiding in her about my marriage, or indeed anything else, if that is what concerns you,' he added pointedly, giving her a look which he hoped would convey exactly he meant by *anything else*.

Lady Dunsforth looked affronted. 'That is not what I meant... I know you would not...' She paused, apparently collecting herself for a moment before reaching out and placing a hand over his. 'I wish only for you to be happy, Robert. That is all I mean to say.'

He nodded, recalling the way that he and Elspeth had last parted. Recalling how he'd warned her to keep her distance from him. Recalling the twin looks of disgust and disappointment on her face as she marched out of his library. Looks which made him feel as far from happy as it was possible to be.

'Thank you, Lady Dunsforth. I can assure you that I am perfectly fine.' He forced a smile, trying to ignore the way that insipid word stuck in his throat. *Fine.* How could he possibly be fine, after kissing Elspeth like that?

'Good,' the older lady replied, although once again, her expression suggested she was far from convinced. 'Now, on to a different topic. We are planning to take our guests to the concert at the Assembly Rooms. It is at the end of the week, on Friday evening. Will you join us? I believe they are playing Beethoven, and I know he is one of your favourites,' she added with a grin.

Robert blinked at her in disbelief. 'You just asked me to keep away from Lady Elspeth, and now you are inviting me out with you all for the evening?'

'I suggested you have less dealings with the lady, not avoid us all entirely,' Lady Dunsforth replied. 'Besides, an evening of music offers little opportunity for conversation. You should find keeping your distance easy enough.'

Robert sighed resignedly. An invitation from Lady Dunsforth was all but impossible to refuse, and as she'd rightly pointed out, he did always enjoy Beethoven. Indeed, given his love of the composer's music, to decline to join them would seem odd, and likely provoke Lady Dunsforth's suspicions further. After all, it was clear that she remained curious about the exact nature of his acquaintance with Elspeth; a curiosity which would not be satisfied by his mysterious absence from their social outing. Better to go, he reasoned, and demonstrate his absolute indifference to the lady. He could do that, couldn't he? He could be polite but aloof, courteous but distant, and not at all consumed by thoughts of her body pressed close to his as they embraced against the bookcases…

'Very well, I shall join you.'

'Excellent!' Lady Dunsforth strode towards the parlour door. 'Now, let us get you away from here before Tilly spies you. I'm afraid that a consequence of your less frequent visits to the house has been to make her more keen on your company than ever. You've become quite the novelty.'

Robert bid Lady Dunsforth a swift farewell, leaving the house and returning to his own before anyone could spy him—not Tilly, and mercifully, not Elspeth, either. He'd seen quite enough of that dark-haired temptress for one day, and truth be told, he needed to spend the next few days giving himself and his considerable ardour a stern talking-to if he was going to get through Friday evening with his sanity intact. But then, keeping his distance would be easy, wouldn't it? Especially if, as her latest rebuke of him had seemed to promise, she was intent upon staying away from him.

He was a book she no longer wished to open, and thank goodness for it. Robert peeled off his coat and cravat, intent now upon going to his outhouse to keep his body and his breath busy and to quieten his thoughts. He had to stay away from her—it was as simple as that. By his reckoning, in a little less than three weeks' time her visit to the Dunsforths would be over. Three weeks and she would be gone from Hallowford for good. He could survive that. He could recover from his lust and allow the memory of her, of that kiss, to fade. He could live with her being next door right up until the day that she wasn't. He could bear the rest of her visit, and he could cope with her departure, just as he bore everything else. What was one more heartache in a lifetime filled with them, after all?

Chapter Eleven

Robert sipped his wine, trying to let the surrounding conversation wash over him as he counted the minutes until the next performance. The first half of the evening had been very enjoyable, with a small ensemble performing Beethoven's Septet against the backdrop of a candlelit room as the audience listened intently. The music had been pleasant and calming, and had reassuringly smothered all opportunities for conversation.

The arrival of the interval, however, had brought the room back to life with movement and chatter as Hallowford Society seized the opportunity to mingle, setting Robert's teeth firmly on edge. Whilst the musicians had played, he'd kept his eyes fixed upon them. Now, standing with the Dunsforths and their guests, knowing where to look was impossible. Because no matter what he did, his eyes kept wandering back to a certain someone, resplendent in that deep purple colour she favoured. His mind wandered too, back to those moments in his library almost a week ago, when he'd ravished her against his bookcase, giving rise to the sorts of thoughts and desires which were absolutely not appropriate in the middle of a candlelit assembly room.

He had to resist looking. He had to resist remembering. He had to continue to do what they'd both done so far this evening—resisting even acknowledging each other's existence. Even if he felt her presence everywhere. Even if the fact that she'd steadfastly eschewed looking at him pained him. Even if he knew that the brittleness of the air between them would not have gone unnoticed by the rest of their party.

'I believe we are to enjoy some of Mr Beethoven's piano sonatas next,' Lady Dunsforth announced approvingly. 'I must say, I find that instrument more pleasing to listen to than the clarinet or the horn.'

'Perhaps that is only because the piano is what you are more accustomed to, Mama,' Melliora said gently. 'You do play so well yourself, after all.'

Lady Dunsforth waved away the compliment. 'Oh, I have barely played in years. But then, neither have you, my dear,' she added pointedly.

Robert found himself suppressing an amused smile as Melliora bristled at that. 'Yes, well, when one is a widow with a child, such pursuits tend to fly out of the window,' she replied, sounding every bit as prickly as she looked.

'And what about you, Lady Elspeth?' Lady Dunsforth continued. 'I imagine you to be a very accomplished musician.'

Robert kept his eyes trained on the rim of his wine glass, but nonetheless he could hear the note of embarrassment in her voice. 'You flatter me, Lady Dunsforth, but regrettably I am not. I do play the piano, but very badly.'

'You are being modest, surely,' Lady Dunsforth replied. 'You have always struck me as a young lady who excels at all she does.'

'Well, no, I...'

Elspeth's hesitant response intrigued him, and before he could stop it, Robert's gaze roamed towards her. A very becoming blush had grown in her cheeks as she clutched her wine glass tightly and looked every bit as uncomfortable as her inability to formulate an answer suggested. She turned her face away from him, as though she'd sensed him looking. As though she did not want her discomfort to be observed. His heart went out to her, then. As much as he knew that Lady Dunsforth would not have meant to embarrass her, nonetheless her clumsy words had had exactly that effect.

'I've always thought that far too much emphasis is placed upon the need for a young lady to be musically accomplished,' he interjected. 'Quite why some skills and talents are ranked more highly than others, I will never know.'

His remark earned him a raised eyebrow from Lady Dunsforth and a barely concealed scowl from the Dowager Duchess. Wonderful. So much for avoiding Lady Elspeth; not only had he acknowledged her existence, he'd wandered straight into the quagmire in her defence. A defence which was rewarded with the briefest glance from her; the first of the evening and one which, he was perturbed to note, made his heart beat a little faster.

This was all his own fault, he reminded himself. His fault for kissing her, for stoking passions which would have been best left to smoulder and die out. His fault for being seemingly unable to hold his tongue and to keep his eyes off her.

'Lord Barden is right,' Melliora said, deciding to join in now. 'In my experience, some of the men who hold musical ability in such high regard when choosing a bride are the same men who would deprive their wives of either the time or the means to play, the moment they are wed. Is that not true, Mama?' she asked pointedly.

Lady Dunsforth looked stunned. 'Well, I…'

Robert grimaced, understanding immediately that the men to whom Melliora referred were likely her own father and the old, dead earl to whom she had been unhappily married. Trust Melliora to decide to kick that particular hornets' nest this evening.

'In my case, I am much better at understanding the

theory of music than I am at executing it,' Elspeth said, adeptly saving Lady Dunsforth from the need to muster an answer. 'Regrettably, I am fairly certain that listening to me play the piano is torture.'

The speed with which she found her voice made Robert wonder just how much she'd understood about the significance of Melliora's words. He already knew that Melliora had told her about Lady Dunsforth's life with her terrible husband. He supposed that he should not be surprised if Melliora had confided in Elspeth about the abject misery of her own marriage. After all, as he knew only too well, Elspeth was far too easy to talk to, and such matters could be discussed without venturing into the murkier territory of exactly who Melliora had turned to for comfort during those dark days, and the consequences that comfort had brought…

'At least if you have the misfortune to be lumbered with a dreadful ogre for a husband one day, you may take your revenge easily enough,' Melliora giggled. 'As long as the brute actually provides you with a piano, of course.'

'Melliora!' The whites of Lady Dunsforth's eyes shone in the candlelight as she stared at her daughter in shock. 'This is neither the time nor the place for that sort of talk,' she hissed, before turning to regard the Dowager Duchess apologetically. 'My daughter means no offence, of course, Anne.'

'Of course not,' the Dowager Duchess replied, although she sounded less than convinced. 'Anyway, if—when—Elspeth marries, her husband will be very carefully selected indeed. There will be no ogres and no brutes.'

The way she levelled her stern and forbidding gaze at Robert as she said those final words left him in no doubt that they were intended for him. Damning, accusatory words which spelled out exactly what sort of man the Dowager Duchess believed he was—but then, from what Lady Dunsforth had told him last Sunday, he ought to expect no less. This was the reputation he had, he reminded himself. A reputation he'd refused to refute. A reputation he'd insisted to Elspeth was justified. He had no right to feel aggrieved when people believed it.

Nonetheless, the Dowager Duchess's remarks caused his temper to flare, and he realised quickly that he was not the only one. As his gaze fell upon Elspeth once more, he saw that now-familiar fire burning in her dark eyes. A look which spoke of her indignance, but more than that—her horror. Horror he fully understood, given what he knew of her feelings about marriage. If he understood that, surely her mother did, too?

'Selected by whom, Mama?' she asked quietly. 'Because you promised…'

The Dowager Duchess looked ruffled, as though

realising she'd said something she'd not meant to articulate. 'Not now, dearest,' she replied, attempting to dismiss Elspeth's concerns with a placatory smile. 'We should take our seats again. It looks like the second part of the concert is about to begin.'

Robert watched as Elspeth acquiesced, and it pained him to observe her fury dissolve into something akin to distress as they walked back towards their seats. He had seen many looks on Elspeth's face during their acquaintance—he'd seen how she looked when he vexed her, disgusted her, disappointed her. He'd seen her look furious with him, and he'd seen her smile. But he had never seen her look so upset, and he was entirely unprepared for how acknowledging her turmoil made him feel. As though he wanted to protect her. As though he wanted to make it all better.

As though he wanted to take her in his arms and kiss all of her distress away.

The thought must have emboldened him—or more likely, caused him to temporarily take leave of his senses, because suddenly he found himself at her side, sitting down next to her. Then, as the surrounding candles were extinguished, dimming the lights for all but the pianist poised to begin upon the stage, he found himself reaching for her hand and clasping it with his own. It was a gesture of solidarity, he told himself. A gesture of comfort and understanding. A gesture of friendship.

It was not, and never could be, anything more. No matter how much he yearned for it, and no matter how much his blood heated at this merest touch.

She ought to have snatched her hand away. She ought to have extricated herself from his gentle grip. And yet, she could not.

Elspeth tried hard to concentrate on the pianist. Tried hard to lose herself in the beauty and complexity of each sonata, just as she normally would. Whilst she had no talent for musical performance, she had always been able to appreciate the skill of others. She had always been able to identify favourites and to relish hearing them played. Tonight, however, she'd managed no such thing. Even during the earlier performance of the Septet, when Robert had sat at a safe distance several seats away, she had struggled to stop her wayward gaze from straying in his direction. The interval, meanwhile, had been pure torment; even though he'd stood across from her and far beyond touching distance, it had been as though she could feel his solid, warm, muscular frame next to her. It had not mattered how often she tried not to look at him, her entire body knew he was there, nonetheless.

It was all that dratted kiss's fault. Ever since their tryst last Sunday, it had been as though her mind had relinquished its mastery over her body, and now every physical part of her was exercising a will of its own.

Her body hummed with an unfulfilled need, as though the feeling of his lips pressed against hers had awoken something within her which did not want to return to its prior state, unstirred and undiscovered. It did not seem to matter how often her mind tried to remind her body that Robert—Lord Barden!—was off-limits. That he was wicked and dissolute, and had only kissed her to prove a point. Her needy body had other ideas—ones which had manifested themselves these past several nights, in fevered dreams at the witching hour. Dreams which had shown her everything that such a delicious and decadent kiss had promised.

Now, despite herself and despite all her powers of reason, she'd fallen willingly under his spell again. Not only had she felt her foolish heart flutter at the way he'd leapt to save her from embarrassment over her woeful musical skills, she'd allowed that momentary kindness to lead her to entertain the idea, yet again, that Robert did have some virtues hidden away, after all. Her resolve to regard him with the disdain he himself had all but insisted he was due had wavered, her guard had lowered, and he must have sensed it. That was why he'd sat next to her and taken hold of her hand. Why he was currently tracing a circle on her hand with his thumb, and even through the fabric of her glove it was driving her to distraction. He was toying with her, just as he had when he'd kissed her. He was showing her that, despite knowing he was wicked, she was susceptible to his charms nonetheless. Susceptible, perhaps even powerless, in the face of his efforts at seduction.

Drat him!

Except, the way he held her hand did not feel quite like that, did it? Loath as she was to admit it to herself, the gesture felt comforting, even tender. Was that what he meant by it? And why? She supposed she might have looked upset at her mother's remarks about selecting a husband for her—remarks which would be challenged in no uncertain terms later, in private. Without doubt, she'd felt upset, not to mention shocked at the strength of her mother's assertion that she would marry, that it was no longer a question of *if*, but *when*. Perhaps Robert had read her correctly once again and had sought only to be kind…

A kind rake. An honourable wretch. The wickedest man in England, but also the one man who she increasingly suspected understood her best of all. Good Lord, she was so confused.

Elspeth startled at a sound coming from behind her; a sound which began as something akin to laughter and ended as a cough. She resisted the urge to glance over her shoulder. Was someone sniggering? How rude. Around them a few people tutted their disapproval; a sea of heads shuffling restlessly, like waves disturbed by the intrusion of a sloop. The movement seemed to discomfit Robert too; she felt him relinquish her hand, and watched as he placed it casually back in his lap. The moment between them, whatever it signified, had passed.

The remainder of the concert passed without incident, and Elspeth managed to concentrate sufficiently even to enjoy hearing her favourite, Beethoven's fourteenth sonata, in all its haunting and dramatic glory. During the third movement, she glanced at Robert and spied him drumming his fingers rhythmically against his knee in time to the music. She found herself wondering if that sonata was his favourite, too, or if his hand was simply restless and itching for her touch. It was a fanciful idea but she entertained it nonetheless, if only to ease her own discomfort at realising just how profoundly her hand ached for his.

When the concert ended and they all got up to leave, Elspeth found herself walking at his side. She hadn't meant for that to happen; if anything, she'd been trying to keep up with her mother and Lady Dunsforth, but had fallen quickly behind them in the crush. She did not speak a word to him, nor he to her, and he did not offer his arm but maintained a polite distance, just as he had all evening. It was as though nothing had changed, as though there had been no strange, tender moment when he'd taken her hand and wrapped his fingers around hers. And yet, that moment had existed, hadn't it? Something between them had shifted; she could feel it in the charged air between them.

In the concerned glances he kept bestowing her way when he thought she was not looking. In the ghost of his touch when he briefly placed a steadying hand upon her arm as they shuffled their way through the jostling crowd.

Then, behind them, there was that sound again. That snigger, although this time no cough accompanied it. Instead, it was punctuated by the animated whispers of two female voices, clearly indulging in a bit of titillating gossip. Elspeth strained to hear, curious to understand what it was that amused them so greatly. As she listened to their words, however, she immediately wished that she hadn't.

'He disappeared into an alcove with her, at the last ball…it's the same lady…she's a duke's sister, or so I heard…he was holding her hand…'

Elspeth felt her heart begin to race at hearing herself and Robert being discussed in such scandalous terms. Next to her, she sensed Robert bristle, and she knew he'd heard the words, too. Despite every ounce of her reason and good sense telling her it would be unwise, Elspeth found herself looking over her shoulder at the two ladies. Both appeared older than her, and prettier, too—especially the willowy blonde. Her attention caused them to chuckle all the more, clearly relishing the amusement they'd gained at her expense.

'He is so wicked,' the brown-haired lady hissed behind her hand. 'They say his wife died of a broken heart, you know, and that he's had one hundred lovers…'

The blonde levelled a spiteful look in Elspeth's direction. 'One hundred and one now, it would seem,' she spat.

How dare they! Elspeth felt her cheeks grow hot at the insinuation and she balled her fists, mustering every ounce of self-restraint she had to stop herself from marching over to them and giving them a piece of her mind. Instead, she gave them both the most withering look she could manage, then forced herself to turn away. She heard one of them gasp, before any further words between them were rendered inaudible by their laughter.

What a pair of dreadful gossips those ladies were! Although they had been correct about one thing—Robert had indeed held her hand, and more than that, she had permitted it. If those ladies had spotted that, then perhaps others had, too…

A wave of panic gripped her then, combining with her fury and making her heart clatter so hard she thought it would burst from her chest. She glanced up at Robert and saw how his posture had stiffened, saw how his jaw had hardened and his green eyes blazed as he pushed his way through the crowd with more determination than ever. He looked angry, too, but more than that, he looked wounded. That expression on his face was the same one she'd spied when they'd spoken in the alcove at that ball, when she'd called him dishonourable and he'd insisted that it was true. A look of hurt, of anger.

Of turmoil.

A look which told her yet again that there was more to Robert's story than he was willing to say. That there were details which remained buried below layers of rumour and reputation. That there was another side to his tawdry tale, and to him. A side which Elspeth wished to fully discover, and to understand. As they left the Assembly Rooms and climbed into the Dunsforths' carriage at last, she made a silent promise to herself—to disregard the gossip, to earn Robert's trust, and to learn the whole story, in his own words. Whether she liked it or not, during these past weeks Lord Barden had managed to get under her skin and dangerously close to her heart. She had to know one way or another whether he was wretched or redeemable—if only to preserve her sanity, to satisfy her suspicions, and to understand if her desire for him was entirely misplaced, once and for all.

Chapter Twelve

Robert leaned his head against his punching bag and closed his eyes, emitting a defeated sigh. The day outside had not long dawned, its bright promise sitting in stark contrast to his mood. He'd been out here for a while now, shirtless and sweating as he kept his limbs busy and tried, to no avail, to quiet his mind. Instead, his head seemed determined to mull over the events of last night, forcing him to continually ask himself the same question: just what on earth had he been thinking? He had sat in that building as it thronged with Hallowford Society, and he'd taken Elspeth's hand and held it in his. He had behaved boldly and recklessly; no matter how dim the candlelight was, or how careful he'd been to conceal their hands as they'd sat side by side, he'd run the risk of the gesture being spied and remarked upon. A risk which had been realised, since it was clear they had been both seen and remarked upon, and in the worst way imaginable.

The thought of Isabelle Stephenson's scurrilous exchange with her companion set Robert's teeth on edge. Not their words about him; as wounding as those were, he'd long since grown accustomed to being spoken about in such terms. No—he was most concerned over their inferences regarding Elspeth. The idea of Hallowford's gossips whispering about her, calling her his lover or his mistress—frankly, it made him feel as furious as he felt guilty. Guilty because if, God forbid, the rumours spread beyond Isabelle and her companion's hushed conversation and Elspeth's reputation was tarnished, it would be all his fault. He ought to have known better; after all, even provincial Society was apt to tease out any tasty morsel of gossip, to invent scandal from the merest hint of indiscretion. And by holding Elspeth's hand like that, he'd been horribly indiscreet.

Not that he could entirely bring himself to regret doing so. Even through the soft fabric of her glove, her hand had felt warm and inviting. And she had not pushed him away, had she? If anything, she'd held on tighter...

Robert gave the bag a firm punch, remonstrating with himself. He had promised himself that he would keep his distance from Elspeth, that he would be indifferent to her, and he'd failed entirely on both counts. Instead he'd succumbed to that overwhelming protective instinct which had gripped him. Not only had he allowed the mask of wicked Lord Barden to slip, but he had behaved in a way which discomfited the man buried beneath the terrible reputation, too. He might not be the depraved sinner which Society believed him to be, but neither was he the sort of man who permitted himself to indulge in tender gestures and warm feelings. His marriage had quickly extinguished any romantic notions he might once have held, and he'd steadfastly refused to recover them since.

As far as he'd been concerned, first as a man scandalously separated from his wife then latterly as a widower, anything which fell outside the scope of a casual liaison could never be an option for him. His reputation had seen to that, and if he was honest with himself, so had his instinct to spare his heart from the sort of pain and suffering his ill-fated marriage had inflicted. And so, he'd sought no deeper connection, taking his pleasure discreetly with women like Isabelle, who were as avowedly disinterested in emotional entanglements as him. Who enjoyed the thrill of being seduced by a man of such despicable repute.

Although, after hearing her gossip so viciously last night, he was starting to regret that brief liaison with Isabelle. Thank goodness he had not revisited that particular dalliance at the ball—even if his choice had meant subjecting himself to some tart words from Elspeth, instead. For once, he almost felt grateful for the way Elspeth could drive him to distraction…

'I thought I'd find you here.'

Startled, Robert spun around to see Elspeth standing in the doorway. Even at this early hour she managed to look breathtaking, her blue day dress a shade lighter than the striking colours she usually preferred, and her hair arranged prettily, if somewhat loosely, around her face. He found himself staring at the stray curls, his fingers tingling with the sudden urge to touch them, and perhaps then, to pull her into his arms and resume what they'd begun in the library…

'Robert?'

Elspeth stepped towards him, folding her arms as a small frown gathered between those deep brown eyes. Robert shook his head slightly, trying to gain mastery over his wayward thoughts. Trying not to lose himself in that stare. She was close enough now for him to see that she was paler than usual, and that those mesmerising eyes were framed by dark circles which betrayed a want of sleep. Clearly, he was not the only one who had had a restless night.

'Elspeth,' he replied, inclining his head in greeting, and startled to realise how hoarse he sounded.

She gave him one of her withering looks. 'I don't recall giving you leave to address me like that.' He watched her eyes dip briefly as they swept over his chest. 'Are you not going to put a shirt on?'

'Oh—right, of course.' He reached for his shirt, pulling it quickly over his head. 'My apologies, *Lady* Elspeth. Although, I would point out that once again it is you who has interrupted me while I was boxing. I did not invite you to join me here.'

She sighed, rolling her eyes at him. 'Oh, for heaven's sake, just Elspeth is fine. And I know you did not invite me, but I think we need to talk, wouldn't you agree?'

'About what?' he asked, feigning ignorance. He could compile a list of guesses as to what she might wish to discuss, but as she stood before him now, he felt suddenly unsure whether or not he was ready for any of those conversations. 'I thought that we'd agreed that I was a book you'd prefer not to open and that you would keep away from me.'

'If I recall, you told me you were a closed book and urged me to stay away from you,' she retorted.

'And yet, here you are,' he replied.

She shrugged. 'I've never been particularly good at doing as I'm told.'

'You astonish me,' he said sardonically, trying hard to suppress his smile as he recalled the way Lady Dunsforth had described Elspeth as determined. That was one word for her, he supposed, although he had many others. Headstrong. Spirited. Enormously clever.

Unconsciously alluring.

His breath caught in his throat as she stepped closer. So close he could reach out and touch those dark curls. So close that he could smell that familiar lavender scent as it began to work its beguiling magic.

'I'm aware of how we parted after we…after you kissed me in your library,' she began. 'But surely you agree that after last night, there are matters we ought to discuss.'

Those dark eyes searched his so intently that in the end, he had to look away. 'On the contrary,' he said, 'given Isabelle Stephenson's rumour-mongering last night, it would be wise for us to avoid each other entirely. Please be assured that I will decline all future invitations from Lady Dunsforth for the remainder of your stay in Hallowford.'

'Is that really what you wish to do?' The perturbed note in her voice made his heart lurch. Of course it wasn't what he wanted to do! Indeed, he had not even contemplated doing that until the words had fallen unrehearsed from his lips. But it was the right thing to do—to quash the rumours before they could truly begin, to preserve Elspeth's reputation.

To save his own sanity.

'What I want does not matter,' he replied, looking at her directly once more. 'I cannot countenance you being tainted by your association with me.'

She arched an eyebrow at him. 'Surely a truly wicked man would not care who he drags down with him. Did you care about the reputations of the other one hundred ladies you've been associated with?' she asked. 'Or is it just me?'

'That number is absurd,' he replied, avoiding the question.

'What about Isabelle Stephenson?' she asked pointedly. 'Did you care about her reputation?'

He felt his face grow hot. 'What makes you think I've ever had anything to do with Isabelle Stephenson?'

'I didn't until you referred to her by name. Was she the blonde or the brunette? I think she was the blonde,' she continued before he could answer. 'The brunette seemed merely enraptured by the whole discussion, whereas the blonde gave me the most spiteful look. Thinking about it now, it was personal for her.'

Robert sighed, begrudgingly impressed by her powers of deduction. 'Yes, she was the blonde. And yes, we were…involved. Once. Very briefly.'

A look flickered across Elspeth's face then. A look he had not seen before. A look which seemed suspiciously like jealousy. Surely not? Whatever it was, she recovered herself quickly, mustering one of her more familiar expressions—abject disapproval.

'The maturer sort of woman who is only too happy to be seduced,' she mused.

He winced at hearing his own words repeated back to him. 'Something like that. Isabelle is happily widowed and I…well, I told you what sort of man I am,' he reminded her, although even to his own ears, his words lacked conviction.

Elspeth eyed him carefully, and he sensed he was being read once again. 'If I've learnt anything about you, Robert, it's that what you say and what you do are two very different things.'

He frowned. 'Meaning?' he asked, although the way his stomach fizzed uncomfortably told him that he knew exactly what she meant. That he knew exactly where this conversation was leading.

'Meaning that at times I feel as though there are two men called Robert Barden, inhabiting the same body. Two opposing and contrary personalities.' She paused, shaking her head at him. 'But then I tell myself that's impossible, which leads me to one simple conclusion—that you are not the man you say you are. I don't believe you are wicked, Robert. It may be that you behaved badly in the past, but I don't think you are that man now. Yet you seem determined that the world should see the worst in you, even though doing so clearly causes you pain. What I do not understand is why.'

Her candour took him aback. He took several steps backwards, then turned away as he tried to find the right words to answer her. The sort of words a truly wicked man would utter. Words which would convince her that he was the man Society believed him to be. Words which were necessary to guard his secrets and to keep Elspeth at a safe distance from him, for both of their sakes. And yet, those words would not come because deep down, he knew, his resolve was wavering, and it had been wavering for some time. Increasingly he yearned for her to know who he really was, and to know that he'd never been rakish or cruel or dissolute for a single day of his life. That he'd been only loyal, honourable, and kind. That his penance for doing the right thing, for setting Lucy free and keeping her secrets had been the utter destruction of his reputation, leaving him no choice but to exile himself into obscurity in the hopes that one day, Society would forget all about the fourth Viscount Barden and his alleged crimes.

'Robert.'

Her voice was soft and searching, and when she placed a gentle hand upon his shoulder, it thoroughly disarmed him. He turned around, and what remained of his defences, of that disguise he'd tried so hard to wear, seemed to disintegrate as his eyes met hers. Still at a loss for words, he took hold of her hand and caressed it thoughtfully in his palm. Then, in the enduring silence of the outhouse, he surrendered entirely to his instincts, tugging her into his arms and placing a tender kiss upon her lips.

This kiss was different to their first one. That kiss had lit a fire between them, one which had burned brightly, promising to engulf them entirely. This kiss smouldered; it was warm and lingering, with neither of them in any hurry to either deepen it or end it. A shiver ran down Elspeth's spine as Robert caressed her cheek with his thumb, before trailing his fingers down to her jaw. His fingers were restrained and gentle, remaining tucked under her chin and not wandering to caress her breasts or bottom as they had last time. There was something touching about that, she realised. Something heartfelt. Something more profound than base lust. It reminded her of how she'd felt last night, when he'd taken hold of her hand—almost as though he might care for her, and she for him. Almost…because that was simply not possible, was it? How could he care for a woman he'd tried so hard to rile and to keep at a distance? And how could she care for him when she could not be absolutely sure who he truly was?

'If you are kissing me again in the hopes you can convince me of your wickedness, then I must inform you, my lord, it is not working,' she said as she finally and reluctantly broke the spell.

'It was worth a try,' he murmured, attempting a smile, although she noticed that there was nothing jovial about the look in his eyes. 'However, you seem to have made up your mind about me. You have simply reached a different conclusion to everyone else.'

'Not everyone,' she countered. 'The Dunsforths do not think badly of you, and since they actually know you, I'd say their opinion counts for a great deal. And

I have reached no absolute conclusions. All I have are my observations and my instincts.' She looked at him pointedly. 'Do you want to know what those are?'

'I have a feeling you are going to tell me anyway,' he replied drily.

'You do have a wicked streak. You like to tease and can be very vexing,' she began, a smile hinting upon her lips. 'But beneath that, you are kind and honourable. You have a genuine affection for the Dunsforths, so much so that a stranger would be forgiven for believing you are a part of their family.'

She thought she saw him bristle at that. 'They are an all-female household, and Lady Dunsforth's son is not nearby. I take a neighbourly interest, that is all.'

'Well, neighbourly or otherwise, that is a decent and honourable thing to do,' she replied pointedly. 'Just as you have so often been decent and honourable towards me.'

'Not always,' he countered. 'Or are you forgetting that I tried to ravish you in my library?'

Elspeth felt her cheeks heat at the reminder. 'Only to prove a point. But it strikes me that you have to try very hard to be wicked, whereas being a good man comes quite naturally. I think that is who the real Lord Barden is. The one who can talk engagingly about mythology. The one who loved his brother and feels his loss keenly. The one who is so worried about guarding my reputation that he would live as a hermit until

I am gone, if it would prevent a scandal. The one who calls me a scholar and not a bluestocking. And the one who held my hand last night—almost as though you sensed I needed some comfort…'

He shrugged, as though the way he'd entwined his fingers with hers had been nothing. 'You were upset—any fool could see that. Little wonder, really, given the way your mother was speaking about marrying you off to the most virtuous bidder.'

The knowledge and understanding implied by his words cut deep. 'I wish my mother appreciated my objections to marrying as well as you apparently do,' she lamented. 'I'm afraid even an exchange of cross words late last night has failed to quite hit the mark. She has decided that yet another interminable London Season is what's required. She has decreed that I am to try once more to find a husband.' She shook her head, her sadness and disbelief rushing to the fore once again as she remembered their fraught conversation. 'As if I have not been dangled above that nest of vipers often enough already. Perhaps I should hope that Isabelle Stephenson does her worst. Perhaps a ruined reputation is exactly what I need. I am almost seven-and-twenty—hardly fresh meat for the marriage mart. If every nobleman in this land were to think me tainted, too…'

'You don't mean that,' Robert interjected sharply. 'I understand that your mother's decree has left you feeling powerless, but trust me—it is nothing compared to the powerlessness you would feel when faced with complete and utter social disgrace. It would destroy your life, Elspeth.'

The frankness of his words brought her to her senses, reminding her of why she'd sought him out in the first place. Not to complain about her own misfortune, but to understand the truth about Lord Barden, once and for all. 'I suppose that is especially true if that disgrace is based on nothing more than vicious speculation,' she ventured. 'If it is baseless. If it is all lies. Although it is difficult to fathom why, in such circumstances, those lies would not be refuted. Unless there was some impediment to simply telling the truth.'

The heavy sigh which Robert emitted was all the confirmation she needed that she had grasped the thread of something significant. She watched as he dragged his hands down his face, as though wrestling with himself over how to answer her, perhaps even over how much of the truth he could bear to part with. He regarded her carefully then, and her heart ached to see the weight of his turmoil darkening that lovely emerald green gaze. Perhaps she had been too persistent. Perhaps she had pushed him too hard.

'Forgive me,' she said quietly. 'I have no right to interrogate you.'

Robert gave her a thin smile. 'I should expect nothing less from the goddess of the hunt, I suppose.'

'Do you want to know why Artemis is my favourite goddess?' she asked.

'I presume it is because of your attachment to remaining unwed, and your fondness for a bow and arrow,' he replied, his expression lightening a little.

She smiled at that. 'In part, yes. But Artemis is also the goddess of bearing and caring for children—which is odd, I think, for a goddess of chastity. But I like that she is so complicated and contradictory. And she reminds me of my brother…'

Robert quirked an eyebrow at her. 'Your brother?'

'Yes—Ted. Before he inherited the dukedom after our eldest brother's passing, he was a physician and a man-midwife.' She grinned mischievously. 'I am not supposed to know about the midwifery part—my mother decreed long ago that such information should not reach my delicate and impressionable ears.'

'Should I presume that you dragged the information from your poor and unsuspecting brother nonetheless?' Robert asked.

She shook her head. 'Not quite. But I have learned over the years that any conversation your family doesn't want you to hear is one you should probably listen to—even if that requires a bit of eavesdropping, from time to time.'

He chuckled at that. 'I see.'

'Anyway, I have never told anyone what I know—well, until now.' She let out a long, slow breath. 'It just seems easier to let my mother think I am blissfully ignorant. Just as it has always seemed easier to live up to my bluestocking reputation—scholarly Elspeth, far too wedded to her books and her learning to ever entertain finding a husband. Better that than allowing her to know that I did have high hopes of falling in love once, until those hopes were crushed by bitter experience…'

Elspeth clamped her mouth shut, taken aback by her own candour. She saw Robert furrow his brow, then part his lips as though poised to speak. Whatever words he'd been about to utter, however, were lost as the sound of Temperance's voice intruded, calling Elspeth's name.

'I must go,' Elspeth said, her panic rising as she hurried towards the door. 'If she finds me in here with you…'

'Of course. But Elspeth…' Robert reached for her arm, tugging her back towards him. 'Would you meet me here tonight, after everyone has retired? I know it is more than I should ask of you, but I would like to talk more.' He regarded her earnestly. 'I'd like to tell you more.'

Temperance's urgent pleas gave Elspeth little time to consider. And really, if she was being sensible and proper, there was nothing to consider. It was bad enough that she'd sought Robert out this morning, but to agree to meet him unchaperoned and after dark—that ought to be out of the question. And yet…

'Yes,' she said quickly, before she could change her mind.

He nodded his appreciation as he relinquished her arm. 'Until tonight, then.'

'Until tonight.'

Then she rushed out of the door and back towards the Dunsforth garden, where an anxious Temperance awaited, on the cusp of assembling a search party. As she batted away her maid's concerns, insisting that she'd been tempted down the lane by the promise of a longer walk, Elspeth reminded herself that she would have to take care that night. A nighttime disappearance could not be so easily explained, and frankly, the consequences of their clandestine meeting being discovered were unthinkable. She was flirting with ruin and taking the biggest risk of her life, all so that she could learn the truth about Robert—a man who, for all she knew, might turn out to be thoroughly wicked yet.

Chapter Thirteen

Robert walked to his outhouse under the cover of darkness, with only a sliver of moonlight to illuminate his way. It was a blustery night, the tall trees which abutted the stables and outbuildings stirring continuously in the wind, their summer leaves rustling loudly in protest. Above him, he spied the bats flitting around as they went about their business, and somewhere in the distance, he heard the hoot of an owl. Other than the creatures of the night, however, no one else appeared to be abroad. There was always the possibility of one of his neighbours' carriages returning late, but for now the horses and those who cared for them were at rest. With a final, wary glance over his shoulder, he slipped through the door, confident that he had not been seen and determined to keep it that way.

Pitch darkness greeted him, and for several moments he fumbled around as he tried to light the lamp he'd brought. The possibility of light drawing attention worried him, although he reassured himself that the single small, shuttered window meant that it was unlikely to be seen. Besides, if they were going to talk, if he was going to tell her at least something of his story, he could not do so in the dark. He had to be able to see her. He had to be able to look into those mesmerising dark eyes, if only to reassure himself that he was doing the right thing.

If she came, of course. Despite her promise that she would meet him, it was possible that she'd had a change of heart. Indeed, he would not blame her—he'd had no right to ask her to take such a risk, especially not after being so insistent about the need to guard her reputation and cautioning her about the destruction which would surely follow if she did not. Elspeth was right; he did say one thing and do another. However, he knew that they needed to finish their conversation. He knew, too, that what he wanted to say could not be communicated during snatched moments at a ball, a concert, or in a parlour, or under the watchful eye of a maid or Lady Dunsforth or Elspeth's mother. Ever since they'd first met, he'd been allowing his mask to slip, bit by bit, but if he was going to tear it away completely, he needed to speak to her alone.

And he was going to tear it away completely—he'd decided that earlier, when she'd stood before him and spoken with such honesty about her own life. About how she, too, had often chosen to wear a disguise, to shield herself behind a formidable façade. About how, like him, she'd desired love once, until painful experience had led her to conclude that it was best to remain alone. He'd glimpsed a side of her he had not seen before; a vulnerable, softer side which she kept well hidden. He understood now that the fierce intellectual and committed spinster with a tart mouth whom he'd got to know during these past weeks was not the full story. He wanted to know more about her, and in turn, he wanted her to truly know him, too. For the first time in a long time, he wanted someone he could talk to. He wanted a friend. Perhaps, for her remaining time in Hallowford, that was what they could be to each other.

'You will need to stop kissing her at every opportunity, then,' he muttered to himself. 'Especially if you can no longer blame the wicked lord for your transgressions.'

That was true. Twice now he'd insisted that those kisses were nothing more than him attempting to demonstrate his wicked credentials. Earlier today he'd managed to restrain his desire for her, but only just. His attraction to Elspeth was undeniable, as was the passion she'd stoked within him every time their lips had met. He would have to take care, especially tonight. He might not be a wicked rake, but he was still a man—one who was clearly not immune to surrendering to his lust, where Elspeth was concerned.

Robert spun around as the door creaked open. In

the dim lamplight he saw a shadowy figure creep inside, wearing a long cloak to obscure their identity. His heart lifted as Elspeth lowered her hood, impatiently brushing a few stray curls of her hair away from her face. Given the risks, it was unwise of her to come, but nonetheless Robert realised just how glad he was that she had.

'I hope you have not been waiting long,' she said in a low voice. 'Mama and Lady Dunsforth took an age to retire tonight, and it turns out that creeping out of the house without being spied by one of Lady Dunsforth's servants is no mean feat.'

'Do you think anyone saw you?' Robert asked, worried now. If a maid had seen her leave, it would not be long until the Dowager Duchess was alerted and all hell broke loose.

'No.' She smiled at him. 'Don't fret. I must confess, that was rather exciting.'

'It won't be exciting if we are discovered together,' he replied, heaving a sigh. 'I am sorry, Elspeth, I should never have asked you to meet me like this.'

She shrugged. 'But you did, and I am here.' She folded her arms across her chest, regarding him carefully. 'You said that you wanted to talk more.'

'I did… I do.' He paused, suddenly feeling at a loss. He'd no idea how to proceed, much less where to begin. 'How are matters between you and your mother?'

'Unchanged.' Elspeth's expression darkened. 'She insists that all she desires is my happiness and says that she cannot understand my opposition to another London Season. Apparently I am obstinate and headstrong and even more difficult than my brother, Ted, was over the matter of getting married.'

Robert frowned. 'But the Duke of Falstone is married now, is he not?'

'He is, and happily so. But Ted was fortunate enough to fall in love.'

'Then perhaps you will, too,' Robert replied, trying not to consider how decidedly off-kilter that particular thought made him feel.

'Now you sound like my mother,' she scoffed.

'I don't mean to,' he protested. 'All I mean is that Society cannot surely be entirely bereft of gentlemen who...'

'Who would entertain a bluestocking for a wife?' Elspeth interrupted, finishing his sentence before he could find the words. 'Who, by some miracle, would not be remotely put off by either my conversation or my temperament?'

'It would not be a miracle, Elspeth. I enjoy your conversation, and I am a gentleman, am I not?' The words fell from his lips before he could think better of them. Before he could think about what they might imply.

In the shadows of the outhouse he saw a look of surprise flicker across Elspeth's pretty features. 'Take care, my lord, that almost sounded like a compliment,' she replied in that familiar tart tone. The tone she deployed whenever she felt the need to muster her defences—he recognised that now. 'Unless, of course, you would take issue with my temperament?'

He gave her a wry smile. 'Well, you are fond of firing arrows in my direction.'

'And you are fond of teasing me,' she countered.

He shrugged. 'I cannot help it. You are a worthy adversary. Like it or not, Elspeth, but we do make quite the pairing.'

'Perhaps I ought to marry you, then,' she quipped drily.

Her words took him aback. How had their conversation strayed this far? How was it that they were standing in his outhouse as the witching hour approached, discussing love and matrimony? Suddenly, this felt like dangerous territory, even more so than the conversation he'd planned to have, about his murky past.

'You would not want a man like me,' he replied quietly. 'You would not want a man with my reputation as a husband. You would not want to spend your life being whispered about, laughed at or even pitied for having the misfortune to be the wicked Lord Barden's wife. Indeed, I could never countenance condemning any lady to such a fate.'

He saw her frown, and it was clear that the rawness of his words had perturbed her. 'I am sorry, that was flippant of me. Obviously, I was not really suggesting that we should marry.'

'Of course not.' He forced a smile, discomfited by how profoundly her words stung him. What the devil had got into him tonight? 'If you do marry, it should be for nothing less than love.'

In the gloomy light he saw her step towards him, and felt her place a tender hand upon his arm. 'Did you love your wife, Robert?'

'Yes, but not in the way I wanted to love her.' Admitting that reminded him at once of all his sorrow, all his regret. 'I cared about her, but it was always as though there was something missing between us. Something I could not understand—not at first, anyway.'

'If there was something missing, as you say, then forgive me, but why did you get married?' Elspeth asked. 'What happened?'

'My father happened.' He paused, trying to swallow down the bitterness which always rose within him, whenever he spoke about the wicked third Viscount. 'As he always did. I was young, barely one-and-twenty, when I was told I was to marry Lucy. She was eighteen, very pretty and accomplished and, most importantly for my calculating and mercenary sire, she came with a handsome dowry. Her father had made his fortune in trade, but like many of his rank, he sought to connect himself to titled, landed wealth through making good marriages for his children. And so, a deal was brokered between our fathers and we were wed. Neither of us had any say in the matter. My father's word was law, and I'd long since learned the hard way that disobeying him wrought consequences not only for me, but for my mother, too. He always took out the worst of his rage upon her, and I could not bear the thought of that. She had already endured a lifetime at the mercy of his temper.'

'Oh, Robert.' Elspeth squeezed his arm sympathetically. 'To have to marry against your will must have been dreadful.'

'It wasn't at first—not for me, anyway. Before our betrothal I'd been rather impulsive when it came to romantic entanglements.' He glanced at her sheepishly. 'Of course, Society took that to be a sign that I was just like my father, but actually, I think at the root of it was a desire to find love. And so, I made my peace with the match and resolved to be a good husband. We might not have chosen each other, but I saw no reason why, given time, our marriage could not flourish. In fact, I was determined that it would, that I would be kind and attentive and never anything like my father. He was unfaithful and so cruel, and my mother both feared and despised him. I swore I would never give Lucy cause to feel that way about me.' He laughed bitterly. 'Ironic, really, when you consider the rumours which subsequently spread about the sort of husband I'd been.'

Elspeth frowned. 'What went wrong?' she asked gently.

He dragged his hands down his face wearily, feeling pained by the memory of it all. 'From the outset, it was clear that Lucy was disinterested in her marriage to me. We spent most of those early months of our union in London, where she seemed content to live a separate life from me, mainly socialising with her circle of female friends. At first I told myself that things would improve as we got to know each other better, that if I was pleasant and charming, then she would warm to me eventually.'

'But she didn't,' Elspeth interjected.

He sighed. 'No, she didn't. About a year after our marriage, my father died suddenly and I inherited everything. We left London to live on the Barden estate with my ailing mother, and that only made matters worse. Lucy hated it there—she missed her friends and resented not being able to so readily escape my company. In time, that hatred and resentment turned into despair. She became reclusive and her health began to suffer, and she developed persistent stomach pains, which she treated with copious amounts of wine and laudanum.' Robert shook his head sadly. 'I felt helpless. I could not understand how I had managed to make her so ill and miserable, and she refused to talk to me about it. None of it made any sense, until...'

He pressed his lips together, unsure if he could bring himself to give voice to this part of his sorry tale. Only three people had ever learned the truth of it: Lady Dunsforth, Melliora, and Rafe, and the latter had taken the secret to his grave.

'You don't have to tell me, Robert,' Elspeth whispered, clearly sensing his hesitation. 'Not if you do not wish to.'

He offered her a grim smile as he slumped down against the wall, as though sitting down might somehow ease his burden. After a moment, Elspeth sat down beside him, and unthinkingly he reached for her hand, clutching it in his. Her skin was warm and reassuring against his, and he found himself drawing strength from her touch.

'About two years after my father's death, my mother also died,' he began again. 'My mother's passing seemed to stir something in Lucy, and we grew closer for a time as she sought to comfort me as I grieved. Her health seemed to improve, as did her mood, and I started to hope that we had begun a new and better chapter of our lives together. Her enthusiasm for Society reemerged, and one day she announced that when I next went to London, she would accompany me.' He shook his head. 'I took this as a sign that she'd begun to enjoy being with me. What a fool I was.'

In the dim light he saw Elspeth's brow furrow, and he could sense that she was working it all out. 'There was something or someone else she sought in London, wasn't there?' she breathed. 'Some ulterior motive for her sudden enthusiasm to join you.'

'There was someone else,' he confirmed. 'Someone I'd been aware of, but had thought nothing of until that fateful day I returned home early from the Lords and caught them together.' He gave her a meaningful look, hoping that was sufficient to convey exactly what such *togetherness* had entailed. 'Suddenly, everything made sense.'

He watched as Elspeth's dark eyes grew wide. 'Lucy had a lover,' she said.

He nodded. 'Yes. Someone she had loved for a long time, and who loved her in return. Someone she had promised herself to, before she was forced into marrying me. Someone she could not bear to be parted from, and whose absence from her life had caused her such intense misery.'

'Who was he?'

'Not he,' Robert replied, meeting that inquisitive dark stare once more. 'She.'

Elspeth remained at Robert's side, her fingers wrapped in his as she listened in an astonished silence to the rest of his story. In truth, she hardly knew what to make of it. It was not that she was unaware of the possibility of women developing tender feelings for other women, it was just that she'd never encountered such ladies in Society before. But then, she supposed, those sorts of liaisons were bound to be clandestine, conducted behind closed doors and beneath the veil of female friendship. Ladies like Lucy, and indeed like herself, were expected to find suitably wealthy and noble husbands, irrespective of their own feelings. To desire anything else was to risk Society's scorn. Spinsters and bluestockings were bad enough, as Elspeth knew only too well, but a lady with a female lover? That was unthinkable to most, and certainly never openly discussed.

In Lucy's case, however, it seemed that suppressing her desires had proven impossible. Robert explained that Lucy and her lover, Frances, had pledged themselves to each other, making plans to live together as spinsters. Plans which had never come to fruition, since their respective fathers had arranged marriages for them, with Frances marrying an extremely wealthy banker not long after Lucy had wed Robert. They'd continued their affair in London in the immediate aftermath of their marriages, until Lucy's removal to the Barden estate had separated them, prompting Lucy's descent into that deep despair which had bewildered Robert for so long. But when Frances wrote to Lucy, informing her that her husband had died unexpectedly and pleading with her to return to London, Lucy had been determined to reunite with her beloved at any cost. The day that Robert had discovered them together had also been the day that they'd been making their plans to run away.

'I am glad I saw them together that day,' Robert concluded with a sigh. 'Otherwise, Lucy would have simply disappeared, and I would have had no idea why or where she had gone.'

Elspeth felt her eyes widen at that. 'Surely she would have left you a letter?' she asked. Until now she'd felt some sympathy for Lucy's plight, but to have simply abandoned Robert like that would have been cruel and thoughtless.

In the dim light, she saw him shake his head. 'I doubt it. I recall looking at her that day and thinking how desperate she was. She would have done anything to be with Frances.'

'What happened next?' Elspeth asked quietly.

Robert laughed bitterly. 'You mean, after I realised my marriage was over? I did the only thing I could do—I decided to let her go. Frances had become a woman of considerable means, with a house in a remote part of Wales and a good income bequeathed to her by her husband. We agreed to a formal separation, whereby Lucy would live with Frances and I would provide her with an annual allowance. We agreed this privately, deciding that, given the circumstances, it would be best to guard the details of our separation closely. Lucy's health had improved, but I was concerned that her state of mind remained fragile—as was Frances. We knew that even the merest hint of scandal would be more than she could bear, and so I sought to protect her. I was naïve really. I thought that a dignified silence was the best way forward. I did not appreciate how easily silence becomes a void into which rumours are seeded and permitted to grow.'

Elspeth nodded. 'Yes, and you quickly became the villain of the story.' She shook her head. 'I remember hearing the tales of how you'd cruelly exiled your wife to the countryside because she'd objected to your philandering ways. How you were just like your father. It must have been awful, Robert, to hear yourself spoken about like that. You must have been tempted to say something, surely?'

'Like what?' He let go of her hand, dragging his hands wearily down his face. 'Husbands and wives do not separate without just cause, and Society will always seek to attribute blame. If I had suggested that the fault was not with me, then people would have either thought I was lying, or worse, they would have blamed Lucy instead. I could bear the scrutiny, but I knew she could not. She might never have loved me, but she was still my wife. I was bound in law and the eyes of God to care for her.'

Elspeth was taken aback by the vehement nobility of his words. 'All these years of being whispered about, of having accusing fingers pointed at you. Of being portrayed as the Devil himself, and yet, none of it could have been further from the truth.'

'I'm not a saint, Elspeth,' he replied quietly. 'I just tried to do what I thought was best. I'm not immune to feeling resentful or angry each time I'm reminded of how the world sees me.'

She shifted uncomfortably, thinking of all the times her curt words to him must have issued such reminders. 'I don't believe anyone could be immune to that. I am sorry for how I have behaved towards you at times,' she whispered.

He smiled at her. 'Don't be. I have spent a good deal of our acquaintance trying to convince you of my wickedness, after all.'

She nodded slowly, one final question weighing heavily on her mind. 'What happened to Lucy, in the end?'

'She died almost four years ago, from consumption,' he replied. 'After about a year in Wales, her health worsened again and never really recovered. Of course, the rumour-mongers hold me responsible for that, too, but in truth it was illness that took her.' In the near darkness Elspeth could see the weight of sadness in his eyes. 'Towards the end she wrote to me, telling me that although she was dying, she was happy, and wishing for my happiness, too. She even told me that once she was gone, I should marry again.'

Unfathomably, Elspeth felt her heart begin to beat a little faster. 'But you won't,' she whispered.

For a moment Robert was silent. Then, before she could say anything more, he wrapped his arm around her shoulder, pulling her close to him. 'No, I won't,' he replied.

Elspeth leaned against him, relishing the shiver which the feeling of his warm breath on her hair provoked. She knew she ought to pull away, that she should not be sitting there like that, with him—indeed, she should not be there, in that outbuilding in the depths of night, at all. And yet, as she cuddled closer to him, enjoying the muscular solidity of his chest beneath her fingers and listening to the beating of his heart, she found herself struck by an overwhelming sense of rightness. Of belonging. Of everything falling into place, just as it was meant to be.

She looked up at him. 'Perhaps you should,' she said. Then, before she could reason with herself, she reached up and kissed him, firmly and intently, upon the lips.

Chapter Fourteen

Elspeth breathed in deeply, greeting the bright and breezy summer's afternoon with a sigh of relief as she wandered down the lane. Quite unexpectedly she had found herself at liberty today. Her mother and Lady Dunsforth had gone out in the carriage to attend a picnic with other ladies of Lady Dunsforth's acquaintance, and they had not protested when she'd asked not to join them. Lady Melliora had already excused herself following her brief appearance at breakfast, looking pale and drawn, explaining that she was feeling unwell. Elspeth had seized the opportunity to do likewise, suggesting she was fatigued and would not be good company.

A suggestion which was not a lie, exactly—in fact, to say that ever since her nighttime meeting with Robert she'd had a lot on her mind would be an understatement. In truth, she was still grappling with it all and still struggling to comprehend how Robert bore the repeated blows which life had dealt him. To be forced into a marriage which had offered him only rejection and betrayal was bad enough, but to try so hard to act rightly and yet still find himself judged so harshly—it was a wonder it had not driven him out of his wits. How he'd managed to meet so much injustice with such stoicism, she would never comprehend. It was clear that the sacrifices he'd made to guard his wife and to keep her secrets had cost him dearly, and yet he had never broken, he had never surrendered. He had tolerated his dreadful reputation with a quiet dignity in self-imposed exile, resigning himself to the necessity of remaining invisible and alone.

Robert Barden was not a saint, but he was honourable, and he was admirable. More than anything, he deserved happiness and he deserved to be loved. That was what she'd meant to tell him when she'd suggested that perhaps he was wrong to dismiss the idea of remarriage—or at least, that was what she had been telling herself she'd meant, ever since. If she was honest, the feelings which had gripped her in the aftermath of Robert's revelations had been as confusing as they were powerful. That night, he'd let down his guard and taken her into his confidence. He'd left her in no doubt as to who the real Lord Barden was; that kind and decent man she'd glimpsed over the preceding weeks had come into full view, and now it was as though she would never be able to tear her eyes from him again. The real Robert Barden made her blood heat and her heart race; he dominated her thoughts and made her long for his touch. Made her long for his kisses.

Oh God, and she had kissed him that night, hadn't she? Right after telling him that he should reconsider his position on marriage, she'd pressed her lips against his for the briefest of moments before bidding him a swift goodnight. In the days since they'd parted, the memory of that kiss had tormented her. Just what had she been thinking, and moreover, just what had Robert made of it? He had kissed her before, of course, but that was different, wasn't it? At least, he'd told her that he'd been trying to convince her that he was wicked then, and nothing more. By contrast, there had been no mischief in her own kiss, only affection.

But then, the way he'd wrapped his arm around her and held her close as they'd sat together in that outbuilding had felt affectionate too, hadn't it? Was it possible that Robert felt something for her, too?

Oh, she was so confused! Elspeth walked faster, as though somehow her feet could outpace her racing thoughts. She'd reached open countryside now, the gentle townscape of Hallowford some distance behind her as rolling green fields and gentle patches of woodland greeted her. This was exactly what she needed, she told herself. A healthy dose of solitude and fresh air never failed to soothe her unquiet mind, and so it would today. These past days, she'd longed to see Robert again and dreaded their next encounter in equal measure. Her fevered imagination had contrived scores of ways their paths might be forced to cross, whilst at the same time fearing that she would betray her hopeless attraction to him in the merest glance. She vowed now that when she did see him again, she would be calm and collected, and not at all vexed or flustered. She would not even think about how she'd kissed him, never mind mention it. And certainly, she would not kiss him again…

The dull thud of hooves as a horse galloped towards her startled Elspeth from her thoughts. She felt her breath catch in her throat as she spied a familiar figure sitting astride on his mount, the wind wreaking havoc with his red-brown hair. Seeing her, he slowed the beast to a gentle canter as he approached.

'Elspeth,' he called as he drew his horse to a halt. 'I was not expecting to see you here.'

Elspeth watched as he climbed down to greet her, trying hard not to feast on the sight of his strong legs in his fawn riding breeches. She lifted her eyes to meet his, praying she was not glowing scarlet. So much for being calm and unflustered.

'I have made my escape,' she replied, covering her wayward thoughts with a mischievous smile.

'I can see that.' He chuckled. 'And without so much as an interminable chaperone in sight. Excellent work.'

She inclined her head playfully. 'Yes, well, perhaps

I ought not stray too far. Mother and Lady Dunsforth are attending a picnic, but I cannot think they will be gone all day.'

'Where are you going?' he asked.

She shrugged. 'Nowhere in particular. I just needed... I just wanted some air, I suppose.'

He gave her a knowing look. 'Yes, me, too.' Briefly he glanced over his shoulder. 'There are some old priory ruins not far from here. Just beyond the woodland, over there.' He looked at her cautiously. 'It's a very pretty, quiet spot. I could take you there, if you like?'

Elspeth hesitated. Crossing paths with Robert was one thing, but deliberately disappearing into the depths of the countryside with him was quite another. But then, had they not already been alone together countless times now? And it hardly seemed likely that they'd be seen by anyone in such a secluded place...

'How long will it take to walk there, do you think?' she asked.

'Oh, um—actually, I was suggesting that we ride,' Robert replied.

'What, together? On your horse?' Elspeth felt her heart begin to race. Suddenly the idea of being pressed up against Robert as they made their way across the fields on horseback seemed both tantalisingly tempting and downright dangerous.

Robert nodded, giving the animal an affectionate rub. 'He's a gentle giant, I promise.'

There were so many reasons why this was a terrible idea. One was that she was not dressed for riding, and therefore could not depend upon the drape of a habit to protect her modesty. A second was that she would have to allow Robert to lift her on to the horse, then sit virtually on his lap, and certainly secure in his arms, as they rode together…

'All right, then,' she said briskly, suppressing that sensible inner voice as she surrendered to the desire to spend time in Robert's company. Besides, she told herself, riding was quicker than walking, and hadn't she always adored a romantic ruin?

Her half-hearted attempts at applying logical thought to the situation evaporated the moment Robert took hold of her waist. She suppressed a gasp as momentarily he drew her towards him, allowing their eyes to meet for an achingly brief moment before raising her so that she could sit sideways upon the horse. Then, without a word, he mounted the horse so that he sat behind her, using his arms to steady her as he took hold of the reins once more. Even on such a warm day, the heat of his body around hers was stirring, provoking feelings like those she'd first experienced in his library when he'd kissed her, and she'd almost lost herself in the ecstasy of his touch.

'Stay close to me,' he murmured, the deep timbre of his voice and the warmth of his breath against her ear sending shivers of awareness down her spine. 'We won't go at more than a trot. You'll be perfectly safe, I promise.'

Elspeth nodded, allowing herself to rest against his chest as they set off towards the ruins. Nothing about this was sensible; if anyone spied her now, nestled against the body of Lord Barden, it would cause a scandal. And yet, the temptation to be with him like this had proven impossible to resist. There was no denying it: she had developed a tendre for this man, one which was now fully outside of her control. She was not used to feeling like this; she was not used to allowing her heart to rule her instead of her head. She was a bluestocking and a spinster and long ago had made her peace with how her life would be. She'd never once considered that a man like Robert might wander into her quiet, orderly, scholarly life and turn everything on its head. That she would find herself craving his company and his touch, and wondering all the while whether it was possible that he felt the same.

'It was a Carthusian priory. Founded in the fourteenth century.'

As Robert dismounted from his horse and held out his arms to lift Elspeth down, he wondered if he'd taken leave of his senses. The chances of them being seen together in the wilds which lay beyond Hallowford were slim; nevertheless, this impromptu outing was unwise and the opposite of keeping the distance he'd previously insisted was necessary to thwart Isabelle Stephenson's gossiping tongue. Even more concerning, however, was how riding with Elspeth pressed against him like that had made him feel. The whole ride had been torture, her proximity stoking his lust and longing, although he'd known to expect that. What he'd been wholly unprepared for, as she'd nestled against his chest, enveloped between his arms, was how he'd been struck by something deeper than base desire. Something tender and far more dangerous. A feeling which went beyond craving her. A feeling which made him wish that she could be his.

A feeling which, if he was honest with himself, had been threatening to overwhelm him since that night in the outhouse. Since he'd poured out his heart to her and she'd listened to him without judgement. Since he'd been unable to resist pulling her into his arms. Since she'd kissed him.

Because she had kissed him, hadn't she? He had not dreamt it. Just as he had not dreamt that she'd suggested that he might be wrong to dismiss the idea of remarriage. In the past days, he'd ruminated on those words again and again, trying and failing to decide why she'd said them. Trying and failing not to let his desires run wild as more than once he found himself imagining what it would be like to share his life with Elspeth, despite knowing that there was no point in thinking about that.

'Carthusian?'

Elspeth breathed her question as he helped her down. He made short work of it, not daring to let their eyes meet or his hands linger upon her trim waist, lest he succumb to the temptation to pull her close to him and draw a line of kisses down her neck.

'Yes.' He tethered his horse to a tree, then offered her his arm as they walked towards the ruins. 'You can still see where the monks' cells were, surrounding the cloister, although many of the walls do not survive above waist height now. The church tower has fared better, though, as you can see.'

'It is lovely,' she replied, lifting her gaze to admire the simple stone structure. 'I must confess, I am not familiar with the Carthusians or their way of life.'

Robert's eyes widened in surprise as he regarded her. 'Have I unwittingly stumbled upon a subject about which Lady Elspeth Scott is not supremely well-informed?' he asked teasingly.

Merriment sparkled in those dark eyes, undermining her efforts to look displeased. 'Even I do not know everything,' She tightened her grip upon his arm, seeming to pull herself closer to him as they made their way towards the church tower. 'So, tell me about the Carthusians.'

'They are a hermitic religious order. Each monk living at this priory had a cell of his own, in which he spent most of his time—praying, writing and studying in solitude and silence.'

Elspeth grinned at him. 'Sounds blissful.'

He chuckled. 'I thought you might say that.' He felt his expression grow serious once more as his eyes searched hers. 'It is possible to tire of being alone, though.'

'I imagine it is.'

She stared back at him for a long moment, and he had the sense that he was being studied once again. This time, however, he realised that it did not trouble him. He no longer felt as though there was anything about himself that he needed to hide.

'I will have to imagine, of course, since I am seldom alone these days,' she continued. 'Although I did manage to evade my social obligations today, so perhaps I should not complain too much.'

'No, I understand. There is such a thing as too much company, too,' he replied.

'Are you trying to tell me something, my lord?' Elspeth laughed, placing a hand on her chest in mock offence.

'Not at all. I don't think I could ever tire of your company.'

Elspeth's smile faded, and for a moment Robert regretted the candour of his words. But then, she squeezed his arm, patting it gently with her free hand.

'I agree,' she replied. 'I don't believe I could tire of your company, either.'

She relinquished his arm, and for several moments they walked in silence, weaving their way around a maze of crumbling walls and into the roofless remains of the chapel. Robert tried to keep his attention firmly on their surroundings, but his gaze wandered to Elspeth as often as his thoughts replayed the words of her compliment. She could not tire of his company, either. Did she mean it? Or had those words been uttered out of politeness rather than sincerity?

He hardly dared to hope that she had meant it. Just as he hardly dared to contemplate the implications for their acquaintance, if she did. It was one thing to confide in her, to foster friendship with her, even to desire her. It was quite another to think that a woman like her might ever entertain the idea of having a man with a reputation like his. Even if she did, could he honestly countenance offering himself to her, when he knew all too well the consequences of such a union? She would be shunned by Society, and forever tarnished by association with him. Her life would be ruined, and all because of him.

The thought of it made his stomach lurch. No—there could never be anything more between them than this. Scarcely more than a week of Elspeth's time in Hallowford remained, and her departure would mark their separation for good. For them, there could only ever have been this summer; it was madness to contemplate anything more. It was futile to dream of a future which could never be, no matter how much he craved it. No matter how much he wanted her.

'I presume that in between all of your social obligations, you have found little time for reading,' Robert said in the end, choosing a safe topic of conversation. Choosing to avoid dangerous subjects like feelings or desires or kisses.

Even though he ached to ask why she'd kissed him that night. Even though he yearned to kiss her again.

She sighed. 'That is correct. I suppose I ought to have stayed at home today and settled down with a book while I had the chance, rather than wandering off into the country.'

'But then you would not have seen me, or this charming ruin,' Robert countered with a smile. 'Even the most diligent scholar cannot study all the time. Besides, it is far too beautiful a day to be anywhere other than outside, enjoying it.'

She inclined her head in agreement. 'True. Still, I fear I will have to return your book about Norse mythology to you unread.'

'Keep it,' he insisted.

He watched as Elspeth's lips parted in surprise. 'But it belonged to your brother.'

'And as a learned man, Rafe would have been delighted for it to fall into the possession of a brilliant and accomplished woman like yourself.'

'That is kind of you, Robert,' Elspeth murmured. 'Thank you. I will treasure it.'

They'd moved to stand in the shadow of the tower now, its tall remains shielding them from the afternoon sun and from prying eyes—not that there was anyone here to observe them. Before he could stop himself, Robert reached out, running his fingers tenderly down her cheek. What he'd said had been the truth; Rafe would have liked Elspeth. He would have been drawn to that sharp wit and clever mind like a moth to a flame. Moreover, he would have seen immediately his older brother's hopeless attraction to her and would have urged him to pursue her. Indeed, if he was here now, he'd be busy admonishing Robert for even considering allowing a woman like Lady Elspeth Scott to slip through his fingers.

'What happened to your brother?' Elspeth whispered her question, taking hold of the hand which had come to rest beneath her chin and lacing her fingers with his.

'He was killed.' Robert pressed his lips together for a moment, collecting himself. He still struggled to articulate what had happened to Rafe, even after all this time. 'It happened in London, not far from the Excise Office, where he'd held a senior position for several years. Apparently he'd been working late and had stepped outside for some air. It seems he walked a little way down the street, when he was set upon—more than likely by a thief. Like me, Rafe was a competent boxer and probably he tried to fight the man off. It's unclear exactly what happened, but the assailant was armed. He drew a pistol and shot my brother once, straight through the heart.'

He watched as Elspeth's eyes widened and her lips parted in shock. 'I am so sorry, Robert. That is dreadful. Was the killer apprehended?'

'No. The air was thick with fog that night, and at such a late hour the street was quiet. As soon as the shot rang out, the assailant fled. There were no witnesses.'

Elspeth shook her head in disbelief. 'To lose your brother like that, and then for there to be no justice… I do not know how you bear it.'

'The same way I bear everything else, I suppose. I try not to dwell on the past, or to think too much about the future. I keep to my quiet life in Hallowford and live one day at a time.'

'Yet you said yourself that you have tired of being alone,' she said softly. 'Do you ever think about leaving Hallowford?'

'And go where?' he asked. 'London Society would not welcome me, and I locked up my country house for good after Lucy left. It contains too many unhappy memories—not just of my doomed marriage, but of my childhood, too. Of living in fear of my father's wrath. Of watching helplessly as he destroyed my mother, little by little.'

Elspeth squeezed his fingers gently, as though to remind him that he was here, with her, and not that small boy again. 'You once said that Hallowford is a place of refuge as well as exile. I presume then that your memories of summers spent here are better ones?'

He nodded. 'Rafe and I only ever came here with our mother. Mercifully, my father never joined us. Every summer, it was as though my mother would come alive again, spending long afternoons taking tea with Lady Dunsforth while Rafe and I ran riot with Melliora and her brother. It was a reprieve for all of us, I suppose. From my father—from his behaviour,' he added carefully.

Elspeth looked at him thoughtfully. 'I suppose Lady Dunsforth and your mother had a lot in common, given what they both had to endure with their respective husbands.'

'I think they supported each other. Certainly Lady Dunsforth was always very good to my mother, and to Rafe and me.'

'It's no wonder you are like family now, then.'

Robert swallowed hard at the truth in Elspeth's statement, thinking immediately of the Great Secret, and of Tilly. He'd shared so much about his life and his past with her, but still, there were some things she could never know. Some secrets which were not his to tell.

'Lady Dunsforth and Lady Melliora know the truth about Lucy, don't they?' Elspeth asked quietly.

He nodded. 'Rafe knew, too, although he died about a year before Lucy did. Her passing would have shocked him—although that would not have prevented him from urging me to fall in love and to remarry. He was a great believer in that.'

Elspeth quirked an eyebrow at him. 'But you are not?'

Robert drew a deep breath. How could he begin to answer such a question, especially when it had been posed by the woman he strongly suspected he was falling for? The woman he yearned for but could not have, because even if she wanted him, in his heart he knew that he could never condemn her to a life spent with him.

'Anyone can fall in love,' he replied, gently withdrawing his hand from hers now. 'Surely the question is whether or not it is wise to do so.'

Chapter Fifteen

Elspeth slipped through the door of the Dunsforth house, trying to be as quiet as she could. She had parted company with Robert before they'd reached the lane, walking on ahead of him in the hopes that they would not be spied together. Passing the stables, she'd seen that the Dunsforth carriage and horses had returned, which meant that so too had her mother and Lady Dunsforth. Drat it. No doubt her mother had already received reports from the servants about her prolonged absence and would treat Elspeth to yet another interrogation, the moment she learned she was home.

Elspeth walked briskly up the stairs, hoping to reach her bedchamber and evade her mother's questioning for a while yet. In truth, right now she did not feel ready to face anyone. She could feel how flushed her cheeks were, how her heart raced and her mind whirred at the memory of the afternoon she'd spent with Robert. Of how, once again, he'd spoken to her so honestly about the past, about his brother. Of how they'd confessed to enjoying each other's company. Of how it had felt to sit nestled against him on horseback; how she'd held his hand as they'd talked, and how he'd sent a delicious shiver down her spine when he'd brushed his fingers down her cheek. She'd held her breath then, wondering if he would kiss her in earnest, just as she'd dared to do that night in the outhouse. Hoping that he would. And yet, he had not.

Elspeth sighed, leaning her head against her bedchamber door. Perhaps, for all their growing closeness, Robert did not desire anything more than friendship with her. Or, if he did, he was determined to suppress those feelings. After all, as he'd said himself, falling in love was not necessarily wise, and certainly, he believed it would be unwise for any lady to love him. The problem was, wise or not, Elspeth was beginning to suspect that she was dangerously close to losing her heart completely to Robert Barden, and she had no idea what to do about it. Her time in Hallowford was coming to an end, and when it did, she would have to leave Robert behind. Could she really face doing that, without uttering a word about her feelings for him?

'Where have you been, dearest?'

The sound of her mother's voice startled Elspeth from her thoughts. She turned to see the Dowager Duchess standing a little way down the hall, a deep frown etched between her eyes.

'I was out walking,' she replied as smoothly as she could. 'Forgive me for being home so late. It was such a lovely afternoon and I must have wandered further than I intended.'

'I see. I thought you said this morning that you were too fatigued to go out,' her mother said pointedly.

'I was, but I read awhile and felt better. I thought that a little air would be restorative.'

Her mother nodded slowly. 'Were you alone?'

The question was so loaded with suspicion that it took all of Elspeth's strength not to shrink beneath its weight. 'Of course,' she said, trying her best to look offended as she gave voice to her lie. 'Lady Melliora was too unwell to join me, and Temperance was accompanying you.'

Elspeth watched with bated breath as her mother's eyes narrowed, just briefly. 'I would prefer it if you did not wander off all afternoon by yourself, Elsie. We are not at Chatton now.'

As tempted as she was to protest at the infantilising nature of such a decree, Elspeth decided that in the circumstances, meek acceptance was best. After all, it was clear that her mother was not entirely inclined to believe her.

'Of course, Mama.'

Despite Elspeth's assurances, those keen blue eyes of her mother's remained narrowed. 'Elspeth, I...' she began.

'Yes, Mama?'

The sound of frantic footsteps above them intruded, causing the Dowager Duchess to startle. 'We will talk more later,' she said, shaking her head. 'Now is not the time. Lady Melliora is still feeling unwell, and now little Tilly and her nursemaid have begun to sicken. Lady Dunsforth is at Tilly's bedside while she awaits the physician's arrival, and a servant has gone next door to fetch Lord Barden.'

'Lord Barden?' Elspeth repeated, hoping she sounded nonchalant. 'Why?'

Her mother shrugged. 'Tilly has asked for him. I'd have thought he would want to keep away if there is sickness in the house, but Lady Dunsforth assures me that he will come.'

Elspeth nodded. 'He will be concerned. As Lady Dunsforth says, he is a good neighbour.'

The Dowager Duchess arched an eyebrow at that, but before either of them could say anything further, Robert came running up the stairs. He attempted a bow as he approached them, although it was plain to see that he was far too agitated for performed politeness.

'Duchess. Lady Elspeth. Forgive the intrusion,' he said breathlessly. 'I presume Tilly is in the nursery?'

Elspeth nodded. 'She is. Come, my lord, I will take you to her.' Spying the look of protest on her mother's face, she added: 'I can see if Lady Dunsforth requires any assistance.'

Hurriedly she turned away, then led Robert up a further flight of stairs towards the nursery. She might as well make herself useful, she told herself. Better that than hiding in her room, ruminating on her feelings, or standing in the hallway at the mercy of one of her mother's lectures.

Lady Dunsforth greeted them both with a grim nod as they walked through the door. She was perched beside the bed in which Tilly lay, her countenance sombre as she regarded her granddaughter anxiously. The child, meanwhile, was pale, her eyes opening and closing as she fought the lure of sleep. Nevertheless the sight of Robert raised a weary smile, and she held out her hand towards him.

'Look, Tilly—Robert and Lady Elspeth have both come to see you,' Lady Dunsforth said quietly.

'How is she?' Robert asked, his tone thick with worry.

'Still a little feverish,' she replied. 'But well enough to resist sleeping and to keep asking for you, which I am taking to be a good sign.'

Elspeth heard Robert sigh with relief, before turning to pull two chairs closer to the bed and beckoning Elspeth to sit beside him. 'And Melliora?' he asked.

'Much the same as she was this morning. The physician has sent word that he will call shortly and attend to them both—and Tilly's nursemaid, of course.' Lady Dunsforth rose slowly from her seat. 'Melliora has asked to see me. Would you mind keeping Tilly company, at least until Evans can spare one of the maids?'

Robert nodded. 'No need to trouble the servants—I am happy to stay for as long as I am needed.'

'As am I,' Elspeth agreed swiftly.

The ghost of a frown appeared momentarily between Lady Dunsforth's brows as she regarded them both carefully, but then Tilly coughed and her attention was diverted back towards the small patient in the bed once more. 'Very well,' she said, stepping towards the door. 'Lady Elspeth, I will inform your mother that you are staying here, with Lord Barden and Tilly.'

Elspeth emitted a deep sigh as she heard the nursery door click shut, announcing Lady Dunsforth's departure. 'Do not be surprised if my mother comes bursting in any moment,' she said, answering the quizzical look which Robert gave her.

'I see,' he replied, glancing at Tilly, who appeared to have finally surrendered to sleep. 'Well, if she does, I will assure her that Tilly is a keen-eyed chaperone and you are in no danger of being ravished by me.'

Elspeth rolled her eyes in mock exasperation, laughing softly and trying not to think about how she'd felt that day in his library, when Robert had played the wicked lord and had done exactly that. Trying not to consider just how often she imagined being ravished by him again.

'What does *radish* mean?'

The sound of Tilly's little voice startled her, and Elspeth looked down to see two bright blue, inquisitive eyes regarding them both. She glanced helplessly at Robert then, unsure how best to answer the child. In reply he shrugged, then offered her an amused grin before returning his attention to the girl.

'I thought you were sleeping, Tilly,' he said.

'Not sleepy,' she replied, even as her eyes began to roll once more. 'I can count to thirty now, Robert. One, two, three…'

'Another time, Tilly,' he whispered softly. 'Once you are feeling better.'

'Is Lady Elspeth your friend?'

The girl's eyes had closed again now, but her question, although uttered sleepily, had a sharp pertinence which made Elspeth flinch. She looked up to meet Robert's gaze and saw that there was an unmistakable warmth there, swirling in those green depths. Her mind immediately wandered to their impromptu outing earlier that day. To the feeling of sitting so close to him as they rode together on his horse. To the feeling of her arm resting against his as they meandered together around the ruins. To the feeling of simply being with him, of talking to him. Warm feelings, certainly, but ones which for her signified more than friendship. She knew that now. Knew it, and could not ignore it.

'Yes, Lady Elspeth is my friend,' he confirmed, a small smile hinting at the corners of his mouth as he held Elspeth's eye.

'You have lots of friends. Me… Mama… Grandmama…'

He chuckled softly. 'I would not say lots. Indeed, Lady Elspeth is the first friend I have made in a long time.'

'Is that why you want to *radish* her?'

Elspeth heard herself gasp, then clapped her hand over her mouth in a bid to stifle her laughter. She saw that Robert's mouth had fallen open, his words clearly failing him as he fell into an uncharacteristic silence. Then he offered her the briefest, most sheepish grin, and she was certain that she could see a hint of red creeping up from beneath his collar. His embarrassment was strangely endearing, and before she could stop herself, Elspeth reached for his hand, placing it in her lap and entwining her fingers with his. They sat like that for several moments, quietly watching Tilly, as mercifully her questioning gave way to sleep once more, and Elspeth found herself imagining a life like this. A life she'd always resisted permitting herself to consider. A life with a home, a husband, and children of her own.

A life spent with Robert by her side, watching their babies as they slept.

Then the door clicked open and the physician walked in, closely followed by Lady Dunsforth and the Dowager Duchess, and their fingers flew apart. Discomfited by her thoughts, Elspeth made a swift retreat, muttering barely discernible excuses and praying that no one would notice the longing and the turmoil which she felt certain was lingering in her eyes.

Robert crept out of the nursery as quietly as he could, conscious that the hour was late and that the Dunsforth household had retired for the night. He'd spent all evening in the nursery by Tilly's side, not even leaving her to take some supper. Instead, he'd accepted Lady Dunsforth's offer to have a tray sent up to him, although he'd found himself picking at its contents, his appetite having apparently deserted him. Little wonder, really; between his concern for Tilly's health and his ongoing struggle with his feelings for Elspeth, he had a great deal on his mind. Thankfully, the physician had seemed confident that Tilly would make a swift recovery, and indeed, despite her evident fatigue, there had been hints of the lively little girl he knew. Nonetheless, he had not been able to bring himself to leave her, and to her credit, Lady Dunsforth had not suggested that he should—until now, at least. At the stroke of midnight she'd appeared in the doorway, telling him in no uncertain terms that he needed to go home and rest and that she would take over for now.

'I will send word if her condition changes,' she'd promised as she'd eased herself into the rocking chair in the corner.

He'd known from the look on the indomitable lady's face that there was little point in arguing. 'How is Melliora?' he'd whispered, rising from his seat.

'Sleeping soundly,' Lady Dunsforth had replied. 'The physician gave her one of his draughts, which seems to have done the trick. Now go,' she'd urged him, waving a dismissive hand in his direction. 'And stop worrying! Tilly is strong, just like her mother.'

'And her father.'

The words had fallen from his lips before he could stop them. He'd left the room then, before Lady Dunsforth could reply. Before she could remind him of everything he was not meant to say. Of everything which was never to be discussed. Tonight, of all nights, he had not wished to hear it.

He tiptoed down the stairs and along the hallway of the second floor, where the bedchambers which Lady Dunsforth kept for guests were situated. He felt his heart beat a little faster as he wandered past the room in which Elspeth slept. She had not reappeared after the physician had left, and in truth, he had missed her company. Missed the feeling of her fingers wrapped around his. The quiet hours he'd spent at Tilly's side had given him far too much time to think—about his feelings for Elspeth, and about what a life spent together would be like. As darkness had fallen and a maid had come in to draw the curtains on the world outside, he'd realised that he'd been lost in a reverie, imagining Elspeth as his wife and the mother of his children. Imagining that empty home next door, transformed by a full nursery and echoing with the noise of chaos and the sound of laughter. Imagining how it would feel to wake up each day at Elspeth's side; to be permitted to love her and to feel loved in return.

He paused at the top of the stairs, heaving a weary sigh. Perhaps Lady Dunsforth did have a point—perhaps he did need to rest. Clearly, the events of the day had left him too overwrought to properly control his emotions. Some sleep, followed by some boxing in the early morning would help him to master them, although he knew that he could not conquer them completely. His longing for Elspeth now ran far too deep for that.

'Robert?'

The hushed sound of Elspeth's voice made him startle. He held up the candle he carried and looked over to see her standing in the doorway of her bedchamber. He sucked in a sharp breath as his tired eyes absorbed the alluring sight of her in her nightgown, her dark hair plaited and draped over one shoulder. He swallowed hard, knowing that if he had any sense, he'd bid her a swift goodnight and hurry back towards the sanctuary of his own home. Certainly, he should not linger here a moment longer, and he absolutely should not walk back along the hallway to speak to her…

Except, that was exactly what he did. 'I was just returning home,' he whispered as he drew closer. 'I am sorry if I disturbed you.'

She shook her head. 'You didn't. I wasn't asleep.' Momentarily she chewed her lip, then glanced nervously along the hallway.

'I should go,' he murmured. 'If your mother sees us…'

'No. Don't.' She placed a hand upon his chest and looked up at him, those dark eyes of hers at once resolute and beseeching. 'Come in—just for a moment.'

He began to shake his head. 'Elspeth, I don't think I should…' he rasped, his mouth feeling suddenly dry.

'Please. I want to talk to you and I cannot do that here.'

One look at the imploring expression on her face and Robert knew he was powerless to refuse. God help him. With a brisk nod he slipped quietly inside her bedchamber, then stealthily closed the door behind them before placing his candle down on a nearby table. He clasped his hands behind his back, determined to be a gentleman and to keep his distance. Determined not to notice the way her nightgown skimmed over every perfect curve of her figure, or the way that several dark curls of her hair had freed themselves from her plait and were now daring him to touch them.

'This is a bad idea,' he breathed, partly to Elspeth but mostly to himself. 'If you wanted to talk to me, why did you not return to the nursery after the physician left? I've been sitting with Tilly all evening.'

'My mother forbade it,' Elspeth whispered. 'After dinner she told me in no uncertain terms that I was to retire to my room for the rest of the evening. She insisted that she would be doing the same, that in the circumstances it was the proper thing for guests to do, but...' She paused then, pressing her lips together tightly, as though she was fighting hard to control her emotions.

Despite himself, Robert reached out and cupped her face with his hand. 'What is it, Elspeth?'

Her eyes met his, and even in the candlelight, he could see the concern swirling in their depths. 'Nothing,' she said after a long moment. 'I just think she might have an inclination, that's all. About us.'

'About us?' he repeated, his voice oddly strained as he withdrew his hand.

'Yes—about the time we've been spending together. About our...friendship.'

He nodded, trying not to ruminate upon how painfully inadequate that word felt. 'We haven't done anything wrong, Elspeth,' he insisted, trying not to allow his thoughts to linger upon how that was not entirely true. He doubted very much whether the Dowager Duchess would regard kisses in his library, or clandestine midnight meetings, or riding with her tucked against him on his horse as innocent markers of friendship.

She gave him a tight smile. 'You're right. Whatever she might think of you, she cannot surely object to us simply getting along well together.' She shook her head at herself then. 'Forgive me, I realise I have not even asked you about Tilly. How is she?'

'She is sleeping. The physician thinks that with plenty of rest, she will recover quickly.'

'That is a relief. Not that illness has prevented her from missing anything.' She gave him a pointed look. 'You'll have to mind your tongue in future, unless you want more awkward questions about *radishes*.'

He smiled. 'She is a clever girl. It really is high time that Melliora began to look for a governess for her...' He paused, shaking his head at himself. What on earth had got into him tonight? 'Forgive me, I should not have said that. It isn't for me to have an opinion on such matters.'

If Elspeth thought the remark odd, then she didn't show it. 'You will hear no disagreement from me,' she murmured. 'If I had my way, all girls would receive the very best education. I cannot think of a single reason why women should not grow up to be as learned as men.'

'I've little doubt that was your singular mission at that school of yours,' he observed.

'A mission which was in vain,' she replied sadly. 'The prevalent opinion was that village girls have little use for classical learning. An opinion which rather missed the point, I think, but after a time I had to accept that I was swimming against the tide.'

The defeated look which swept momentarily across her pretty features was disarming, and before he knew what he was doing, Robert had placed his hands gently upon her shoulders, pulling her towards him. 'I know you will have done your best,' he murmured.

Elspeth came to him willingly, wrapping her arms around him and tucking her head against his chest. For several minutes he stood there, holding her close to him, smoothing his fingers softly over her hair. The moment was tender and intimate, and it threatened to overwhelm him completely. He knew that he should retreat, that embracing Elspeth like this in the depths of the night was dangerous. That if he surrendered to his passions and allowed his lips to touch hers, the embers of his longing would burst into flames once more…

'I really should go,' he whispered, releasing her.
'Don't.'

She looked up at him then, her gaze dark with an

unguarded desire which matched his own. With her hand she cupped his cheek, then raised herself on to her tiptoes and placed the softest, most searching kiss upon his lips. The last vestiges of his resolve were vanquished by her touch, and he gathered her into his arms once more, the feeling of her tempting form pressed against him stoking his ardour as he deepened the kiss. He heard her moan her encouragement as his hands explored every curve, from the swell of her pert breasts to her slim waist and rounded bottom, and before he knew it, she was urging him further into the room and towards her bed. It was only when they collapsed down together on her soft sheets that he came, briefly, to his senses.

'Elspeth, are you sure about this?' he began. 'I can leave. We do not have to…'

In the dim light, he saw her smile as she ran her fingers over his chest. 'I know—but I want to. That is, if you want to…'

He caressed her cheek. 'I do. More than anything.'

It was the truth. As they kissed, as clothes were shed and they melted together in the heat of their embrace, Robert realised that he had never felt quite like this. As though this signified far more than desire, far more than the base pleasures of the flesh because, he knew, his heart was involved, too. Amongst those heady feelings of lust, he realised, lurked other, more profound emotions. A sense that this was entirely right. A sense that he belonged with Elspeth, and she with him.

A sense that this was what it was like to fall in love.

Chapter Sixteen

Elspeth nibbled on her hot roll, keeping her eyes fixed upon the table in front of her and trying to ignore the way her heart clattered and her entire body thrummed with nervous excitement. This morning the breakfast room was quiet, with illness or fatigue meaning that most of the household had remained in their rooms. Only Elspeth's mother had joined her, sitting down opposite her a short while ago to her tea and toast. A heavy silence hung between them as they ate, and every so often Elspeth felt the weight of her mother's scrutinising gaze upon her. She dared not meet it, fearing that if she did, her mother would know everything in an instant. She would read the look on her face and know what had happened last night.

She would know that Elspeth had invited Robert into her bed and had permitted him to know her completely.

Elspeth felt her cheeks grow warm as memories of those hours they'd spent together in the darkness flooded back to the fore. Heady, revelatory hours during which Robert had shown her pleasure and satisfied a need which she had not truly understood that she'd felt. She had not been entirely naïve about such intimacies, at least in a theoretical sense. She'd perused enough of her brother Ted's medical books to understand the mechanics of it. But the way Robert's touch had made her feel, and the sensations which had overwhelmed her as they'd joined together—no book could have prepared her for that.

When, reluctantly, Robert had left her bed and crept out of her room, she'd felt bereft, and even now, hours later, that ache remained as potent as ever. She knew that she ought to be sensible, that she ought to allow her head to rule her and not her heart. That she would do well to remind herself that taking Robert to her bed like that had been impulsive and reckless, that she really had only intended to talk to him. She'd planned to say so much—about her feelings for him, about the future. About whether their growing closeness might amount to more than friendship. About whether he might care for her, too. And yet, at the crucial moment her confidence had faltered; for the first time in her life, her words had failed her, and she'd allowed her actions and her passions to speak for her instead. Now there was still so much to say, and so much which had to be resolved. But still, there was reason to hope.

After last night, it was clear Robert shared her desires. Perhaps he might share her other feelings, too…

'We need to talk, Elsie.'

The clatter of the butter knife which accompanied the Dowager Duchess's words made Elspeth jump, and she forced herself to meet her mother's eye. 'We do? About what?'

Her mother sighed. 'I know what has happened, dearest, and I cannot remain silent about it any longer.'

Elspeth's heart descended into the pit of her stomach, and she prayed her cheeks were not glowing scarlet. Yesterday she'd had the discomfiting sense that her mother was suspicious about the nature of her acquaintance with Robert, but surely she could not know how far matters between them had gone. Surely she could not know that they'd been intimate, could she?

She swallowed hard. 'What do you mean, Mama?' she asked, forcing a frown and trying her best to sound genuinely perplexed.

However, it was clear from the severe look on her face that the Dowager Duchess was not going to be fooled. 'I am talking about you and *that man* who lives next door,' she hissed. 'I warned you, Elsie, after you danced with him at that ball. I saw the way he looked at you then, and…well, I told you to keep away from him, didn't I? I told myself that you're a sensible young woman, far too clever to fall for the charms of a man like that! Far too clever to court scandal with such a libertine.' She shook her head, pushing her plate away. 'How wrong I was.'

'Mama, it is not like that,' she began to protest. 'Lord Barden is not what you imagine him to be…'

'You're the talk of Hallowford, Elsie.' Her mother's usually bright blue stare was uncommonly dark and unrelenting. 'You have no idea how horrified I was, to overhear ladies gossiping and to realise that they were talking about my daughter.'

'What?'

'I heard a few of them discussing you at the picnic yesterday.' The Dowager Duchess shook her head in disbelief. 'There was a lady there, a Mrs Stephenson, whispering about how you'd been seen with Lord Barden at the Beethoven concert we attended—about how you'd allowed him to take your hand. They were speculating that you are his…his latest…'

Elspeth felt every bit of colour drain from her face. 'His what?' she whispered, although she hardly needed to ask. It was clear that Robert's fears about Isabelle Stephenson's rumour-mongering had been realised, and that they were at serious risk of being engulfed by scandal.

'His mistress, Elsie,' her mother hissed. 'The latest in a long line of women he has seduced for sport, without intending to wed a single one of them.' She shook her head. 'Thankfully Agnes had gone to speak to her driver and did not hear what was said. I'm not sure I could have borne the humiliation…'

'I am no such thing,' Elspeth protested, her heart pounding so hard that she could barely hear herself speak over the noise of it. 'Lord Barden has not…he would never…he is not like that, Mama!'

'Oh, Elspeth, how could you, of all people, allow yourself to be duped by that man?' Her mother pressed her eyes closed, as though she was unable to bear witness to the words she was about to say. 'Tell me there is no truth in any of this. Tell me you have not allowed him to take liberties with you. Tell me that you have not…'

Elspeth swallowed hard, thoughts of last night running unabated through her mind. There had been no seduction—at least, not on Robert's part. After all, she'd been the one to invite him into her room, and into her bed. She'd behaved impulsively and acted upon her passions, but she had done so freely. She had not been duped.

'I've done nothing I'm ashamed of, Mama,' she replied carefully. She knew that she could not be truthful, but she did not wish to lie, either.

The Dowager Duchess rested her head in her hands and sighed. 'We're leaving,' she said. 'As soon as possible.'

Elspeth stared at her mother, aghast. 'But we're not due to depart for another week,' she protested.

The Dowager Duchess looked up, her expression grave. 'We need to get you away from here. You must see that, Elsie. I spent half of last night thinking about it, and I can see no other way. I will inform Lady Dunsforth that our plans have changed.'

'But where will we go? Viscountess Millington is not expecting us until next week...'

'We are going to London,' her mother announced, her tone resolute. 'I've received word from your brother that he and Charlotte are to travel to the London house too, as Ted must do his duty and attend the Lords whilst all this unpleasant business with the Queen is going on. He said that we are welcome to join them, and so I will write to the Viscountess and explain. Cecily will understand. Indeed, given the circumstances I suspect that she will likely be in London too, before long.'

Elspeth shook her head, the heat of tears stinging her eyes. She blinked furiously, refusing to let them fall. 'And I suppose, since we will be in London, I will be forced to endure an endless stream of balls and dinners where you parade me in front of every suitable unmarried man the *ton* has to offer in the hopes that one of them will finally take me off your hands? How fortuitous for you, Mother,' she added, her voice thick with sarcasm. 'How well everything has turned out.'

The Dowager Duchess looked affronted. 'I only want what's best for you, dearest.'

The chair scraped harshly against the wooden floor as Elspeth stood up. 'Yet you've never once considered that the person who knows what is best for me, is me!'

Before her mother could say another word, Elspeth marched out of the breakfast room. Her head was spinning, and her stomach threatened to expel the single hot roll she'd managed to swallow. She leaned against the wall in the hallway, attempting to take several deep breaths. She needed to calm herself. She needed to think straight, to formulate a plan. She needed to see Robert, to warn him about the impending scandal. To tell him that she was being dragged away from Hallowford against her will. To confess what she felt for him and to find out if he felt the same way, too.

Perhaps he would say that he did care for her. Perhaps, together, they could tell the Dowager Duchess the truth about Lucy, about just how undeserved his reputation as the wicked lord was. Perhaps then her mother would understand, and would permit Robert to court her properly...

Seized by a renewed sense of hope, Elspeth hurried towards the Dunsforths' front door. Just as she was about to open it, however, she was distracted by the sound of raised voices, coming from the parlour. Two voices, she realised, as she crept back towards the closed door, listening carefully.

Voices belonging to Lady Dunsforth and to Robert, and they were arguing.

* * *

'I am not trying to interfere, Lady Dunsforth. I can assure you, I mean only to help.'

Robert raked an agitated hand through his hair, at a loss to understand how this conversation had deteriorated so quickly. A conversation, he reminded himself, which he had not even intended to have, but somehow an enquiry about Tilly's health had led to other topics and had got very much out of hand. He'd called at the Dunsforth house this morning with a very different purpose and a very different sort of conversation in mind. He'd hoped to speak not with Lady Dunsforth but with Elspeth, and he'd intended to offer himself to her in marriage. A course of action which he'd agonised over during a long and sleepless night, but one which he knew he had to take. Contrary to what the world believed about him, he was an honourable man, and honourable men did not bed maidens—and the sisters of dukes, no less—with impunity.

Although, if he was honest with himself, honour was not the only factor in his decision. Last night had been so far removed from all those casual liaisons with worldly widows; it had been heartfelt and profound, confirming beyond all doubt that he had fallen for Elspeth. That he wanted to spend his life with her. That he wanted to make her his wife. Honour bound him to offer himself to her, but he could not deny that his heart desired it, too. And so, he'd come today to declare himself, to confess his feelings and to try his best to set aside his guilt. Guilt at knowing that by asking for Elspeth's hand, he was offering her a life of being tainted by him, by his reputation, and by his very name. A life of being whispered about and ostracised. A life on the fringes of Society. But after last night, and given everything he felt for her, he had to ask her. Didn't he?

'This is hardly the time for a conversation about Tilly's education.' Lady Dunsforth's sharp tone brought Robert's mind back to the present discussion. 'Mother and child are still convalescing. Besides, Melliora has made her feelings plain often enough. She does not wish to employ a governess yet.'

'I appreciate this is not a good time, and that it is Melliora's decision. However, I want you to know that if the impediment is financial in nature, then I…'

'You know well enough that it is not, Robert,' Lady Dunsforth interrupted, her nostrils flaring as she regarded him. 'You know that Tilly is well provided for—by us, and by the late Earl's family.'

Robert must have bristled at that, because before he could say a word in response, Lady Dunsforth was glaring thunderously at him.

'You know how things must be, Robert,' she hissed, taking a step closer. 'You know what we all agreed, long ago—as far as Society is concerned, Tilly is the late Earl's child. You can never be more than a family friend and a neighbour to her. You must make your peace with that and hold your tongue or we shall all suffer—Tilly most of all.'

He nodded briskly. 'I am well aware of what is at stake,' he replied, his tone stern and unyielding. 'I want only what is best for Tilly, and in my opinion that is a good, classical education, with no limits placed upon her learning simply because she is a girl.'

Lady Dunsforth arched an eyebrow at that. 'We would like Tilly to marry well when she is of age, Robert, not become a bluestocking.'

'There is nothing wrong with a woman being learned, Lady Dunsforth,' he countered. 'It is a foolish man who does not want an interesting, educated woman for a wife.'

'Hmm,' Lady Dunsforth mused, giving him a pointed look. 'And one has to wonder if you have a particular interesting and educated woman in mind. Perhaps a young lady with whom you've spent a good deal of time, this summer.'

He bristled again, thinking immediately of his purpose in visiting. Of his planned proposal. 'I do not know what you mean.'

'I'm sure you do not.' Lady Dunsforth held his gaze, apparently seeing right through his protestation. Then she let out a heavy sigh, her face brightening as she regarded him in her usual affectionate way. 'Let us have no more cross words between us. I must join the

Dowager Duchess and Lady Elspeth in the breakfast room, and I'm sure you will want to see Tilly. Although, as I said, she is much improved this morning.'

'I am relieved to hear it, but on reflection, I think it would be best if I leave her to rest now,' Robert replied, offering Lady Dunsforth a tight smile. 'I can call again later.'

With a swift farewell, Robert made his way out of the parlour and towards the front door. It was clear that his plan to speak to Elspeth could not be realised whilst she was at breakfast with her ever-watchful mother. He would have to bide his time and seek another opportunity. Perhaps if he could find some way to get a note to her, he could ask her to meet him in the outhouse…

As he hurried down the steps, intent upon returning home, a familiar figure caught his eye, standing in the gardens across the street. A figure whose back was turned, but who was unmistakable in every way, from the purple of her gown to the mass of dark curls arranged neatly upon her head. Robert felt his heart begin to thrum faster in his chest as he crossed the street to greet her. Now that an opportunity had presented itself, he knew he had to seize it. Nonetheless, the prospect of proposing to her felt suddenly very daunting indeed—he was going to lay his heart bare before her, and he had absolutely no idea what she would say, or if she would accept him.

'Elspeth,' he said softly as he approached, hoping not to startle her. 'I was hoping to speak with you.'

'Really? What about?'

She did not turn to look at him, instead staring straight ahead, her arms crossed defensively over her chest. Her cool response served only to make his heart beat even faster. Last night, as she'd kissed him and led him towards her bed, she'd seemed so certain—was it possible that she now regretted it? Had she awoken this morning, filled with panic and shame, and resolved to pretend it had never happened?

'About last night,' he replied. 'About us.'

He stepped round to face her, trying to meet her eye. Still she averted her gaze, but he could see now that her usually pale and flawless skin was red and blotchy, and his heart descended into the pit of his stomach as he realised that she had been crying.

'Elspeth, what is wrong?' he whispered, resisting the overwhelming urge to reach out and caress her cheek. To pull her into his arms. 'If you are worried about what happened between us, I promise you that I am an honourable man. In fact, I want to ask…'

'You are no man of honour,' she hissed, lifting her gaze now as she found her voice again. She shook her head at herself, her lip trembling. 'My mother was right—I have been duped. I am such a fool. Why did I not see it before?'

Robert frowned. 'See what? What do you mean, Elspeth?'

'I know the truth, Robert,' she said, glaring at him. 'I heard you talking with Lady Dunsforth. I know that Tilly is your daughter.'

For a moment, Robert felt as though every last ounce of breath had been knocked from his body. He cast his mind back to that heated parlour conversation. They had indeed referred to the Great Secret, and clearly those few, careful words had been overheard and misconstrued.

'No,' he began, shaking his head slowly as he tried to gather his wits. 'It is not as you think. I am not…'

'Do not insult my intelligence, Robert.' She swiped angrily at her watering eyes. 'The way you dote on Tilly, your concern for her—it is all so painfully obvious that I am ashamed I did not see it before. Your daughter is the reason that you remain in Hallowford, and why you are so close to the Dunsforths. Tell me, was Lady Melliora just one of your many dalliances? Just another of your skilful seductions? I'm sure she was quite the prize—disarmingly beautiful and unhappily married. An irresistible target for a rake.'

Her accusations made Robert's temper flare. 'Is that really what you think of me?' he growled. 'After everything I've told you about my life and about my past, you would still so readily believe me capable of such wickedness?'

'What am I supposed to think?' Elspeth retorted. 'I heard what Lady Dunsforth said to you,' she continued, keeping her voice mercifully hushed. 'I heard her say that the late Earl was not Tilly's father and that you have to content yourself with being a family friend to Tilly and nothing more.'

'Lady Dunsforth is right—I do,' he replied. 'But I am not Tilly's father.'

'Then who is?'

Robert felt his breath catch in his throat at the question. Rafe's name was on the tip of his tongue and yet, he knew, he could not utter it. 'I cannot say,' he replied quietly. 'It is not my secret to tell.'

He could tell immediately by the look on her face that she did not believe him. 'How convenient,' she spat, walking away from him and back towards the gate.

'It is not convenient—it is the truth,' he called after her.

She turned back then, just briefly, shaking her head at him. 'I do not know what the truth about you is anymore,' she said. 'And it no longer matters. I am leaving Hallowford imminently. Our paths will not cross again.'

'Imminently?' he repeated. 'But I thought you had another week here?'

Elspeth slipped through the gate, closing it behind her, creating a barrier between them. 'My mother has decided that we need to leave now,' she announced as she glowered at him through the iron bars. 'We are to go to London. She wants to get me far away from you, and for once, I daresay that she is right. Goodbye, Robert.'

With those parting words, Elspeth turned and marched back towards the Dunsforth house, leaving Robert staring after her, wondering if the pain in his chest was the feeling of his heart breaking. This morning he'd allowed himself to hope, to contemplate a future with Elspeth, only to have any prospect of happiness snatched away by the ghosts of a past which was not even his. Life was unfair, but then, he knew that. It was a lesson he'd been forced to learn over and over again, alongside another: that love would always elude him, and that he would spend the rest of his life alone.

Chapter Seventeen

Eight weeks later

It was raining—again. Elspeth greeted the heavy droplets which rolled down the enormous windows of the British Museum with a sigh, then continued up the grand, ornate staircase, following the echo of the curator's voice as he conducted their group's tour of the museum's extensive collections. To her side walked her brother, Ted, and Charlotte, her friend who'd also become Ted's wife in recent months. It had been Ted who'd secured tickets for their tour today, and there was little doubt in Elspeth's mind that her older brother had done so for her benefit. It was a fact frequently acknowledged in their Mayfair home that Lady Elspeth Scott had smiled little since her arrival in town, and that she seemed to be very much out of sorts. It was also a fact that the entire household had made valiant efforts to cheer her up, but to no avail. Although she was loath to admit it, Elspeth was all too aware of the awful malaise which continued to hang over her, much like the rain clouds which seemed to linger incessantly in the autumnal London sky.

'I believe we shall see the Parthenon sculptures next,' Charlotte said once they reached the hallway. 'What a marvel! Especially for you, Elspeth, given your love of everything Greek.'

Elspeth nodded, forcing herself to mirror her friend's bright smile. They continued into the next gallery, Charlotte resting her hand against her swollen belly as Ted stayed protectively at her side. Upon their arrival in London, Elspeth and her mother had learned the happy news that Charlotte was with child, and that the Duke and Duchess of Falstone's baby was expected in the new year. The Dowager Duchess had been overjoyed, of course—so much so that even weeks later, she still talked of little else and continued to fuss over Charlotte as though she was made of porcelain. For Elspeth, meanwhile, her happiness had been marred by something which felt uncomfortably like jealousy. She loved her brother and Charlotte, and she was delighted for them, but being confronted with their unbridled joy each day served as an unwelcome reminder of what might have been. Or at least, what she'd deluded herself into believing she could have.

A life with Robert. A husband and children of her own.

What a reckless, foolish woman she had been!

But at least her dalliance with England's wickedest lord had resulted in no lasting consequences, beyond wounded pride and, if she was honest with herself, a broken heart. The worst possible consequence, the one which had dawned on her during that long, nauseating journey south, had not come to pass. After an anxious wait, the arrival of her monthly courses had confirmed that her belly would not ripen with a child. She would not have to confess to her mother what had happened, or face the prospect of being sent away to bear the child, or contemplate the possibility that her brother would force the wretch to marry her. Instead, she could pretend that night had never occurred. She could forget how she'd invited him into her bed and given herself freely.

Except—she couldn't, because she could not stop thinking about it. She could not stop thinking about him.

And worst of all, she could not stop wondering if she'd made a dreadful mistake. If she'd jumped to the wrong conclusion. If she'd been unjust in her accusations and in her refusal to believe him. She'd had time to reflect now—too much time, perhaps—and the more she thought about what she'd heard that day, the more she'd begun to doubt her interpretation of it. One question she kept returning to concerned his close friendship with both Lady Dunsforth and Lady Melliora—if he had behaved so badly, would they really have forgiven him? She supposed it was possible that they had, at least for Tilly's sake, but still—something about that did not quite add up. What plagued her above all, however, was the fact that he had been so adamant that he was not Tilly's father. So insistent that it wasn't true. And yet, how else could she explain Lady Dunsforth's words?

'As far as Society is concerned, Tilly is the late Earl's child. You can never be more than a family friend and a neighbour to her.'

Words she'd scrutinised so often that she feared she'd drive herself mad, and still she could come up with no alternative explanation for them. Robert was Tilly's father—he had to be. He was the wicked lord that Society whispered about, because only a notorious rake would bed an earl's wife, get her with child and then not even have the decency to wed her after they were both widowed! And for that matter, it was entirely possible that the story he'd told her about his late wife, Lucy, had been a fabrication, and he had banished her so that he could philander with wild abandon. The evidence was stacked against him, and it suggested that Lord Barden was guilty as sin.

So why was she having such a hard time believing it?

Perhaps because of the hurt she'd spied, lingering in his eyes as she made her accusations. Perhaps, too, because of the steely vehemence of his denial…

'It's Dionysus,' Charlotte whispered beside her.

Elspeth felt herself flinch at the word. At the memories it provoked of that sunny morning, when she and Robert had first spoken about their favourite gods and goddesses. The same morning that she'd spied his scandalously shirtless form as he'd boxed in his outhouse and had struggled to tear her eyes away.

She cleared her throat, brushing off the thought. 'Pardon?'

'The statue.' Charlotte inclined her head towards the stone figure in front of them. 'That's what the curator said. He was—oh, now, I always forget this one… Isn't he associated with festivity?'

Elspeth gave a brisk nod, casting an eye over the male figure which reclined decadently before them. 'The God of wine and a good time,' she replied, wincing as she heard herself say those words. Heavens, she was even quoting Robert now.

Charlotte smiled at her. 'Aptly put.' She sidled closer then, threading her arm through Elspeth's and giving her a knowing look. 'There was a time when visiting a place like this would have enthralled you. Yet today you seem to be barely here with us. I know I have said this before, but I am here if you wish to share your burdens.'

Elspeth felt her heart lurch, and instinctively her gaze slid towards her brother, who thankfully, stood at a safe distance, engaged in conversation with the curator. If Charlotte was going to speak to her frankly, the last thing she wanted was for Ted to overhear.

'I don't know what you mean,' she replied.

Charlotte tilted her head sympathetically. 'I think you do. You are not yourself, and have not been since you came to London. I know that something happened in Hallowford. I can tell by how tight-lipped your mother is whenever your time there is mentioned.'

Elspeth had to concede on that point. Halfway to London, the Dowager Duchess had decreed that no one—no one!—was to say the name *Lord Barden* ever again. It was to be as though he did not exist. As though the events of the summer had not occurred.

'If anyone asks, we stayed with Lady Dunsforth for a short time and were not acquainted with that man. We must ensure that no hint of scandal follows us to London,' she'd said. 'We don't need any inopportune whispers from the provinces destroying your prospects for making a good match this Season.'

Elspeth had been unable to resist rolling her eyes at that final part. Her mother remained determined in her quest to find Elspeth a suitable husband, as though somehow this Season the right sort of man would fall miraculously from the sky and into a Mayfair ballroom. The sort of man her daughter might fall in love with—charming, handsome, clever, and thoroughly enamoured with having a bluestocking for a bride. The sort of man who, in her experience, did not actually exist. For a time, she'd believed she'd found him in Robert, until she'd listened at the parlour door that day and learned just how badly she'd deluded herself.

'Nothing happened in Hallowford,' she assured Charlotte, the lie tasting sour in her mouth. 'And as for my mother—she is displeased with me, that is all, because I won't play along with all her ridiculous efforts to match me with every unmarried, high-born man who happens to wander into a ballroom.'

'Ah—yes, Ted did mention your announcement at the last ball you attended.'

Elspeth grimaced at the reminder. The travails of pregnancy had kept Charlotte away from that event, and so mercifully she had not witnessed Elspeth tearing her dance card from her wrist, handing it to her mother and informing her that she was retiring for the night to wait amongst the wallflowers. Not her finest hour. The problem was, what little patience she'd ever had with the marriage mart was well and truly spent. She could no longer tolerate its rituals—the performed politeness, the endless dancing, the insipid conversation. The need to conceal who she truly was because years of bitter experience had taught her that most gentlemen regarded bluestockings with, at best, curious amusement, and at worst, utter derision.

Except for one gentleman, of course. The gentleman who'd intrigued her, enraptured her, and shattered her in turn. The gentleman she needed to stop thinking about quite so much. She allowed Charlotte to lead the way as together they sauntered along, following the curator's voice as they left the Parthenon statues behind and wandered into the next gallery, where more ancient treasures surely awaited.

They rounded the corner and entered through the door, where, much to Elspeth's horror, they walked straight into the path of Lord Barden.

The sight of Elspeth standing in front of him took Robert's breath away. She was as lovely as ever—perhaps even lovelier than the image he conjured of her in his dreams each night. These past weeks his thoughts, waking and sleeping, had been haunted by his memories of her, as his mind and his heart grappled with her sudden absence from his life. In his head he'd replayed the most precious scenes of that summer—working closely together in his library, holding her as they waltzed at the ball, riding with her nestled against his chest as they travelled to the priory ruins. Clutching her hand in his during the concert. Going to her bed in the depths of the night.

As time had marched on, however, those visions of her had become increasingly ethereal, as though he was losing his grip on them. As though they were fading beyond his reach. As though his heart might be taking those first tentative steps towards accepting that she was lost to him forever. Yet now, here she was, made flesh again and standing mere steps away—frozen to the spot and staring at him, whilst a red-headed lady stood at her side, regarding them both in confusion.

'Lady Elspeth.' Somehow he managed to find his tongue, inclining his head politely as he spoke.

The sound of his voice seemed to startle her back to life. 'What are you…?' she began, shaking her head. 'Why are you in London?'

He shrugged. 'The same reason as everyone else—to attend the Lords for the Queen's trial.'

That much was true. Despite his reluctance to do so, in the end he'd surrendered to his sense of duty and had made his way to London in time for the trial's beginning in mid-August. He'd attended the Lords diligently while the case for the prosecution was heard, but had kept a low profile otherwise, avoiding the *ton*'s balls and soirées like the plague. But with the trial adjourned for the past few weeks, he had grown restless at home, and had found himself venturing out a little more—not to socialise, but to keep his mind and body occupied. It was with this intention that he'd come alone to enjoy a tour of the British Museum's collections today—until the fates had conspired to give him far more than he'd bargained for…

'My brother tells me that the trial will resume next week, and the case for the defence will be heard,' Elspeth said. 'I am sure you will be praying for a swift conclusion to the whole business.'

He nodded. 'And a just conclusion, of course.'

She arched an eyebrow at him. 'The sort of just conclusion which acknowledges that the rules are different for men and women—that women must be beyond reproach, whilst men can do as they please?'

Robert's heart sank as he heard those words. Words he'd uttered weeks ago, when he'd been playing the part of the wicked lord. Words he had not meant, but which he'd spoken in an effort to reinforce his dreadful reputation. A reputation which, it was clear, Elspeth believed in more than ever. Despite everything he'd told her, despite how close they'd grown during their time together—still she had chosen to think the worst of him, and evidently had clung to that version ever since they'd parted.

'Are you enjoying your visit to the museum?' he asked, changing the subject rather than tackling her barb. 'I always like coming here. Where else in London can you find so many treasures from antiquity lying under one roof?'

For a moment, the expression on her face appeared to soften. 'I quite agree,' she said, although there was a lack of conviction in her voice which struck him as odd. Out of character, even. 'It has been a lovely visit,' she added, offering her companion a thin smile.

Unthinkingly, he took a step closer. Close enough

now to spy the dark smudges beneath her eyes, which betrayed a want of sleep. Close enough to note that she was a shade paler than he recalled, and her face a little thinner, too. Subtle details, but telling ones. Ones which worried him.

'Forgive me, Lady Elspeth, but are you quite well? Only...'

'I am fine, my lord. Not that it is any of your concern.' Those deep brown eyes blazed at him as she took a step back. 'We must get on,' she continued stiffly. 'We spent far too long lingering over the Parthenon statues. I'm sure you must like those—especially the one of Dionysus. I'm sure that he very much meets with your approval.'

Another cryptic barb. His gaze shifted briefly to the red-haired lady, still standing at Elspeth's side, her lips parted in consternation. It had not escaped his notice that Elspeth had not troubled herself to introduce him to her companion—an oversight which was no doubt intended to wound him as well. He suppressed a sigh, stiffening his resolve and determined not to appear openly provoked by her hostility. If the situation demanded that he speak in riddles too, then so be it.

'Since I would prefer to go home without half a dozen arrows planted in my chest, I think I will take my leave. Good day, Lady Elspeth.' He tipped his hat curtly. 'Please accept my best wishes for the Season. I hope it brings you everything you desire.'

Robert turned and walked away, hoping that neither Elspeth nor her companion had been able to discern just how devastated he felt. These past weeks, he'd permitted himself to imagine the day that their paths might cross. Indeed, if he was honest with himself, it was part of the reason he'd come to London. The lure of knowing she was residing in the same city as him, that by placing himself in her orbit he might manage to tempt the fates to conspire to throw them together once more had been irresistible. In his mind's eye, such a reunion had been passionate and heartfelt, reigniting the fire which had burned so brightly between them during the summer. In this ideal world he'd conjured, he'd been able to tell the truth about Tilly, to reconcile with Elspeth, and to declare himself to her. He'd been able to finally ask Elspeth to marry him, and of course, because it was a dream, she had said yes.

Today's encounter had shown him just how far from reality that dream had been. Nothing about her response to him suggested that she'd reconsidered her opinion of him. If anything, the passage of time appeared to have only served to condemn him further in her eyes. As far as she was concerned, Lord Barden was a wicked sinner, a man who'd toyed with her, who'd sought to dupe her into believing he was an honourable man, before his past had caught up with him and his true colours had shone through at last. At the museum she'd been hostile to him, but there had been a fragility about her, too. As though what had happened and how they'd parted had caused her pain. As though perhaps, she was hurting also.

He marched out of the museum and into the pouring rain, his heart racing as the sting of hurt combined with the unbearable thought that what she'd overheard, and what he'd failed to explain that day in the gardens, had continued to plague Elspeth, too. And yet, what could he do? To tell her the truth would mean betraying Melliora, and he could not do that. He could not share secrets which were not his to tell—no matter how much he wanted to make things right. No matter how much he yearned to have Elspeth back in his life.

Besides, he reminded himself, the truth would probably never be enough, even if he did reveal it. Elspeth would probably not believe him. After all, she'd told him as much herself, hadn't she? How those words she'd uttered that day in the gardens had haunted him.

'I do not know what the truth about you is anymore...'

Robert huddled into the collar of his greatcoat, watching the rainwater spill ceaselessly over the brim of his hat as he hurried down the street. Damn this weather. Damn London. Damn its Society and its whispers. Damn other people's secrets.

Damn himself for coming here. The sooner he could leave town and return to his sanctuary in Hallowford, the better.

Chapter Eighteen

'So, he's merely someone you were acquainted with in Hallowford?'

Charlotte wrinkled her freckled nose delicately—a sure sign, if Elspeth ever needed one, that her friend did not entirely believe her. The carriage journey from the museum to their home in Mayfair had been a discomfiting one, with Charlotte trying to make tactful enquiries about the scene she'd witnessed and Elspeth trying her best not to answer them.

She shrugged at her friend's question. 'He was a neighbour of the Dunsforths, that's all.'

Charlotte nodded slowly. 'And does this neighbour have a name? Only, you did not introduce us.'

Elspeth shifted uncomfortably on the cushioned seat. That had been rude of her, and she didn't doubt that Robert had noted the oversight, too. But then, almost everything about their brief interaction had been impolite, bordering on hostile—on her part, at least.

She glanced warily at her brother, who until now

had paid little attention to their conversation. 'His name is Lord Barden,' she replied.

'Barden?' That name caught Ted's notice, and a frown gathered between his dark eyes. 'I've seen him in the Lords a good deal of late. An enigmatic fellow, keeps to himself, mostly. Mind you, with a reputation like his...' Ted shook his head, his frown deepening. 'Sorry, did you say he was at the museum?'

'He was,' Charlotte answered before Elspeth could say a word. 'He spoke to Elspeth while you were still chattering away to the curator.' She gave Ted a quizzical look. 'What do you mean, about his reputation?'

'Oh, it's just some ancient gossip about his marriage. His wife died a few years ago, but they had long since separated. Society maintains that he is a libertine, and that he abandoned her,' Ted explained, giving Charlotte a sceptical look.

Elspeth quirked an eyebrow at her brother. 'You don't believe it?'

He shrugged. 'I tend to be wary of gossip, that's all. The truth is often far more complicated than rumours would suggest. To be honest, I know nothing about the man, and that in itself makes me doubt the veracity of the whispers about him.'

'What do you mean by that?' Elspeth felt her heart begin to race. She trusted Ted's instincts, perhaps more than she trusted her own at present. She'd questioned the rumours too, and when Robert had confided in her about his marriage to Lucy, she'd believed him wholeheartedly and without hesitation. That is, until she'd listened at the parlour door that day. Until what she'd overheard had seemed to throw everything else into doubt...

'What I mean is, our dearly departed brother was one of Society's most dissolute gentlemen. A rake, a gambler, a drinker—if it was a vice, Perry indulged in it with wild abandon. Over the years he kept some fairly infamous company, and yet, I never heard him so much as utter the name of Lord Barden.' He paused, wincing. 'Trust me, Perry was never shy about sharing a tawdry tale, and he had plenty of them. But never any about that man.'

'Our brother could hardly be called a reliable witness,' Elspeth countered. 'And he did not know everything about everyone. Just because Perry never told you that the man was wicked, does not automatically make him a saint.'

She held her brother's eye, trying not to flinch at how irritated she was by his logic. Logic which, if it could be proven to be correct, would mean that she'd been horribly wrong, and terribly unfair.

Ted grinned at her. 'Lord Barden has really got under your skin, hasn't he?' She watched his amusement turn to curiosity as he regarded her carefully. 'Did you see him often during your time in Hallowford? I am surprised Mother permitted it, given what is said about him…'

Elspeth felt her cheeks begin to colour. 'For goodness sake, he was just a neighbour!'

'Just a neighbour who seemed to vex you greatly,' Charlotte interjected thoughtfully. 'And what did he mean, when he started talking about having half a dozen arrows in his chest?'

Elspeth looked out of the window, avoiding her friend's eye and avoiding the question. She could see that they'd just turned on to Grosvenor Street and were moments from home. Where, no doubt, this conversation would continue and would be made all the more excruciating by the presence of the Dowager Duchess. Suddenly, home felt like the very last place that Elspeth wished to be.

'I think I shall walk from here,' she announced. 'It is no longer raining, and I would benefit from some air. You know how much travelling by carriage disagrees with me,' she added, rubbing her stomach for dramatic effect.

'What! On your own?' Charlotte's lips remained parted in surprise.

'This is Mayfair, Charlotte, not Seven Dials. I will be perfectly safe.' She banged loudly on the carriage roof, signalling for their driver to stop. 'Besides, I have decided that I refuse to be chaperoned to the end of my days. I have come to the conclusion that it is a wearisome punishment meted out to spinsters in the hopes that it will persuade them to marry,' she added, a little too forcefully.

Ted smiled knowingly. Unlike Charlotte, he knew there was little point in arguing with Elspeth once her mind was made up. 'And what should I tell Mother?'

She shrugged. 'Tell her that you tried to dissuade me from my folly but to no avail.' She offered her brother a tight smile. 'I will walk to the park and no further. You have my word.'

The carriage stopped and Elspeth hurried out of it, relieved to be able to breathe at last. Relieved to be liberated from what had begun to feel like an interrogation. She walked along the straight, immaculate street at a pace, barely noticing her surroundings as her mind remained deep in thought. Guilt gnawed at her as she reflected upon her behaviour at the museum. Once again, she'd allowed that tart mouth of hers to rule her, and the hurt in Robert's eyes had been plain to see. That troubled her, no matter how often she tried to remind herself that it shouldn't. No matter how often she told herself that Robert had deserved her ire, because of how he'd deceived her. Of how he'd played her for a fool. Because he had, hadn't he? Unless she really had got it all so very wrong. Unless there was another explanation for what she'd overheard that day as she'd lingered outside the parlour.

Elspeth strode into Hyde Park, still plagued by the

feeling that she was missing something as her thoughts turned to what Ted had said about Robert in the carriage. Her brother was right—Robert was an enigma, and the truth about his life, whatever it was, was almost certainly complicated. Perhaps she'd been wrong to assume that his involvement with Lady Melliora had been little more than a frivolous seduction. After all, Lady Melliora was a great beauty, and they'd been friends since childhood. Perhaps, for a time, their mutual affection had developed into something more passionate between them. That would certainly explain how their fondness for each other had endured, in a way that a more calculated seduction would not. Perhaps Lady Melliora had loved Robert once, and perhaps he'd been in love with her.

Perhaps he still was.

She gasped as a carriage raced past her, startling her and forcing her to realise just how far she'd wandered, and just how much her errant thoughts had strayed. She supposed that she ought to turn back and go home before her family grew concerned, but still she could not quite face them. She shuddered, contemplating the likelihood that Ted and Charlotte had already reported her encounter with Lord Barden to the Dowager Duchess. No doubt her mother would be apoplectic...

'Hello, Elspeth.'

The deep timbre of Robert's voice interrupted her

spiralling thoughts, and she looked up to see him standing in front of her, cutting an imposing figure in his hat and woollen greatcoat. Around them a cold wind blew, whipping the fallen leaves into a frenzy. She resisted the urge to shiver as she wished she'd worn a warmer pelisse. As she wished she hadn't walked as far as the park, and into Robert's path.

As she wished that the ground would open up and swallow her whole.

She nodded curtly. 'We meet again, my lord.'

She saw his jaw harden at her brittle politeness, but he made no remark upon it. 'Have you evaded your chaperone's clutches again?' he asked instead.

'Charlotte—the Duchess of Falstone—was not my chaperone,' she countered. 'She is my sister-in-law and my friend. I do not require a chaperone.'

He raised his eyebrows at her. 'Because you are an old maid who does as she pleases now?'

She bristled at his attempt to tease her. 'If you say so, my lord,' she replied hotly.

He took a step closer. 'My lord be damned,' he growled. 'It's Robert, Elspeth. And you are no old maid. You will never be—not to me.'

Elspeth felt her breath hitch as she gazed up into those green eyes, and despite herself she began to recall how much darker they'd looked in the candlelight, as she'd led him towards her bed. 'You forget yourself, my lord,' she replied, pushing the memory aside. 'You forget that you have deceived me. You forget what a fool you made of me, this summer.'

She heard him sigh deeply. 'The only time I deceived you was when I tried to convince you I was a wicked man. When I said and did things which are not a true reflection of who I am,' he insisted.

'Oh, really.' She quirked an eyebrow at him. 'Such as?'

'Such as all that nonsense I spouted about this awful business with the King and Queen, about the different rules of conduct for men and women. Quite frankly, hearing you repeat that back to me in the museum earlier set my teeth on edge. And for that matter, I do not care for Dionysus, either. That day when I told you he was my favourite God, I…well, I suppose I was simply saying what you expected a wicked man to say.'

'I see.' She folded her arms across her chest. 'Well, you certainly did try hard to convince me. I have not forgotten how you kissed me in your library, just to prove your point,' she added, alarmed to feel her cheeks heat at the memory. Drat it—could she not find it within herself to remain unflustered, just this once?

'Trust me, that kiss was about far more than proving a point. I kissed you because I wanted to.' He paused, pressing his lips together and glancing warily to the side as a pair of ladies sauntered past, casting inquisitive looks in their direction. 'I swear to you, Elspeth, that everything I have told you about my marriage and about Tilly is the truth,' he continued, lowering his voice now.

'It is really none of my business, my lord,' Elspeth replied huffily, trying her best to sound indifferent. Trying not to notice how the sound of her pounding heart seemed to echo in her ears. Trying not to ruminate on his confession that he'd wanted to kiss her in the library that day, or on what else that kiss might have signified. What any of their kisses, or indeed that night they spent together, might have signified. 'It hardly matters now.'

'Of course it matters!' Robert took another step closer, taking her gloved hand in his, and God help her but she could not bring herself to snatch it away. 'It matters because I care about you, Elspeth. It matters because I miss you. I've missed you since the day you left Hallowford. I don't think I will ever stop missing you.'

Robert relinquished Elspeth's hand and dragged his fingers down his face. He had not meant to be so blunt, to speak so honestly, but there it was—a declaration, of sorts. An indication of how he felt about a woman who'd departed from his life, but had never been far from his thoughts. A woman who had thus far greeted his outburst with silence, her dark gaze searching his, as though trying to determine if he spoke in earnest. Out of the corner of his eye, he noticed that the same pair of ladies who had walked by moments ago were sauntering past again, this time in the opposite direction, and this time making it plain that they were straining to hear every word.

He cleared his throat. 'We are attracting unwelcome attention,' he said quietly.

'I'm sure you are used to that.'

'Regrettably I am, but you are not. I should go. It was bad enough that we became fodder for the gossips in Hallowford. The last thing you need is to be whispered about in London.'

She rolled her eyes at that. 'Well, it would certainly present a further obstacle to my mother's matchmaking plans.'

'Ah yes—of course.' Robert pressed his lips together for a moment, trying not to dwell on just how much the thought of Elspeth being paraded on the marriage mart stung him. 'Have you, er, have you met anyone suitable?'

'What do you think?' she asked, giving him a withering look. 'Anyway, I thought you were going?'

'I was,' he replied, struck then by just how much he did not wish to leave her. He had a sense that in these last few moments a crack had formed in the ice between them. Sensed, too, that if he stayed, if he continued to talk to her, he might find his way to making that ice thaw. 'But I am in no hurry to go anywhere. Perhaps we could walk together for a little while?'

Momentarily she frowned at him, and he braced himself for one of her infamous rebukes. But then, to his surprise, she inclined her head in agreement. 'I suppose I am in no hurry, either.'

Together they set off in the direction of the Serpentine. Robert maintained a polite distance, clasping his hands behind his back in an effort to resist offering her his arm. Thankfully the park was not particularly busy, the earlier torrential rain having persuaded most of London's ladies and gentlemen to forego their afternoon promenade. Even so, he was conscious of just how unwise it was, to be spending time with Elspeth alone like this, in broad daylight and for all to see. And yet, he knew he could not let the opportunity pass him by. In the coming week he would be embroiled in Lords' business once again, and once that was concluded he would return to Hallowford. For all he knew, their paths may never cross again...

'I have not spoken to anyone about what I heard that day,' Elspeth said, breaking the silence which had fallen between them. 'Not even my mother. The secret, whatever it is, is safe with me.'

'I do not doubt it.' He shook his head at himself, emitting a deep breath. 'What you heard—the situation with Tilly—it is complicated.'

He saw her glance at him, a small frown creasing her brow. 'My brother said something similar earlier. Something about how the truth is always more complicated than rumours. He was referring to the chatter about your marriage, of course, but it made me think that perhaps you and Lady Melliora…well, it had not been so much a seduction, but a love affair. That perhaps you had been in love with her. After all, I know that she was trapped in a miserable marriage to the Earl, and you were separated from Lucy. Perhaps you were both lonely, and one thing led to another, and…'

'I have never been in love with Melliora, Elspeth. I have never been anything more than her friend. And I am not Tilly's father.' He drew a deep breath as he stopped walking and turned to meet her eye. 'I do not know what else I can say to prove that to you, other than ask you to believe me. I wish I could tell you everything, but I cannot.'

'Because it is not your secret to tell—I know.' She gave a small nod, although it was hard to discern from her expression whether she believed him or not.

'I promised years ago that I would take it to my grave,' he replied. 'Trust me, that was not an oath I took lightly. It weighs on me at times, the thought that Tilly may never know the truth. But that is Melliora's decision, not mine.' He smiled sadly. 'It is not always easy to do the right thing, or indeed to know what the right thing is. So I do my best, I take an interest, and that little girl will always have a protector in me, should she have need of one.'

Elspeth offered him a cautious smile. 'Then Tilly

is fortunate to have you. Especially since her father, whoever he is, would appear to have no interest in doing anything for her.'

'On the contrary, he would have adored Tilly. If only he had...' Robert pressed his lips together, swallowing down his words. Instinctively he'd leapt to his brother's defence, and in doing so he'd said far more than he should have.

'Would have?' He could already see Elspeth's clever mind was hard at work, trying to answer the riddle. Trying to decipher the clues which had just fallen from his clumsy tongue.

'Yes, he would have.' Robert cleared his throat, then turned around, poised to retrace their steps. 'We should go back now. We have walked far enough, and your family will be wondering where you are. The last thing you need is to provoke your mother's wrath.'

She quirked an eyebrow at him. 'Are you trying to be my protector, too?' she teased.

Her remark brought a smile to his lips, and this time he dared to offer her his arm. 'Always.'

Momentarily Elspeth appeared to hesitate, looking warily at the sleeve of his greatcoat. But then, to his surprise, she threaded her arm through his, and together they began to walk back towards Mayfair. Robert tried hard to concentrate on putting one foot in front of the other, and not to dwell upon how it felt to have Elspeth holding on to him, so close at his side. To do so was dangerous, as even through the thick wool of his coat, her touch was overwhelming. He knew that he'd missed her; knew that he'd felt her absence keenly. But he had not appreciated until that moment just how profoundly he'd missed the feeling of her. Just how desperately he yearned to be closer to her, to pull her into his arms, to kiss her and to never let her go.

'I am sure they will be missing you—Lady Dunsforth, Lady Melliora, and Tilly—while you are in London. Tilly especially.' Elspeth looked up at him, her dark gaze pensive. 'I am sorry for what I said in the gardens that day. For suggesting that you seduced Lady Melliora. The way I spoke to you, it was unforgivable—and not particularly rational, either. I doubt that Lady Dunsforth would look so favourably upon you if you had behaved like that, and Lady Melliora certainly wouldn't.'

Robert chuckled softly. 'That is true enough.' He felt his face grow serious again as he regarded her. 'Tilly's father did not behave like that, either. As I understand it, he and Melliora loved one another very much. If life was less cruel, they would be married now, and he would be the one helping Tilly to learn her numbers, not me.' He let out a slow breath. 'There, I have said enough. Too much, perhaps.'

They'd reached the gate now. Time to go their separate ways once more, which was just as well, because he had the discomfiting feeling that if he kept talking to her like this, he would break his promise completely and he would tell her everything. As it was, he suspected that Elspeth would work it out—not today, perhaps, but given time, the truth would eventually dawn on her. She was far too intelligent for it to be any other way.

'My house is this way,' he said, pointing in the direction of St James's as he relinquished her arm. 'Unless you'd like me to accompany you back to your home first? I know you do not require a chaperone, but still…'

She let out a small laugh. 'Thank you, Robert, but I fear my mother is displeased enough with me already. I daresay seeing us together would be the last straw.'

His heart warmed to hear her use his name. 'Then I will bid you farewell,' he said, tipping his hat politely. 'I hope that we part on better terms than we did in Hallowford. I fear that neither of us was feeling very rational that day, given everything that had happened between us. I know that I certainly wasn't.'

The way her cheeks coloured slightly told him that she'd grasped his meaning. He took a step closer to her then, suddenly possessed by the urge to talk about that night. To explain what it had meant to him. To tell her what she meant to him. Yet something about the guarded look in her eye dissuaded him. Reminded him that whilst the ice between them had begun to thaw, she might not wish to reignite the fire which had burned so brightly during the summer. Indeed, that she might regret their intimacy and not wish to be reminded of it.

'Goodbye, Elspeth,' he whispered instead, before turning away and taking a handful of footsteps towards his home. His heart already felt heavy with the weight of their parting, just as it had on that summer's day, when he'd watched at his window as her carriage had taken her away from Hallowford for good. He'd boxed in the outhouse for hours afterwards, until finally, hungry and exhausted, he'd had to admit to himself that no amount of physical exertion could exorcise Lady Elspeth Scott from his thoughts. From his dreams. From his heart.

'Robert?'

He spun around to see that she was still standing on the same spot, staring after him.

'I have missed you too,' she said.

Then, before he could utter a word in reply, she turned away, and all he could do was watch as she strode purposefully back towards Mayfair, her deep purple skirt swishing all the while.

Chapter Nineteen

Elspeth surveyed the raucous scene from the safety of her corner vantage point, her hot breath clinging uncomfortably to her skin thanks to the white mask which adorned her face that night. As usual, the Viscountess Millington's masquerade ball had been an enormous success, with most of the *ton* turning out in their finest costumes for the event. Every inch of the splendid, gilded ballroom seemed to be covered with all manner of characters, from harlequins to highwaymen, to Roman emperors, Cleopatras and Queen Elizabeths, each wearing a mask to complete their disguise. Each enjoying the liberation which came with concealing one's identity, just as much as they enjoyed the copious wine which flowed from the Millington cellar as they chattered and danced beneath the glow of glittering candelabras.

'Ted and I are going to leave soon,' Charlotte murmured beside her.

Elspeth inclined her head in acknowledgement. The Duchess of Falstone had come as a flower girl tonight, wearing a mask which covered only her eyes and a cream gown which, as a talented embroiderer, she'd embellished herself with intricate floral motifs. She rested a weary hand against her growing belly, as though to remind Elspeth of the reason for their early departure. As her pregnancy advanced, Charlotte found the evenings increasingly tiring, and Ted, ever the attentive husband, was always keen to get her home to rest.

'Then I will come with you,' Elspeth replied, deciding to seize the opportunity to retire, too. As balls went, masquerade balls were an enjoyable spectacle, but even so she was in no mood to stay and enjoy the revelry. So far, she'd managed to avoid the dancing, sticking close by Charlotte's side and far away from any prospective partners. If Charlotte left and she remained, however, she would have no excuse not to participate.

Charlotte shook her head slightly, her red curls shimmering in the candlelight. 'No. Your mother says you must stay.'

Behind her mask, Elspeth felt herself frown. 'When did she say that?'

'Before we left home. She said she knew you would try to make your excuses.' Charlotte touched Elspeth lightly on the shoulder, giving her an apologetic squeeze. 'She says she will be staying, and so must you.'

Elspeth looked over to where her mother stood, resplendently dressed as a medieval queen and deep in conversation with Viscountess Millington. She suppressed the temptation to sigh. Wonderful. Since learning about her daughter's encounter with Lord Barden in the museum a week ago, the Dowager Duchess appeared to have intensified her efforts to find Elspeth a suitable husband. Apparently, hearing that the *wicked lord* was in town was bad enough, never mind that he'd had the audacity to speak to her daughter in public! Elspeth had listened obediently to her mother's warnings about the threat posed to her virtue, nodding in all the appropriate places and trying not to consider what her mother would say if she knew the whole story. If she knew how they'd walked and talked in the park. How the cold, blustery air around them had been warmed by the frankness of their conversation. How she'd taken Robert's arm and confessed that she'd missed him…

How she knew now that he cared about her, and that he'd missed her, too. She also knew that he had been truthful with her. One look into those earnest green eyes of his had been enough for her heart to know it. Her head had taken longer to understand, but the realisation had dawned upon her later that night as she'd ruminated upon his words.

'He would have adored Tilly...if life was less cruel, they would be married now...'

Lady Melliora had indeed had a love affair, but not with Robert. The affair had been with someone close to Robert; close enough for him to know that they were in love, that they would have wed. The raw, defensive way he'd spoken about Tilly's father in a past tense which seemed so absolute had led her to one conclusion: the affair had been with Robert's poor, dead brother, Rafe. That was why he was so close to the Dunsforths, and so affectionate and protective towards Tilly. She wasn't his daughter—she was his niece.

She'd spent half the night lying awake then, cursing herself for being such a fool. She'd been so determined to assume the worst that she'd jumped to the most obvious conclusion and had clung to it for weeks, even in the face of her growing doubts. Even while knowing that it did not entirely make sense. For someone who'd always prided herself on being a scholar, she'd failed to examine the situation critically, or to properly consider other possibilities. Instead, she'd indulged her sense of betrayal, and in doing so she'd hurt herself, and she'd hurt Robert, too. When they'd spoken in Hyde Park she had apologised to him, but now, in light of everything she'd come to understand, those words did not feel quite enough.

But what would be enough? And would she ever

get the opportunity to say it? Her heart ached to realise how unlikely it was that their paths should cross again. Robert was not a wicked lord, but when it came to London Society, he was a reclusive one. He would not be here tonight, or at any of the many balls she'd be forced to attend before the Season was over. Standing there now, Elspeth was struck suddenly by an overwhelming yearning to see him again. To talk to him. To dance with him.

To kiss him.

'Uh-oh. I can sense your scowl burning through your mask, sister. I presume Charlotte has informed you of our mother's decree?'

Ted gave Elspeth a sympathetic look before slipping his arm around Charlotte. He'd come as Galen tonight, wearing a long robe and cap which looked vaguely Grecian. Elspeth had little doubt that the choice to dress as one of antiquity's great physicians had been a deliberate nod to his own past life as a medical man. At least Ted had been able to choose his own attire, she thought sourly. Her desire to dress as Artemis had been thwarted by her mother, who'd been horrified by the idea of her daughter turning up in a loose robe, with a sack of arrows draped across her back. After much thought, her mother had concluded that she should go as Susanna from *The Marriage of Figaro*, a decision which had left Elspeth wearing a rather fussy-looking pale blue gown in last century's style, its low neckline conspiring with the very tight stays she wore beneath it to show off far more of her bosom than she was comfortable with.

'I think I should warn you that I saw Mother pointing you out to Baron de Wold a little while ago,' Ted continued when Elspeth did not answer. 'I think he intends to ask you to dance.'

Elspeth could not stifle her groan at that. Baron de Wold was at least twenty years her senior and an insufferable bore who thought that talking was the sole preserve of men. Ladies, in his opinion, were not made for thinking, never mind for expressing their thoughts. Of course, Elspeth had always begged to differ with his views and had hoped that her sharp tongue and her deliberately clumsy footwork had put the man off from pursuing her several Seasons ago. Clearly not.

She lifted up her mask so that she could bestow her brother with one of her most fearsome stares. 'Is Mother trying to provoke me?' she asked. 'Is she trying to drive me to despair?'

'I suspect she is rather hoping that the threat of dancing with de Wold will motivate you to dance with some of the other gentlemen in this room,' Ted answered. 'If I were you, I would consider doing just that, if only as a means to avoid him for the rest of the night.'

After apologising several more times for leaving her, Ted and Charlotte both bid her farewell. Drawing a deep breath, Elspeth pulled her mask down over her face once more and took several steps backwards, hoping beyond hope that the Viscountess Millington's richly decorated red walls might somehow be able to conceal her. Even as she did so, she could see the tall, thin figure of a half-masked Baron de Wold making his way towards her, poised to add his name to the empty dance card which dangled from her wrist. Oh drat…

'May I have this next dance?'

A voice intruded—a male voice, deep and familiar. Elspeth heard herself gasp as she glanced to her side to see a tall, broad figure standing there, resembling a medieval knight in his costume—a belted tunic emblazoned with the cross of St George, worn over fitted fawn pantaloons. Like her, his face was entirely concealed by a mask. Nonetheless, she knew exactly who was beneath it. Knew, too, exactly how she wished to answer him.

'Of course, my lord,' she replied as calmly as she could, trying to ignore how her heart suddenly raced.

The knight held out his hand to her. Without hesitation she accepted, placing her fingers in his palm and allowing herself to be whisked away before the dreaded Baron de Wold could reach her, never mind open his mouth to speak.

Holding Elspeth while they waltzed brought back memories of Hallowford. Memories of a different ball, of arguing with her in an alcove before taking her in his arms for the first time. Of being struck by the potency of his longing for her as he fought the overwhelming desire to kiss her. He held her closer to him tonight; closer than was proper, really, but he could not seem to help it. He tried to attribute his lack of inhibition to the disguise he wore; tried to convince himself that, like everyone else around him, he was simply enjoying the liberation of a masquerade ball. Everyone knew that on nights like these, lines became blurred and rules were broken. That for a brief moment in time, the world could be turned upside down in the name of a night's revelry, before order was restored in the light of a new day.

However, he knew that for him, it was far more than that. It was true that he'd enjoyed his anonymity tonight, that the absence of furious whispers and scandalised glances in his direction had come as a relief. But that wasn't why he dared to hold her close, or why he allowed himself to gently caress her arm with his fingers as they danced. By coming here, by donning a costume and venturing into Society, he'd broken his own rule, and he had done so with one single purpose—to seek Elspeth out. To seek the opportunity to show her—indeed, to tell her—what she meant to him. To make his feelings clear, just as he'd intended to do in the summer, before words were overheard and misconstrued. Before everything had gone wrong. He'd despaired after that—despaired of ever repairing the damage between them. Despaired of finding happiness or love. But then fate had intervened—or at least, that was how it seemed to him. Their meeting in Hyde Park days ago had felt like a second chance; one which he had not entirely grasped at the time but, by God, he was going to seize it now. He could not know how Elspeth would respond, and did not dare to guess whether or not she felt the same way. But he had to tell her nonetheless. He could remain silent no longer.

'It took me far too long to find you,' he whispered to her. 'I was looking for a lady dressed as Artemis.'

'My mother would not permit it. Apparently such a costume would have sent the wrong message.' She rolled her eyes. 'I refrained from pointing out that I believe a bow and arrow to be exactly the right sort of message for the likes of Baron de Wold.'

He chuckled. 'I did notice him making his approach.' He felt his laughter die in his throat as a dreadful thought occurred to him. 'Surely your mother is not considering him for you? Quite apart from the age difference between you, the man is, well…'

'Odious? Yes, I know.' He heard her sigh. 'At this juncture, I can barely understand what my mother is considering. Dressing me up like this, insisting that I show off my *attributes* while no doubt hoping I will keep my mouth shut…'

'You look beautiful,' he interjected, forcing his wayward eyes to remain locked with hers and not allowing them to dip to admire those *attributes* which his less gentlemanly thoughts had already been drawn to, more than once. 'Although…'

'Although?'

'I am used to seeing you wearing purple. When I think of you, it is always in purple.'

'When you think of me,' she repeated. 'And do you think of me often, my lord?'

'You must know that I do.' He caressed her arm again, wishing he could say more but not quite prepared to take the risk in the middle of a bustling ballroom. 'So, who are you dressed as?'

'Susanna from *The Marriage of Figaro*. Presumably from the part of the opera where she pretends to be the Countess, since Mother did not insist that I dress as a maid.'

He nodded. 'Strong-willed and clever Susanna. She suits you.'

'And you are clearly a knight,' she observed, and he sensed that behind the mask, she was smiling. 'Although, you have no chain-mail or armour.'

'I'm not sure it would be possible to dance wearing either,' he retorted. 'Besides, I did not come here tonight to do battle.'

'No? Then what did you come here for?'

Their eyes met, and for a moment Robert was

gripped by the urge to tear their masks away and to press his lips against hers. To let his actions speak instead of his words and to make his feelings plain. He drew a deep breath, trying to calm the tide currently raging inside of him. His blood was too hot, his heartbeat too rapid, and it would not do. He had to get this right. He had to leave her in no doubt about his affection for her. His love for her.

Because that was what this was, wasn't it? It was love.

He was in love with her.

'I came for you,' he said in the end. 'I came because I…'

The waltz ended, and Robert's words were cut off as the crowd jostled around them, moving frantically to change partners before the next dance began. Reluctantly he relinquished Elspeth from his arms, and together they moved away from the throng as he grappled with the knowledge that another moment had been lost and wondered how he could stay with her a little longer. He supposed he could ask her to dance with him again. Doing so was not without risk; dancing together a second time might provoke comment, as it would be viewed as a declaration of his intention to court her. Although, of course, that relied upon him being recognised, and he was quite confident that so far he'd managed to slip amongst the crowds unnoticed.

'Elspeth,' he began. 'Would you do me the great honour of…?'

'Pardon me, but I think it is my turn now.'

The nasally voice of Baron de Wold intruded, cutting across Robert's words. He watched as Elspeth flinched, and although he could not see it, he could sense the expression of dread which was doubtless etched upon her face.

She turned slowly to face the man. 'Apologies, my lord, but I have already promised this next dance to this chivalrous knight,' she said pleasantly, although her words were firm enough.

'But you have just danced with the knight,' Baron de Wold objected. 'He cannot monopolise you all evening. That is not proper.'

'Ah, but you see, he is of the medieval world, my lord. The rules are different there,' Elspeth replied quickly. 'Have you not heard of courtly love?'

Baron de Wold shook his head in confusion. 'I do not see quite what…'

Robert sucked in a sharp breath as he saw Elspeth's mother, the Dowager Duchess, draw closer. The half mask she wore did nothing to disguise the concerned expression on her face as her gaze flitted from her daughter, to the Baron, then finally to him. A heavy dread pooled in his stomach as he saw how she watched him carefully, as though she was trying to peer behind the mask. As though, perhaps, she had already worked out who he was.

If Elspeth noticed her mother standing there, then she did not show it. 'No, my lord, I am sure you do not,' she replied to the Baron, before turning away and taking hold of Robert's arm. 'Now, if you'll excuse me…'

Apparently, Baron de Wold was not willing to give up so easily. 'Who is this knight, anyway?' he demanded. 'Who is my rival? I must know!'

Before Robert could say a word, the Baron had launched himself at him, reaching for his mask and pulling at it. For such a lean man he was surprisingly strong, and the string holding Robert's mask in place was no match for his brute force. In the midst of the commotion, Robert felt the flimsy strings give way, watching in horror as the mask fell from his face and landed on the wooden floor of the ballroom.

Around them, a collective gasp went up. Bodies stilled and gazes shifted until Robert could have sworn that every pair of eyes in that room rested upon them.

'Barden?' Baron de Wold hissed. 'Lady Elspeth, what the devil are you doing with a man like *him*?'

Robert felt his temper flare at the man's disparaging tone. His fists began to curl as the overwhelming temptation to plough one of them squarely into the Baron's sharp jaw possessed him. The Baron continued to look down his nose at him while around them,

Robert sensed the simmering of the crowd as they watched and whispered. As they waited, no doubt, for him to fulfil their expectations. To be the wicked man about whom mothers warned their daughters and whom fathers prayed their sons would not emulate. Or, perhaps, they awaited the moment when he would flee, when he would return quietly to his place of sanctuary and leave them to their gossip and their speculation.

Yet, as he stood there with Elspeth close at his side, he realised that tonight, he would do neither. That he could no longer bear to answer his dreadful, undeserved reputation with stoical silence. That he wanted to show the world something of the man who Elspeth had seen in the summer; the man who she'd insisted did exist even when he'd deployed every possible tactic to convince her that he didn't.

'You do not know me, my lord,' Robert said, before glancing at the gathered crowd. 'Indeed, none of you know me.'

'I think we all know enough, Lord Barden,' the Baron scoffed. 'You have quite a nerve, coming here tonight and using your disguise to fool Lady Elspeth into dancing with you. Goodness knows what sort of scandal you planned to draw this poor, unwitting young lady into!'

Robert opened his mouth to retort, but before he could say a word, Elspeth stepped forward, looking every bit as furious as he felt. 'You speak as though I have no mind of my own, my lord,' she said. 'Perhaps you believe that all ladies are merely empty-headed ninnies, or perhaps it is that you wish them to be, so that you may find it easier to convince one of them to marry you.' She paused, curling her lip at him, and Robert noticed how Baron de Wold appeared to shrink under the weight of her steely, dark gaze. 'I am not unwitting, and I have not been fooled. Nor am I some feeble creature to be pitied. I know my own mind well enough, and I knew exactly who I had chosen to dance with.'

Baron de Wold bristled at that, before drawing himself up straight once more. 'Then I'd suggest you require further schooling on what constitutes a worthy and suitable gentleman, Lady Elspeth.'

Robert felt his breath catch in his throat as Elspeth glanced at him, a smile teasing the corners of her mouth. 'On the contrary, my lord, I am able to recognise such a gentleman, when I see one.' She stepped back then, taking hold of Robert's arm. 'Lord Barden is one of the very best of men. He is right—none of you know him. None of you understand anything about the man you have insulted for all of these years.'

'But really, Lady Elspeth, I must insist…' Baron de Wold began to bluster.

Elspeth let out a small laugh. 'You may insist upon nothing, my lord. You are not my father, or my brother, and you will certainly never be my husband. Now, if you will excuse me, I rather think that I need some air.'

Her subtle tug on Robert's arm as she said those words was all the indication he needed to know that she wanted him to accompany her. After casting one final glare in Baron de Wold's direction, Robert turned away and began to escort Elspeth towards the garden, his heart pounding with a potent mix of fury, pride and exhilaration, and with his head held high.

Chapter Twenty

Elspeth hurried through the garden doors of Viscountess Millington's home, sucking in a deep breath as the cool night air greeted her. Her head was swimming with the events of the last few moments. One minute she'd been dancing with Robert, indulging herself in the feeling of being held by him, of the delicious shivers which had run down her spine each time she'd felt his fingers caressing her arm through the sleeve on her dress. Indulging, too, her temptation to ask him searching questions and daring herself to make her feelings plain. The next minute, Baron de Wold had intruded and—well, she'd let him know exactly what she thought of him, in front of everyone. She'd let Society know what she thought of Robert, too. She'd contradicted popular opinion; she'd cast doubt on years of gossip and speculation, and in doing so, she'd aligned herself with him in no uncertain terms. There would be further talk now—about them, about the nature of their acquaintance. Noses would twitch, desperate to detect the whiff of scandal.

In short, Elspeth had broken just about every rule concerning what it was to be an unattached lady in polite Society. And yet, she did not care a jot because she'd spoken from the heart. She'd spoken out of love, because she was in love with Robert. She understood that now. The feelings she'd grappled with these past months; the growing attraction, the consumption of her thoughts by him, the passionate desire which had led her to invite him into her bed, and the misery she'd felt following their sudden parting—all of it had led to now. To a realisation which had struck her like a lightning bolt as she'd seethed at Baron de Wold's insults and leapt to Robert's defence as well as her own. The realisation that this avowed spinster had lost her heart to the man who Society called wicked, but who she knew was anything but.

Wordlessly she traversed the terrace and descended the steps which led to the neat, formal gardens, still holding on to Robert's arm as she wandered on to the gravel path, lined with shrubs. Few torches had been lit here, meaning that apart from the silvery light of the moon, they were bathed in near darkness. Still, she walked on, wishing to be neither seen nor overheard. There were things which needed to be said; feelings which needed to be declared. Perhaps Robert sensed this too, since he walked quietly at her side, allowing her to lead the way without question. It was only when they reached the furthest point in the garden, marked out by a stone bench situated within a spiral of tall conifer plants that she stopped.

'We are alone now,' she declared, swiftly surveying the scene all about her. 'At least, I think we are.'

'Yes, we are, but—do you think that this is a good idea?' Robert asked uneasily. 'After what just happened...everyone was listening, Elspeth, including your mother.'

She turned to face him, relinquishing her grip on his arm and trying not to think about her mother. About what she would say. About whether she was currently searching the gardens for her, ready to drag her away in disgrace. She suppressed a shudder.

'I will worry about my mother later. First, I think we need to talk. There are things I need to say to you, and...' She slumped down on the bench, feeling the cold dampness of the stone through her skirts and becoming suddenly aware of the chill seeping through the fabric of her gown. 'Now I do not know where to begin,' she finished with a sigh.

She must have shivered, because in an instant Robert had sat down at her side. He wrapped his arm around her, pulling her close to him. 'You have no shawl, and I do not have a coat to give you,' he said. 'Perhaps we ought to go inside and go our separate ways for tonight. I could call on you tomorrow, if you wish me to, and we could talk then?' He groaned. 'Although, I doubt your mother would permit me. We could meet instead, perhaps in Hyde Park?'

She shook her head vehemently. 'No—it has to be now.' She gazed up at him. 'I know the truth about Lady Melliora and Tilly. I know that your brother, Rafe, was Tilly's father. I know that you are her uncle.'

Robert gave her a grim smile. 'I knew you would work it out. In truth, I think a large part of me wanted you to.' He emitted a deep breath, and Elspeth watched as it clouded in the cold night air. 'Rafe and Melliora had fallen for each other when we were all still young. I think he'd hoped to marry her, but then her father had arranged her betrothal to old Lord Westhaigh, and that was that—or so I thought, at least.'

'But they found a way to be reunited,' Elspeth said quietly.

He nodded. 'They did. In London. I will never forget the day that Rafe confided in me about their affair, and that the child Melliora carried was his. She found out she was with child mere weeks after her husband died. They'd planned to marry, once Melliora was out of mourning and the baby had been born. Rafe knew that he could never acknowledge the baby as his, that everyone had to believe he or she was the Earl's or else there would be a scandal. But he was prepared to do that—to do anything, for them both.' He shook his head sadly. 'But then he was killed. He never got to marry the woman he loved, and he never got to meet Tilly.'

'I am truly sorry, Robert,' Elspeth whispered. 'For all of it. For your brother. For doubting you. For accusing you...'

'You have nothing to apologise for, Elspeth,' Robert insisted. 'You overheard something and you drew a logical conclusion.'

'I jumped to the wrong conclusion, and in doing so, I hurt you. You'd confided in me about your marriage, and I repaid your trust by assuming the worst of you. Worse still, I clung to that version of events, even after my doubts began to set in. I insisted to myself that it must be true even when my heart kept telling me that there was another explanation. For someone who prides herself on being intelligent, I have been intolerably stupid of late. Whether you think I should be or not, I am sorry—for all of it.'

'You are not stupid, Elspeth. Far from it.' He hugged her tighter to him. 'I will admit that I was hurt. But I must share some of the blame, too. For all my insistence that I wasn't Tilly's father, I refused to tell you who was. I cannot blame you for doubting me, when I would not explain myself properly. When I would not explain that I am Tilly's family—just not in the way that you believed.'

'You were keeping your word to Lady Melliora,' Elspeth insisted. 'You were doing the honourable thing and protecting them both.'

Robert sighed. 'Yes, well, I have been far too quick to dispense with my sense of honour tonight. Turning up here, waltzing with you, and then there was that scene with de Wold…'

'Baron de Wold made that scene—not us,' she countered. 'And there is nothing dishonourable about asking me to dance. I am glad that you came tonight. I am glad we danced, and I do not regret a single word I said to the Baron. He deserved every last syllable.'

Robert chuckled softly at that. 'He certainly did.' In the moonlight she saw him regard her cautiously. 'But you also spoke up in my favour. Very stridently, I might add. Society will draw its conclusions from that, as I am sure you must realise. Everyone will assume that there is some sort of attachment between us. They will make a scandal out of it, I have no doubt about that.'

'I could not care less what Society thinks, Robert…'

'You may say that now, Elspeth, but trust me—it is no fun being on the wrong side of the *ton*'s good opinion.'

'I am sure it is not, but I am also sure that any misery Society can inflict pales in comparison to the misery of being without you,' she blurted. 'Because, believe me, these past weeks of being parted from you have been intolerable. If I am honest with myself,

I think that is why I was so desperate to cling to the story I'd told myself about you seducing Lady Melliora. I knew that the alternative meant accepting that I'd got it all wrong, that I'd made a mess of everything. That I'd lost you. That I'd condemned myself to remaining alone until the end of my days.'

She watched with ragged breath as the truth of her words dawned on Robert. As the implications of what she'd said were realised. For a long moment he pressed his lips together, searching her gaze carefully in the moonlight. Searching for his answer. Searching, perhaps, for a way to let her down gently, to tell her that despite everything that had happened between them, he was not looking for a wife.

'I thought you wanted to remain alone,' he began cautiously. 'I thought that you decided long ago that you would not marry.'

'I did, but…'

Lord, she could hardly breathe. She forced the cold night air into her lungs, reminding herself that this was it. She had to speak up now, no matter the consequences. She had to tell him how she felt. After tonight, there might not be another chance.

'That was before I met you,' she began again. 'That was when I believed the only choices before me were the likes of Baron de Wold. That marriage would cost me my true nature, that I would be required to suppress my interests and my scholarly inclinations, indeed the very essence of who I am, all to please a husband. But you have never once made me feel like that, Robert. You have teased and provoked me, you have conversed with me and confided in me, and through all of it I have felt as though I have met my match. I love you, Robert—unequivocally and with absolutely no regard for what Society thinks about it. I love you.'

She saw his eyes widen in what looked like surprise. 'Elspeth, I…'

Gently she put her finger to his lips. 'Please, let me say one thing more or I fear I will lose my courage entirely. I'd like to marry you, Robert, if you will have me. I will accept it if you do not feel the same way, but I cannot go home tonight without telling you that I would love nothing more than to spend the rest of my days with you.'

For a long moment Robert simply stared at her, unable to speak. Were it not for his very tangible awareness of her body leaning against him, of the way her heat contrasted with the surrounding cold air, then he would have believed that he was dreaming. That yet again he'd been lured into one of those many fantasies he'd entertained in the lonely weeks since they'd parted in the summer. But no—this was real. Elspeth really had told him that she loved him. That she wanted to marry him.

'Robert.' She nudged him. 'Say something.'

He blinked, shaking his head in disbelief. 'I, er… I've never received a marriage proposal from a woman before. That was…unexpected.'

In his arms, he felt her shoulders slump. 'Oh, I see. Well, as I said, I will understand if you do not wish to…'

Robert did not give her the chance to finish that sentence. In an instant he cupped her cheek with his hand and pressed his lips against hers, stemming the flow of her words and offering none of his own, but hoping to convey his answer with a kiss instead. Immediately Elspeth melted against him and he held her closer, savouring all those details he'd craved so desperately these past weeks, from the delicate softness of her mouth, to the way she tasted. The last time he'd kissed her it had been the middle of the night as they'd lain together beneath her sheets and he'd struggled to tear himself away from her. This kiss, like that kiss, grew quickly passionate; before he knew it, her tongue had greeted his, and his wayward fingers had trailed a path from her jaw to her collarbone, before caressing the swell of her breasts in that temptingly low-cut gown…

There was no denying their mutual attraction, or their desire for one another. There was no ignoring the fire which had been reignited between them, and there was no refuting that he loved her just as much as she loved him. But marriage? He wanted Elspeth as his wife, more than anything. But he had to be sure that she truly wanted him as her husband, that she understood what binding herself to him would actually mean.

'Of course I want to marry you,' he breathed when finally their lips parted. 'I love you, Elspeth. I spent the summer falling in love with you. That final day we spoke, in the gardens—I was going to ask you to marry me that day.'

In the dim light he saw those dark eyes of hers widen. 'You were?'

'Of course.' He smiled. 'Despite my reputation, I am not the sort of dishonourable wretch who makes a habit of ruining maidens.'

'So asking for my hand was simply a matter of honour?' she asked.

He pulled her close to him again, dropping a kiss on the top of her head. 'Trust me, there was nothing simple about it. That night we spent together felt like a commitment to me. I knew then beyond any doubt that I'd fallen in love with you. So yes, asking you to marry me was a matter of honour, but it was a great deal more than that. I knew then that I wanted to spend my life with you.'

She rested her head against his shoulder. 'I understand what you mean about that night. I had only planned to talk to you, but once we were in my room and in the darkness, it was as though my words failed and my feelings took over. I never could convince myself that I should regret it, even when I convinced myself that you'd duped me, that you were wicked. Still, I didn't regret it. Still, I couldn't stop thinking about it, or about you.'

He chuckled softly. 'I don't think I've been able to stop thinking about you since we first met. I lost count of how many times I told myself I ought to know better than to let myself be so drawn to you, or to allow myself to surrender to my passions like I did in my library that day.'

She looked up at him, arching an eyebrow. 'I thought you were merely trying to prove a point?' she teased.

He smiled, smoothing a stray curl away from her face. 'You already know it was more than that.'

'I know. And you weren't the only one surrendering to their passions that day. Mine rather got the better of me, too.' She grinned sheepishly. 'I did effectively dare you to kiss me, after all.'

'You did,' he agreed, 'and I was absolutely not prepared for the fire that kiss lit between us. I don't think a kiss had ever made me feel like that before. I suppose I should have taken it as a warning, really.'

'A warning?'

'Yes, a warning that what was occurring between us was something far more serious than I think either of us could have bargained for.' He frowned, hesitating for a moment. 'You know the reason why I have chosen to be alone, Elspeth. Why I have never sought to marry again. Quite apart from the fact that I believed no woman would have me for a husband, I knew I did not wish to sully a woman's reputation by giving her my name. Discreet dalliances with widows like Isabelle Stephenson were one thing—I did not wish to live like a monk, after all. But marriage was quite another.'

Elspeth furrowed her brow at him. 'So what are you saying, that you want to marry me but you will not?'

'No, I am simply saying that what worried me the day after our night together when I planned to ask for your hand, is the same thing that worries me now. I fear that connecting yourself with me will taint you. That you'll be ground down by being whispered about and pointed at until the end of your days.' He regarded her carefully. 'I just want you to be sure this is what you want—that is all.'

Elspeth nodded, running her fingers down his cheek. 'It is,' she replied, without even the merest hint of hesitation. 'I actually do not believe that your bad reputation is as set in stone as you think it is. My brother, for one, doubts its veracity, and if he does then there will be others who do, too. Perhaps we will find that the more you venture into Society, the more Society revises its opinion of you. But ultimately, if Society rejects us both, then so be it. I really could not care if we never set foot in London again, Robert. I would happily live out my days in Hallowford, or on your estate, if you ever wish to return to it. Indeed, I would live anywhere, as long as I am with you and our children.'

'Children?' he repeated, a note which sounded suspiciously like hope resonating in his voice.

She nodded, then planted a firm, brief kiss upon his lips. 'Yes—children. At least, I hope there will be children. You are a wonderful uncle to Tilly, Robert, even if she does not know that is what you are. I am convinced you will make an equally wonderful father. Besides, you are a viscount. Surely it has occasionally occurred to you that you might need a son to inherit your title and estate?'

He laughed at that. 'To be honest, after Rafe died I decided it could all go to some distant cousin, just to spite my dreadful father.' He hugged her close again, resting his chin against the top of her head. 'But your plan about sons sounds far more sensible.'

'So, is that a yes, then? Are we getting married?'

For a moment he paused, his breath catching in his throat as he teetered on the cusp of answering her question in the affirmative. Of accepting her proposal. Then he shook his head, relinquishing her from his arms as he got to his feet. 'No—sorry, this isn't quite right,' he said gravely.

Elspeth looked up at him, her eyes wide—half in

horror, half in disbelief. 'What on earth do you mean?' she said, rising from the bench and planting her hands on her hips in that now-familiar, formidable pose.

At once a smile broke across his face, and he reached for one of those hands, clutching it in his. 'I mean that as a gentleman, and as a chivalrous knight, I should be the one to propose,' he replied playfully. Then his smile faded, and he held that dark gaze with all the solemnity the moment deserved. 'Lady Elspeth Scott,' he said softly. 'Will you do me the great honour of becoming my wife?'

Elspeth laughed, throwing herself into his arms, although not before he could spy what he was certain were tears gathering in her eyes. 'Will you ever cease to enjoy vexing me, my lord?' she asked as he held her close to him.

'Is that a yes then?' he prompted her, chuckling.

She kissed him softly on the cheek, then draped her arms around his neck as she held his eye. 'It is a yes,' she answered him, and now the tears were flowing in earnest. Tears of happiness. Tears of joy. The only sort of tears he would ever give her cause to cry.

'Of course it is a yes,' she repeated, her voice a whisper this time. 'Yes. Now and forever—yes.'

Chapter Twenty-One

The Tatler about Town,
November 1820

As all of London reels from the sensational events in the Lords last week and digests the news that a certain Bill was withdrawn and a royal divorce thus thwarted, this faithful correspondent hopes readers will forgive her for neglecting this story in favour of another, perhaps even more surprising matrimonial tale. It has reached the keen ears of this Tatler *that a certain notorious Lord B— has brought both his widowhood and long exile from Society to an end through his marriage to Lady E—, the beautiful and accomplished sister of the Duke of F—.*

The wedding took place on Monday at St. George's Church, Hanover Square, the banns having been read thrice and without objection. It appears the happy couple felt no need to evade public awareness of the forthcoming nuptials by means of a special licence or a drawing room ceremony. It also appears that Lady E—'s family had given the match their blessing and were content to attend the event, with the Duke of F— giving his sister away in the traditional fashion. A goodly number of our illustrious haut ton were there to share in the couple's joy, although this Tatler *must observe that more than a few will have struggled to suppress their surprise as they perched upon their pews on that chilly late autumn morning.*

Indeed, as this loyal correspondent feels duty-bound to note, it is a match most confounding even in a year which has, from the outset, been laden with the unexpected. Lord B— is a man who has been hitherto most scandalously described and yet, this Tatler *understands, he has been prone to defying all of the usual adjectives of late. Perhaps it is the years spent in the wilderness which have reformed certain reputed ill manners in favour of more gentlemanly conduct. Or perhaps, as some have begun to speculate, no reformation was ever required at all. This* Tatler *will, of course, leave readers to determine their own opinion on the matter, but if the recent royal wrangling in the Lords reminds us of anything, it is that what is truth and what is rumour may often be difficult to decipher, even by the noblest in our land.*

What is generally agreed upon, however, is that the impeccable Lady E—, now Lady B—, is a lady of great wit and formidable character. If one were to ask a certain Baron d— W—, one may also learn that she does not suffer a fool gladly. This faithful correspondent therefore rather suspects that Lord B—, irrespective of the current nature of his character, has more than met his match. As this most disharmonious year draws to its close, this Tatler *finds herself wishing the newlyweds every happiness in their union—while remaining with her pen poised, as always, to report upon any fresh scandal which reaches her ears.*

Epilogue

Late Spring 1821

Elspeth strode along the beach, the pale purple skirts of her dress skimming across the golden sands. The day was fine and bright, with a gentle breeze which carried the tentative promise of warmer days to come. As she walked, she bent down periodically to collect shells which had caught her eye. It was a habit she'd established, not long after arriving with Robert at the Barden country estate as the winter had ebbed into the spring. She would walk, and she would collect, and then she would return home, where she would consult various natural history books retrieved from the extensive Barden library to learn whatever she could about her specimens. Robert would always come too, enjoying the sea air and watching her with amusement as she examined her latest findings with a critical eye.

'At this rate, we are going to have to open our own

museum,' Robert said, chuckling as he watched her pick up another pair of shells.

Elspeth groaned as she stood up straight, tucking the shells into her reticule with one hand as she clutched her swollen belly with the other. 'At this rate, I will have to start asking you to collect the shells on my behalf,' she replied. 'I feel as though I have doubled in size this week.'

Robert laughed again, then put his arm around her shoulder and pulled her close to him before kissing her softly on the cheek. Elspeth was fairly certain that he'd been smiling ever since the moment when she'd told him she believed she was with child. Falling pregnant so soon after their wedding had come as a surprise, although logically, she knew that it shouldn't have. After making their vows at the altar of St George's on that freezing cold November day, they had spent a great deal of those early weeks of their marriage ensconced in the master bedchamber of their townhouse in St James's, making up for lost time.

'You look beautiful—as always,' Robert murmured, caressing her cheek. 'The sea air clearly agrees with you.'

Elspeth had to concur with that. A glance in the mirror each morning confirmed that her complexion was rosy, and now that the sickness which had accompanied the early weeks of her pregnancy had abated, she had a healthy appetite, too. Life here on the Yorkshire coast was peaceful in a way that her life at her family's Northumberland estate had always been. The large, centuries-old Barden Hall which sat at the centre of Robert's considerable estate was perhaps not as comfortable as Chatton House, and for now they had confined themselves to its most modern wing whilst renovations were arranged and undertaken. But the part of the house they occupied was warm and comfortable enough, and besides, they'd agreed that it was right that they come here. It was right that Robert should end his prolonged absence, that he should attend personally to his duties to his estate whilst giving Elspeth the opportunity to begin her role as its mistress. And it was right that their first child was born at Barden Hall. This was a new chapter of their lives, after all. A new, better, and altogether happier chapter.

'I discovered how much I adore the seaside not long before going to Hallowford,' she mused. 'Before visiting the Dunsforths, Mother and I visited another friend of hers, Lady Salmesbury. She has five unmarried and very lively daughters, so it was hardly a peaceful visit, but nonetheless walking along the beach each day brought me a great deal of joy. I will confess, I rather missed it when we moved on to Hallowford.'

'Then on behalf of my beloved landlocked, provincial town, I feel I must apologise to you,' Robert replied, a teasing glint sparkling in his green eyes. 'I do hope that your stay there was not too displeasing.'

She quirked a playful eyebrow at him. 'Oh, it was very displeasing. And as for some of the people I met! There was this one gentleman, you know, he was so provoking and disagreeable...'

'Oh, was he, indeed?' Robert laughed, kissing her on the tip of her nose. 'Did he really have nothing to recommend him?'

'Hmm,' she mused, feigning thoughtfulness. 'Well, I did once see him boxing shirtless in his outhouse. I suppose that did redeem him somewhat, in my eyes.'

'Ah—a handsome wretch, then?'

She nodded. 'A very handsome wretch. One who turned out not to be quite so wretched, once I got to know him.' For a long moment she gazed up at him, vaguely aware of the sound of the waves licking the shoreline as she studied the swirling, green depths of his eyes. 'What about you—do you think the sea air agrees with you? Does being back at Barden Hall agree with you?' she asked searchingly. Although Robert had willingly agreed to return, she was always keen to reassure herself that he was as content living here as she was. For Elspeth, this was a brand new home, but for Robert, it was a place which held a lot of unhappy memories.

He nodded. 'Actually—yes, it does.' He glanced down, picking up a large shell and running his fingers over it thoughtfully. 'I will admit that I expected the house to trouble me. That I would imagine the ghost of my father stomping down its halls, or wander into a room expecting to spy Lucy, weeping on the sofa with a glass of wine in her hand. And yet, most days, I hardly think about them. The house feels…changed. Its air is different.' He shook his head at himself, still rubbing that shell. 'It is hard to explain it.'

'Perhaps it is due to the renovations,' she remarked. 'I know there is still a good deal to be done, but the house already appears to have been transformed.'

'No—it's more than that. The house has a lightness about it that was never there before.' He smiled at her. 'That is entirely down to you. To us.' He ran his fingers gently over the outline of her swollen belly beneath her gown. 'To our happiness. My only wish is that my mother and brother could have met you. They would have adored you.'

She grinned. 'Oh, like my mother and brother adore you?'

Robert laughed, then gave a casual shrug as he took hold of her hand and they began to walk once more. It was certainly true that Barden Hall was not the only thing to have undergone something of a transformation in recent times; the Dowager Duchess's opinion of Robert had also changed beyond recognition. Although, much like the house renovations, it was not a change which had been brought about suddenly, or with particular ease.

The Dowager Duchess's initial reaction to the news of their betrothal had been one of abject horror, and Elspeth had not been able to quickly forget the way her mother's face had paled as they'd emerged from Viscountess Millington's moonlit gardens that night to inform her of their decision. Only her acute awareness of the eavesdropping ears of the *ton* had prevented her from voicing her objections at that moment, but in the privacy of their own home she'd expressed her opinion of the match in no uncertain terms.

'You are of age and old enough to know your own mind, Elsie, and if this is what you desire then I cannot prevent it,' she'd said. 'But for the life of me, I do not understand why you wish to marry that man. You know well enough what people say—you must think about the sort of husband he will make. I urge you to reconsider. It is not too late...'

'I meant what I said at the ball, Mama—you do not know him,' Elspeth had replied obstinately. 'None in our Society truly know him. But I know him. I know exactly what sort of man he is, and I know that I love him.'

'Teddy, please, talk some sense into your sister.' The Dowager Duchess had turned to the Duke then, pleading for his intervention. 'Surely you understand my concerns?'

Fortunately for Elspeth, Ted had been inclined to take a more reasoned, balanced view of the matter. 'To be frank, I never thought you would be inclined to marry anyone, sister,' he'd said as he'd sat down at her side. 'So I cannot help but think that Lord Barden must have done something fairly extraordinary for you to have decided to accept him. If he has truly earned his place in your affections, then that matters far more to me than any rumours or speculation about him.'

'Ted—really!' Her mother had begun to object. 'You cannot mean to…'

'Let me finish please, Mother,' he'd interjected, an amused smile playing on his lips as he'd turned to face Elspeth once more. 'However, it would be remiss of me as your brother and the head of our family if I did not seek to assuage our mother's fears about the match.'

Elspeth had frowned at that. 'And how do you propose to do that?' she'd asked.

'With a straightforward conversation,' Ted had replied. 'I will invite Lord Barden to the house to discuss your betrothal, and to get to know the fellow better. I will ask him directly to address the rumours about his previous marriage, and hopefully I can get a better sense of the man's character.'

'But Teddy, do you really think you can do all that in a single meeting with him?' the Dowager Duchess had countered.

Ted had got to his feet then, raising a knowing eyebrow at his mother. 'I daresay that I can. I think that after all of my years of dealing with my dearly departed older brother, I am quite good at knowing a dissolute gentleman when I see one,' he'd replied.

The meeting had taken place the following day, in the parlour of their Mayfair home. Elspeth had never been so anxious in all of her life; not because she feared Robert would fall in any way short in tackling her brother's interrogation, but because she hated the thought of him being under such scrutiny, and of him being forced to spill his most painful secrets in the name of securing her hand in marriage. In the end, she need not have worried. Robert had behaved admirably throughout, addressing Ted's questions honestly and sincerely, and taking no offence at any cross-examination by her mother. He had spoken candidly about his marriage to Lucy, about her unhappiness and their mutual agreement to separate, and about how she had lived the rest of her life in Wales with Frances, and with his support.

'Lucy cared for Frances in a way that she could never care for me,' he'd concluded carefully. 'I hope you will appreciate that in the circumstances, I was keen to maintain privacy over the matter and to shield her from scrutiny. Frances still lives in Wales, and keeps away from London, as far as I know,' he'd added. 'Nonetheless, I would ask that what I have told you today remains confidential—for her sake.'

'Of course, you have my word,' Ted had answered him, rubbing his chin thoughtfully. 'And I am sorry. It does seem that you have had to endure a great deal—not least from Society's gossips.'

'Unfortunately I learned that discretion and silence come at a cost,' Robert had replied, inclining his head politely. 'But I did what I believed was right and honourable, to protect my wife. You have my solemn vow that I will always do the same in regards to your sister.' He'd smiled then, turning his gaze towards Elspeth. 'I will care for her, I will protect her, and I will love her, just as I do now.'

Elspeth could still recall the enormous relief she'd felt when Ted had subsequently given his blessing to the match. Her mother had been right; she was more than old enough to make her own choices, but even so, she did desire her family's approval. The Dowager Duchess's reservations had been harder to overcome, and even as Ted had walked Elspeth down the aisle towards her betrothed on that frosty morning, Elspeth had been aware of her mother's lingering concerns. Thankfully, a family Christmas spent together in London had given ample opportunity for the Dowager Duchess to get to know her new son-in-law better, and to his credit Robert had wasted no opportunity to be the kind, decent, and thoroughly charming gentleman with whom Elspeth had fallen in love. By Twelfth Night her mother's icy demeanour had entirely thawed, and Elspeth's heart had sung when her mother had taken her aside and quietly confessed that she'd judged Robert unfairly, and that she was happy for them both, after all.

'We should invite your mother to visit soon,' Robert said after a long moment. 'And Ted, Charlotte, and the baby, of course, once they feel able to travel.'

'I should think it'll be a while before they're ready to do that,' Elspeth replied. Ted and Charlotte had been safely delivered of a son and heir, named Edward after his father, in January. To date they'd remained in their Mayfair home with the Dowager Duchess and had given no indication that they were ready to brave the long journey back to their Northumberland estate. 'For that matter, I am not quite sure we're in any position to entertain yet either! Not unless you plan to hold dinners on a building site.'

'Point taken,' Robert conceded with a chuckle. 'I will need to see what I can do to speed up some of the work in the house, I think. At the very least, I've no doubt your mother will want to visit when our little one makes his or her appearance.'

'She will, but as long as we can have a guest bedchamber ready for her in our wing of the house, I think we will manage.' She grinned at him. 'So there's no need to sacrifice any of your grand plans.'

'Ah yes—speaking of grand plans, I've been thinking that we should have some frescoes painted in the drawing room.'

Elspeth quirked a curious brow at him. 'Frescoes? Of what?'

'Oh, you know, scenes from the classical world. Representations of myths, of the gods and goddesses.' His expression was serious as he regarded her, but Elspeth could detect the amused sparkle playing in his green gaze.

'And do you have any particular gods or goddesses in mind?' she asked, suspecting that she already knew the answer.

'How about Artemis with her bow and her arrows on one wall, and Dionysus and his wine and his revelry directly opposite her?' he asked, now struggling to suppress his grin.

'Well, I suppose if you want to make us the talk of Society all over again…' Elspeth replied, feigning disapproval with one of her very best withering looks.

As news of their betrothal had quickly spread, Society had, without doubt, thoroughly relished the opportunity to speculate about what had been swiftly deemed the most surprising match of the year. But they'd also appeared to forget about it quickly again, too, especially once the wedding was over. In the end, even the most seasoned gossip had found little to chew over regarding a wedding which had taken place publicly, without incident and with none other than the Duke of Falstone giving the bride away. Clearly there was little fun in discussing a union between two people who were very obviously in love, especially when without doubt, there were a myriad of scandals to sniff out elsewhere.

'I can imagine the reports in print now,' she continued. *'Lord and Lady Barden and their most decadently decorated drawing room...'*

Robert laughed, wrapping his arm around her shoulder and kissing the top of her head. 'I doubt the scandal sheets are interested in reporting upon some frescoes, and even if they were, they would likely misunderstand them anyway.'

'Oh, probably. For a start, the parallels between Dionysus and your past reputation would be impossible for them to resist,' Elspeth remarked, rolling her eyes. 'And I'm sure they'd be only too happy to rake over last year's scene with Baron de Wold, when comparing me to Artemis.' She grinned at him. 'Although I am not sure I would complain about that.'

Robert chuckled again, then kissed her cheek as together they continued their stroll along the sandy beach, warmed by the sun sitting high above them in the sky. Elspeth rested her hand against her belly, feeling the baby moving beneath her fingers and quietly contemplating all the transformations which were to come—in their home, and in their lives together.

In the years which stretched ahead of them like the golden coastline along which they walked, filled with beauty, mystery, and possibility.

Robert glanced down at her belly, then brought his hand to rest over hers. 'Society and the scandal sheets could say whatever they pleased, for all that I care,' he said quietly, lifting his gaze to meet her own. 'We would know the truth—just you and I, together—and that is all that matters, in the end.'

*****

If you enjoyed this story, then you're going to love Sadie King's previous Regency romances:

Spinster with a Scandalous Past
Rescuing the Runaway Heiress
Hastily Wed to the Duke

Watch out for more stories from Sadie King, coming soon!

MILLS & BOON®

Coming next month

DARING TO DREAM OF THE DUKE
Lauri Robinson

Book 1 in Brides for Sworn Bachelors

There was something in Michael's eyes, the way he was looking at her, that was stealing the air from her lungs. Making it hard to breathe and impossible to look away. It felt as if time stopped. As if the world forgot to keep turning.

She had the strangest sensation that he wanted to kiss her. Or maybe those were her thoughts. For that was exactly what she wanted. With every part of her body.

His finger was still beneath her chin, and his thumb was caressing her cheek and sending a thrilling heat through her face, down her neck. Her lips were tingling, her heart was pounding, and the rest of her had the greatest desire to rise on her toes so her face was closer to his.

She'd never wanted something so badly. So completely. An unusual excitement was growing stronger and stronger at the mere idea of kissing him. Of his lips touching hers. She could imagine that it would be better than dancing with him. Better than anything she'd ever known.

Just as she was giving in, about to rise onto her toes, a piercing sense of reality struck. This was Michael. The one man she'd always dreamed of kissing and the one man she couldn't kiss. Couldn't ever let him know about the dreams she'd had for years. He'd merely been being kind to her this weekend, watching out for her, because as Nora had mentioned that first day, he thought of her as another sister. Someone he had to protect. Nora had said that would never change, and he certainly hadn't done anything to make Rosemary believe otherwise.

She'd been the one wishing it would change, and she shouldn't have. It wouldn't matter what she wore—he would never see her as a woman he could be interested in for something more than friendship.

Coming to her senses, she jerked her head backwards, and knowing that wasn't enough, she took a step backwards, too, all the while struggling to catch her breath.

The hand that had been touching her face fell to Michael's side, and it suddenly felt like she'd lost something precious.

He stared at her for yet another stilled moment, and she wished with all her might that she could read his mind. She couldn't, so all she could do was hope that he hadn't realized how badly she'd wanted him to kiss her.

Continue reading

DARING TO DREAM OF THE DUKE
Lauri Robinson

Available next month
millsandboon.co.uk

Copyright © 2026 Lauri Robinson

COMING SOON!

We really hope you enjoyed reading this book.
If you're looking for more romance
be sure to head to the shops when
new books are available on

Thursday 26th March

To see which titles are coming soon, please visit
millsandboon.co.uk/nextmonth

MILLS & BOON

FOUR BRAND NEW BOOKS FROM
MILLS & BOON MODERN

Indulge in desire, drama, and breathtaking romance – where passion knows no bounds!

OUT NOW

Eight Modern stories published every month, find them all at:

millsandboon.co.uk

TWO BRAND NEW BOOKS FROM
Love Always

Be prepared to be swept away to incredible worldwide destinations along with our strong, relatable heroines and intensely desirable heroes.

OUT NOW

Four Love Always stories published every month, find them all at:

millsandboon.co.uk

LET'S TALK
Romance

For exclusive extracts, competitions and special offers, find us online:

- **f** MillsandBoon
- **X** @MillsandBoon
- **◉** @MillsandBoonUK
- **♪** @MillsandBoonUK

Get in touch on 01413 063 232

For all the latest titles coming soon, visit
millsandboon.co.uk/nextmonth